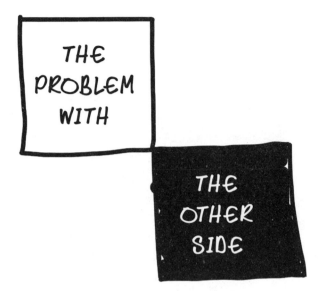

THE PROBLEM WITH

THE OTHER SIDE

THE PROBLEM WITH

THE OTHER SIDE

KWAME IVERY

**CW: Acts of racism and bigotry, racist language,
and gun violence are portrayed in this novel.**

Quotes from *The Good, the Bad and the Ugly* © 1966 P.E.A. Films, Inc.
All Rights Reserved. Courtesy of MGM Media Licensing.

Published in the United States by Soho Teen
an imprint of Soho Press, Inc.
227 W 17th Street
New York, NY 10011

Library of Congress Cataloging-in-Publication Data
Names: Ivery, Kwame, 1972- author.
Title: The problem with the other side / Kwame Ivery.
Identifiers: LCCN 2020019803

ISBN 978-1-64129-205-4
eISBN 978-1-64129-206-1

Subjects: CYAC: 1. Dating (Social customs)—Fiction. 2. Racism—Fiction.
3. School violence—Fiction. 4. Brothers and sisters—Fiction.
5. High schools—Fiction. 6. Schools—Fiction. 7. Elections—Fiction.
Classification: LCC PZ7.1.I98 Pro 2021 | DDC [Fic]—dc23
LC record available at https://lccn.loc.gov/2020019803

Interior design by Janine Agro, Soho Press, Inc.

Printed in the United States of America

10 9 8 7 6 5 4 3 2 1

For Janet S., Suzanne B., and Heather C.
(They know why.)

THE
PROBLEM
WITH

THE
OTHER
SIDE

PART

1

COLLINGSWOODCOURIERNEWS.COM

June 19 | Weather: 74, partly cloudy; rain expected tomorrow

NEWS

Breaking: 2 Students Killed at Knight High School

FOR MORE ON THIS STORY, CLICK LINK BELOW

 School Election Tragedy: Eruption of Violence on Inauguration Day

February

In this world, there are
two kinds of people . . .
—Blondie, *The Good,
the Bad and the Ugly*

| ULY

I'm in love because a clown got handcuffed to a nun.

Last November I was in this dumb-ass school play called *Hostages and Hot Plates* where this rich Connecticut girl holds a whole restaurant hostage until her parents agree to let her marry this penniless-as-hell guy she's mad thirsty for. The parents are okay with the dude being poor, but they're not okay with him being from Neptune (yep, the planet). So the girl holds everybody at the restaurant—her parents, her little brother, her aunt (who's a nun), a snooty middle-aged businesswoman, a squabbling elderly couple, a clown, a magician, and me (I play the damn waiter)—at gunpoint until her parents are okay with Neptune. Of course, hijinks ensue. At one stupid point, the clown and the magician—who are there for the little brother's birthday party—get into a fistfight because the clown thinks he knows more tricks than the magician who thinks he's funnier than the clown and during their scuffle the magician bumps into the snooty businesswoman who accidentally pours cranberry juice all over my white uniform. For some reason, that makes me faint. I especially hated that part, by the way. I've never fainted before in my life. For those of you who don't know: black folks don't faint. I'm not sure why; we just don't. Evidently the playwright missed that memo and forced a brother to faint every night in front of administrators, teachers, and fellow schoolmates. Anyway, after a while the hostage negotiator persuades the girl to let all the hostages go, but her aunt—the nun—decides to stay with the girl, and the clown—feeling guilty about some real disturbing shit he's done over the years (it's a long-ass list that I don't have time to get into right now)—refuses to leave the nun alone with the girl so he handcuffs himself to the nun. The hostage negotiator eventually breaks into the restaurant and, seeing me unconscious on the floor in my cranberry-juiced white suit, thinks the girl blew me up and is about to lock her up for life, but then I wake up and the police chief ends up locking her up for eleven months (the girl's parents are really tight with city council).

And the girl's parents end up still not being okay with Neptune. So the girl went through all that drama for nothing.

But I went through all that drama for something. If it hadn't been for that heap of horse-vomit that had the nerve to call itself a play, I wouldn't be in love right now. So as much as I hated that play, I can't think and talk about it enough, even though it ended three months ago. My grandfather (R.I.P.) used to say, "Even the most beautiful gardens start with shit." At the time, I didn't know what he meant. Now I do.

It started at the end of a quick last-minute dress rehearsal just a couple of hours before our grand opening-night performance. Friday night. The clown and the nun were handcuffed to each other, as usual; but this time, nobody could find the key to uncuff them. Stuart Baldwin, our props guy, was an incompetent asshole even on his most bacon day and he'd misplaced it. It didn't take long for Panic to be the thirteenth member of our twelve-member cast. Everybody started scurrying around our handcuffed nun & clown, whipping back and forth across the damn stage, frantically checking under tables and chairs and heavy curtain folds. It wouldn't have been so bad if our opening night wasn't less than two hours away, but it was. Even Ms. Rothstein, who's normally so calm she could probably have a picnic lunch on a flying missile, was starting to look pale and anxious. Looking even worse were Lori McCormick—the clown—and Harriet Jennings—the nun. There had been rumors swirling around that they wanted to split each other's head open—something to do with Harriet Instagramming a selfie she'd taken with Lori's boyfriend a couple of weekends earlier and Lori body-shaming Harriet by Tweet a couple of days later; I don't know if any of it was true but the quiet, intense way those two girls stared at each other while the rest of us scampered around told me that we needed to find that key sooner than later, feel me? I swear I'd never seen a clown and a nun look so angry.

So, just to lighten the mood, I shrugged, pointed at their handcuffs, and said, "Looks like y'all are gonna need a train to come by soon."

The Magician (I forget the name of the kid who played him) gave me a confused look and asked, "Train? What do you mean?"

I said, "You don't know that movie?"

"What movie?" he said.

I looked at some of the other cast members and asked them, "Y'all don't know that movie?"

They blankly shook their heads "no." Even Ms. Rothstein was looking at me like I was some mile-long quadratic equation handwritten in Sanskrit on paper made of Juicy Fruit gum.

Before I could feel like even more of an alien, Jerry Hoyt the stage manager yelled, "Found it!" The key. It was under one of the seats in the front row of the audience area. We all put our heart attacks back on the shelf and Ms. Rothstein finished giving us the final notes.

During the performance, toward the end of the play, the snooty businesswoman, as usual, handed me a folded dollar and said, "Here you go, young man—this should help with the cleaning bills."

And, as usual, I frowned at the folded dollar and said, "Thanks; this'll go a long way toward cleaning the left lapel."

Sallie Walls, the girl who played the snooty businesswoman, always gave me an actual dollar (which, of course, I always returned to her after the play). But on this particular night, she gave me the dollar with a purple Post-it note attached. I didn't notice the Post-it until minutes after the play when we were all backstage. I took the folded dollar out of my pocket, saw the purple edge peeking above the bill's right side, unfolded the dollar, and saw this message on the Post-it:

The Good, the Bad and the Ugly?

I found myself smiling at the note. Then I looked up and tried to find her in the crowd, my eyesight slicing past patches of still-costumed cast members, moving past the magician, moving past the damn clown, moving past the nun, moving past the hostage negotiator, and finally landing on the fifteen-year-old blond girl, make-upped to look forty-five, still in her businesswoman suit. She was leaning against the big dressing room's wall, alone, staring at the floor with one hand idly cradling her neck, looking the way an apple might look in a room full of bananas. The apple knows it's surrounded by fellow fruit, but what do you talk about? You're round and red, they're long and yellow; you have skin that everybody eats, they have skin that nobody eats; you have seeds, they don't. I knew that look because that was the way I felt the whole time I did that play; shit, that's the way I feel the whole time I'm at this school.

I made my way through the wilderness of the weirdly dressed, holding the purple Post-it note higher and higher as I got closer to her.

Pointing at the Post-it, I nodded at her and said, "Tuco is handcuffed to the guard—"

"—and he tells the guard he has to go to the bathroom," she said, smiling.

"But they can't go to the bathroom 'cause they're on the train," I said.

"So the guard gets up and opens the train door so Tuco can let it fly from the train's doorway," she said.

"But instead of lettin' it fly, Tuco grabs the guard and pulls him off the damn train," I said.

"And they both roll down this gravelly hill—" she said.

"—And Tuco slams the guard's head against this big rock over and over, killin' him—" I said.

"—But then he remembers that he's still handcuffed to the guard . . ." she said.

"And who wants to spend the rest of his life, draggin' around a dead prison guard?" I said.

"Not me," she said.

"So then he tries to break the handcuff's chain—" I said.

"—with the handle of his gun," she said.

"But that doesn't work—" I said.

"—so then he tries stretching the chain as hard as he can, but it still won't break," she said.

"Then he looks up and sees the train tracks, and he gets this idea . . ." I said.

"He lays the guard in the middle of the track and lies down on the other side of the track and waits for the next train to come . . ." she said.

"And then the train comes speedin' by . . ." I said.

"And the train's wheels slice through the chain . . ." she said.

"And now he's free . . ." I said.

"And he runs after the train and hitches a ride on the back of it," she said.

We both laughed. It kind of felt like we should've given each other a fist bump or a high-five or something, but a fist bump felt too brotherly and a high-five felt too corduroy. So we kept our hands at our sides. I said, "That was bacon as hell."

She nodded. "Totally."

There was a pause while we stared at each other.

Then I said, "Oh, and here's your Georgie." I handed her dollar back.

"Oh, thanks," she said, pocketing the bill, still staring at me.

"I'm mad impressed you know about that movie," I said, then motioned back at the nun, magician, clown, etc. "You're, like, the only one who got it."

She said, "It's my favorite movie."

My eyebrows went up. "Real talk?"

She nodded.

"Damn," I said. "It's mine too."

Now it was her eyebrows' turn to go up. "Really?"

I said, "How badass was Eli Wallach in that movie?"

She said, "Oh my God, he *so* made that movie!"

I nodded. "Real talk. I mean, I know Eastwood was the star and everything, but Wallach *owned* that shit! It's hard as hell to be sociopathic and funny at the same time, but my man pulled it off!"

Sallie said, "Completely. I mean, he took this, like, completely despicable, immoral character and made him the most likeable guy in the movie! Blondie and Angel Eyes were supposed to be the better guys, but if I was throwing a party or something, Tuco would be the only one I'd invite. I mean, I'd have to hide everybody's jackets and wallets before he came of course, but I'd still want him to come."

I laughed. I couldn't believe I'd never noticed that her smile was brighter than the room's dozen lights.

She said, "Oh, and you know another cool thing about that movie? Okay, we know Blondie is the Good, Angel Eyes is the Bad, and Tuco is the Ugly. But I think the movie was trying to say that each of them was really all three things. I mean, Blondie did some things that were bad and ugly, and Angel Eyes did some things that were good and ugly, and Tuco definitely did some things that were good and some things that were bad."

After giving what she said some mind time, I said, "Wow, I never thought of it that way. You're right."

Behind me our fellow cast members were getting louder and louder, playing some game with a foam Frisbee.

Sallie threw a distracted glance at them then moved her eyes back to me and said, "Hey, you wanna get outta here for a while—like, go out to the staircase or something? I can't hear myself think in here."

I nodded. "Bacon."

When we got to the staircase, Sallie sat on the top step and I stood two steps down from her and leaned against the railing. She took off her black pumps and sighed, "I've gotta take these off. Never wear heels—they're murder."

"I'll keep that in mind," I said.

Looking at the pumps, she shook her head and said, "Dressing like a businesswoman for the last seven weeks has taught me that the one thing I never want to be is a businesswoman."

I chuckled and said, "You've been doing a pretty good job, actually."

Massaging her foot, she said, "Oh, thanks. You too. By the way—all due respect and everything, but is this play bullshit or what?"

I half laughed and said, "I was thinkin' the same thing!"

Sallie said, "I mean, the girl's parents won't let her get married so she holds up a restaurant?! Who does that?!"

"I know!"

"And the guy she wants to marry is from Neptune?? I never said anything, but you know what's been bugging me the whole seven weeks about that? Neptune is a planet made completely of gas: How can somebody live there?! Maybe it wouldn't have bothered me as much if it was a rock planet like Venus or Mars or

Mercury—with rock there's land, and with land you have something you can build stuff on: schools or supermarkets or whatever the hell. But there's not much you can do when your planet is made completely of gas, except dream about moving to another planet. I mean, if the whole point was to make the guy strange, why not just make him be from Iowa or something?"

I nodded. "Truthanasia."

Sallie said, "I guess you're thinking I'm a hater, but I really don't complain a lot, I swear. I think it's these shoes. They've been strangling my soul for the last seven weeks and I guess I just need to let stuff out."

I said, "No, I feel you. I hate that I have to faint all the time."

She looked surprised. "But you've been doing a good job with that."

I said, "Real talk?"

She nodded. "Definitely. I mean, I know it's weird to tell somebody they're a good fainter, but you're a good fainter."

"Thanks, but I don't like it. I feel like I'm being fake."

She said, "But it's a play; we're all being fake."

I said, "Yeah, but I mean . . . See—black folks don't faint."

Her eyebrows went up. "Really?"

I nodded. "And I think the audience knows I've never done it before, and when they see me doing it, they can tell I'm trying too hard. You know how it is with acting—when you're doing it right, the faking is so fake it seems far from fake, even when you're fainting."

Sallie said, "Wow, try saying that ten times real fast."

"No thank you."

She said, "Are you sure black people don't faint?"

I said, "I'm sure as hell. Think about it: Have you ever seen a black person faint?"

Sallie thought a moment. Then she said, "You know something? I haven't. But then again, I've never seen a Korean person faint or a Latinx person faint or a Russian person faint, but I'm sure they've all fainted. I mean, that's what people do. Faint."

I nodded. "I feel you on that, just not black people."

She kind of squinted and said, "Why do you think that is?"

I shrugged and said, "I'm not sure. I think it could be because we've seen so much shit as a people that not much can surprise us on a Fainting level anymore. It's kinda like when you go to a gym and work out for the first time—your muscles and bones get all sore because your body's like, 'Yo, what's up?! What're you doin' to me?! You've never done this before! Stop!' and you end up hurting all over the next day. But the more you work out, the more your muscles and bones get used to all the trauma to your body and they just get numb to the pain, and instead of knockin' you down they start focusing on buildin' you up. And I think black people and fainting are the same way. Overcomin' was put in our DNA hundreds of years ago and I guess it just gets handed down from generation to generation."

Sallie said, "Wow, I never thought of it that way. See, now you got me really curious. All I wanna do right now is find a black person and see if I can make them faint. Isn't that terrible?"

"Kind of," I said.

She pointed at me and said, "Wait a minute—you're a black person!"

"What gave it away?" I said.

She said, "I'm gonna try to make you faint right now."

"Good luck," I said.

She said, "Oh! but before I do—I gotta tell you something that I just remembered. You've got to swear not to tell anybody else."

I wasn't expecting this. I nodded and said, "I swear."

She motioned for me to lean closer to her.

I did.

She looked around to make sure we were still alone, then she turned back to me and whispered, ". . . I heard that Ms. Rothstein is attracted to you."

After a moment, I grinned and said, "Nice try."

Sallie slapped her thigh and said, "Damn! I so thought that was gonna put you flat on your back!"

I said, "I'm tellin' you—black people don't faint. But that was a nice try, real talk."

Massaging her other foot, she said, "Oh God, I can't wait till this play is over. I only did it 'cause I was bored and Ms. Rothstein talked me into it."

I said, "I only did it 'cause my sister kept buggin' me about how I need to start taking more extracurriculars because that's what colleges are gonna be looking for and how I did nothing during freshman year and how tenth grade isn't too early to start."

Sallie gave a knowing nod and said, "Yeah, my stepmom pretty much said the same thing. But I hate sports, so theater was the only thing that seemed interesting."

As Sallie and I continued talking on that staircase, I found myself realizing something.

I was attracted to her.

Like, *legit* attracted to her. The kind of attracted where things in your body that are normally slow speed up . . . and things *on* your body that are normally soft get very firm, if you don't mind me being up-front about the front.

It was so strange to be feeling like this about her. It was like I was meeting her for the first time, but I'd known her since last year when we were both in the same freshman English class. And just to stay in Real City: I thought she was pretty back then. I think it's her eyes. She has these dark, dark eyes—two tiny round pools of chocolate pudding—that form an interesting clash with her blond hair. And she has this deep, anchorwoman voice that makes her sound older than her fifteen years. She had it even as a freshman last year. Whenever she raised her hand to answer one of Mrs. Lorimar's questions, I always found myself kind of hoping my classmates would stay quiet so I could hear her voice.

So I've always thought Sallie Walls is pretty.

But it wasn't till that staircase conversation (and the stuff that happened right before it—the Post-it note, Tuco & the handcuffs, etc.) that I realized that Sallie Walls is . . . sexy. For those of you who aren't feeling me on that, pretty & sexy aren't necessarily the same jam. You can be pretty but not sexy. And you can be sexy but not pretty (though most times you are—let's not front). I mean, check it out: Beyoncé is pretty. But Rihanna is sexy. Feeling me yet? A sunrise can be pretty, but you wouldn't want it next to you in bed. You want to wake up *with* it, not *to* it. The good news is that pretty can turn into sexy overnight. You can go from pretty to sexy just by staring at someone a certain way. But, for some reason, it's rare for Sexy to get downgraded to Just Pretty. I guess it can happen; I just hope it never happens when I'm around. Pretty fades. But Sexy usually stays.

And Sallie definitely turned from pretty to sexy on that staircase. And it really surprised me.

See, I'm gonna tell you something about white girls, and I'm saying sorry in advance because some of you might get offended by this, but I gotta keep it 100: I've found a lot of white girls attractive . . . but I'm usually not *ATTRACTED TO* them. Before Sallie, I just never really found white girls sexy. I know there are some mad exceptions out there, but a lot of the white girls I've known— mainly here in school—are just too played-out and corduroy to be sexy. Either they're stuck-up or they're fake or they're spaced out or they dance when they know they can't or they worship Nutella or they wear UGGs or they like Justin Bieber or they talk with that annoying vocal fry at the end of every damn sentence.

But not Sallie Walls. She's the apple in a land of bananas. She's funny. She's interesting. She's nice. And she knows how a train can rescue you if you're ever handcuffed to a dead prison guard.

But you know what's really interesting, though? At first, I thought Sallie was sort of racist. While Ms. Rothstein was making announcements and giving us the post-rehearsal notes, I'd always catch Sallie giving me this kind of uptight glance every ten seconds like she was worried I wasn't going to give her dollar back to her. And when I gave it back, she'd take it and smile quickly with her face turning slightly red the way people do when you catch them being someone you weren't supposed to see—like a shoplifter. Or a cheating spouse. Or a bigot.

"Oh, *there* you two are!" the nun said when she spotted us on the staircase. "We were wondering where you were. Ms. Rothstein is about to give her notes."

"Okay, we'll be there," Sallie told her.

The nun walked back into the dressing room.

Sallie and I smirked at each other, then she sighed and said, "Well, I guess all good things really do come to an end."

"Yeah," I said.

She put one of her pumps back on.

On an impulse, I reached down for her other pump and held it toward her like I was offering a gift. "May I have the honor?" I asked.

She smiled and said, "Sure."

She extended her foot toward me and I slowly slipped the shoe back on her.

She said, "Thank you. You're not a freak or anything, are you?"

I laughed and said, "What kind of question is that?"

She said, "No, it's just—the only guy who offers to put a girl's shoe back on her is a shoe salesman, or a freak."

I said, "You left out a third possibility—Just A Nice Guy."

She said, "Some of the freakiest freaks are nice guys. They're usually nice guys Thursday through Saturday and freaks Monday through Wednesday."

"Well you're in luck: today is Friday," I said, then I reached down to take her arm so I could help her off the step.

She gave me her arm and let me lift her up. "Wow, how 'nice' of you," she said with a grin.

"Well, I try to—"

She suddenly gasped and grabbed my shoulder. "Oh shit!" Her face had turned instantly red and there was a terror in her eyes I hadn't seen before; she seemed to be looking at something just over my shoulder.

My heartbeat starting to hammer, I said, "What?"

She quietly said, "Oh my God . . . Don't move . . ."

"What is it?" I said, trying to keep my voice steady.

She slowly said, ". . . There's a rat on that step just two inches behind your head . . ."

I looked at her for a moment, then smiled and said, "Nice try."

"Damn!" she said.

"I told you—BPDF, baby!"

She looked confused. "Huh?"

"Black People Don't Faint," I said. "When are you gonna learn?"

"I think I'm learning," she said as she walked with me back to the dressing room. Every few seconds I could feel our shoulders brush against each other's and every time they did, I felt a kind of lump form in my throat . . . something that happens whenever I'm standing or sitting or walking right next to someone I'm mad Into.

That was my first official conversation with Sallie Walls, and by the time it was over I was in love with her. That's how romantically gangsta she is. There's a song from the 1970s that my grandfather liked—"It Only Takes a Minute to Fall in Love." Pre-Sallie, I'd always thought that song was bullshit.

By the time we got back to the dressing room I realized I had a new problem on my hands: I wasn't sure if she felt the same way about me.

But Hope gave me a shout-out when Sallie asked for my phone number right before we said Goodnight. I gave her mine and she gave me hers.

We spent a big part of that weekend talking on the phone and FaceTiming and learning more stuff about each other. Besides loving *The Good, the Bad and the Ugly* and the other two Clint Eastwood spaghetti westerns (*A Fistful of Dollars* and *For a Few Dollars More*), we found out we both also had mad love for watching stand-up comedy shows on Netflix. And not only that, we both broke out the hate-orade for stand-up comedians who sing or play music during their performance.

"I can't *stand* that shit!" I told Sallie over the phone.

"Me neither!" she said. "Why can't they just stick to comedy? I mean, if I want to hear music, I'll go to Spotify or something."

"Truthanasia," I said. "Singers don't tell jokes in their songs; why do comedians have to sing?"

"I know! Can you imagine Taylor Swift stopping in the middle of a song to say, 'So a priest, a rabbi, and a lawyer walk into a bar . . .'"

I laughed. Actually, that still makes me laugh, and she said it three months ago.

On Monday and Tuesday Sallie and I met after school at Knight Park across the street and sat on a bench and watched *A Fistful of Dollars* and *For a Few Dollars More* on my phone. We'd already seen both movies a hundred times, but that was on our own; we wanted to watch them together so we could comment on different things. It was cold in that park—November was doing its thing—but it didn't really bother me; most of the time, I didn't even notice the cold—I was too busy wondering if this beautiful, funny girl sitting just two inches away was feeling me as much as I was feeling her.

As I tapped my way toward Netflix to pull out *A Fistful of Dollars* Sallie said, "I wonder why they call them 'spaghetti westerns.' Nobody ever ate spaghetti in any of the movies, or did I miss something?"

I said, "I read somewhere that it was because all the movies were made with Italian production companies. That's actually kind of an insult, though. I mean, if I was Italian and somebody called my movie a Spaghetti movie, I'd be offended as hell. I mean, that's kinda like calling a Tyler Perry movie a Fried Chicken & Biscuit movie. Or a Jackie Chan movie a Moo Shu Pork movie."

Sallie said, "Oh, yeah." She was quiet for a moment. Then she said, "I never thought of it that way."

As the whistle and smacking whips of the movie's opening music started our shoulders touched; she didn't move hers away, and I didn't move mine away. My heartbeat slipped into Speed mode again.

"Is this music bacon or what?" I said, trying to keep my voice steady and arousal-free.

She nodded. "It's so lit. I love that whistle. I read that Ennio Morricone—y'know the composer—used the whistle because it was an instrument that made him think of being by yourself; being alone. And Eastwood spends a lot of time by himself in these movies. Well, maybe not so much the other two, but definitely this one."

As the movie ended—my boy Eastwood on his horse, casually riding away from the three corpses on the ground—our shoulders were still touching.

"Now *that's* how you end a cowboy movie," Sallie said. "No sentimental stuff. Just ride away after doing what you needed to do. It's tough, just like the cowboy's way of life. Brutal and true."

I said, "Yeah. Oh, and look at that—no closing credits: just *The End*."

Sallie said, "Yeah. It's like the director was saying, 'You want closing credits? Fuck you. Life during this time was too tough for closing credits. All you're gonna get from me is *The End*.' Tough and to the point."

Watching *For a Few Dollars More* the next day was slightly

disappointing, with a nice-sized slice of promising. Disappointing not because of the movie (Sallie and I agree that it's better than *Fistful* but not as bacon as *Good/Bad/Ugly*), but because our shoulders didn't really touch this time. Now for the Promising: when the bank explodes Sallie put her head on my shoulder. I acted all cool of course, like everything was normal, then I kind of panicked when I realized she might've been dozing off and had put her head on my shoulder simply as part of the accidental affection you give the person next to you when you're falling asleep—no matter whether that person is Mom or Manson.

Trying to keep my voice panic-free, I said, "You asleep?"

"No," she said. "Just comfortable."

By the time Eastwood rode away with the six corpses in his carriage—and the $100,000 in his bag—and *The End* popped up on the screen, I began to think that maybe Sallie liked me just as much as I liked her.

Things only got better over the next two months. We texted each other in class. We ate lunch together. And on the weekends when we didn't have a heavy homework load or an upcoming test we got together and hung out: sometimes we'd take the bus to Cherry Hill Mall or to the Cherry Hill Loews movie theater; sometimes we'd ride the PATCO to Philly to run up the Rocky steps; sometimes we'd stay local and walk around Newton Lake. And every day after school we continued meeting at Knight Park to sit on our bench and watch videos: sometimes Netflix stuff, sometimes YouTube.

During all this I got to learn more things about her. Her middle name is Diana. She was born and raised in Collingswood, New Jersey where our school is. She and her older sister Leona lost their mother when she was four years old. Their father remarried when Sallie was nine but, unfortunately, he passed when she was eleven, leaving her and her sister with the stepmother, who—fortunately—is the Coolest Stepmother In The World, to quote

Sallie. Her favorite dessert is cherry pie with vanilla ice cream. Her favorite candy is Skittles. And though she likes Nutella, she doesn't love it. (Thank God.)

And I guess that brings me to February, where we're at now. Some of you might be wondering if we've kissed yet, and as much as I'd like to say yes, I gotta stay in Real City and say no. We hug hello and hug goodbye, and our shoulders stay glued when we watch videos and there's been some flirty arm-touching and face-touching. But no kiss yet. I'm not sure why we keep putting it off. There have been times when, right after our goodbye hug, she's given me this "Anything else for the Cause?" look but I didn't go in for the kiss because . . . I don't know. Maybe I was nervous. Or it was out in public, and I've never been down with PDA. And there have been times when I wanted to go in for the kiss but she seemed like she wasn't ready. I mean, check it out: What if I go in for the kiss and she pulls back and says, "Whoa, what're you doing?! We're just friends"?

The closest we've come to kissing was last month, and our lips weren't even involved. We'd finally got around to watching *The Good, the Bad and the Ugly* together after putting it off all through December. I guess the delay was because we both knew the movie is mad long and we wanted to wait till both of our schedules were clear so we could watch it unbroken; we both hate having to pause a movie till the next day. So on this one after-noon that was so warm it was like January had gotten whacked in the head by Mother Nature's skateboard and forgotten how to be itself Sallie and I sat on Our Bench, hit up Netflix, and watched our favorite movie together. When we got to the Tuco & the Train scene, it happened: Sallie put her hand on my hand. And I looked at her and smiled. And then I put my hand on her hand. And my heartbeat turned into an Olympics track star again.

I can't believe I just wrote that. If some other guy wrote that and I was reading it, I'd tease the hell out of him for getting all mushy and wack and sprung and poetic over a girl. I mean—doing the hand sandwich on a park bench? It doesn't get more corduroy than that. But here's the thing: You know what my problem is? Deep down, I'm a damn romantic. And that comes straight from Real City. I was one of those losers who welled up when Kate realized Leonardo had frozen to death in the middle of the Atlantic but my insecure ass actually had the nerve to make fun of my cousin Cora for crying all through the second half of the movie when I watched it with her. I'm a damn romantic. There are a billion mofos out there—why did Cupid have to go and add *me* to his cave of captives? I hate being a romantic. You know why? Because the engine that a romantic runs on is the heart. And just like an engine, it breaks down. Or even worse: it just breaks. And then you're nothing but a bus going nowhere, stuck in a bad neighborhood, with nothing to look at but condemned buildings, brick walls, and broken hopes.

So anyway: a hand sandwich with cheese—that's the closest Sallie Walls and I have come to a kiss.

Until today.

It happened this afternoon, during Period G when we both have a Study Hall.

We'd each asked our teachers for a pass to "go to the bathroom" so we could squeeze in a quick nice-to-see-your-face chat.

As Sallie and I were walking down a staircase—not Our Staircase but another one in the school—I suddenly slipped on something that felt like a sheet of paper and down my ass went. I fell back and probably would've cracked my head against one of the steps if Sallie's arm hadn't been a buffer that kept my body closer to 90 degrees than 180. But her arm cushion still couldn't stop me from landing on my back about three steps down.

"Oh my God, Uly, are you okay?! Are you okay?!" Sallie asked as she scrambled down toward me. She had the same terror in her eyes that she'd had that night when she used the invisible rat to test the BPDF theory; but this time the terror was real.

"Yeah, I'm cool," I grunted as she took my arm to help me up.

"Are you okay?" she asked again when I was on my feet.

"Yeah, I'm cool," I said, trying not to wince too hard from the pain that was shooting back and forth in my lower back.

She slightly squinted at me and said, "I don't believe you."

With my best reassuring smile, I said, "I told you—I'm cool."

Her face still rocking the skeptical squint, she said, "Bend to the left."

I bent to the left. "See?"

She said, "Now bend to the right."

I bent to the right. "See? I told you—it's all bacon." And it was true. The pain was actually starting to get lost.

She said, "Now swivel your torso."

As I swiveled I said, "If you want me to strip, why don't you just come out and say it."

She laughed and playfully punched my arm. "Shut up."

She kept her eyes on me as her smile dissolved into something more complicated—the way people look when they have two million things to say but only two minutes to say them in. But she didn't say anything. Instead she stepped closer to me and gave me a kiss on the cheek. The kind of cheek-kiss that's walking distance from the lips and car distance from the ears.

Then she stared at me, like she was maybe waiting for me to finish what she started. It was the perfect moment to go in for the Kiss. But I just couldn't bring my damn self to do it yet.

Instead I broke our staring spell by looking at the steps to see if I could find the thing that made me fall. I said, "What was that . . . ?" Then I spotted a firetruck-red flyer lying up on the second step. I pointed at it and said, "Oh, there it is." I noticed that the flyer showed the smiling face of a familiar-looking girl. "Hey, isn't that your sister?"

Sallie picked up the flyer, which read:

COMING ATTRACTION: VOTE FOR LEONA WALLS THIS JUNE!

Staring at the flyer, Sallie said, "Wow, looks like she's really going to do it. She kept talking about running, but with her you never know sometimes."

I glanced up at the walls of the staircase and noticed, for the first time, that nearly every inch of every wall was plastered with the red flyers of Sallie's smiling sister. And every flyer said the same thing.

Sallie must've been looking in the same direction because she said, "Damn, how many flyers did she put up?"

As we continued going down the stairs, I realized that Sallie hadn't talked much about her sister since we started hanging out. "You and your sister get along?" I asked.

She shrugged. "We do okay. If I had to give her a Hotel Rating, she'd get about a six."

"Six?"

She nodded. "Six hours—the longest I could be trapped in a hotel room with her before I lost my mind."

I chuckled.

She said, "How about your sister? What's her Hotel Rating?"

I said, "About a three."

She said, "Three hours before you'd lose your mind, huh?"

I said, "Are you kiddin'? Three *minutes*."

Sallie laughed.

As we left the staircase to walk down the first-floor hall I suddenly had an idea. I said, "Hey, why don't we ditch Newton Park tomorrow and go to the Franklin Museum instead?"

Most people go to museums to learn—and normally, that would be me too—but this time I wanted to go for only one reason. To kiss Sallie. I think what's been holding me back all this time is that mofos are constantly all around us—mofos who know either her or me or both of us—and knowing that one of them could stumble across us and catch us kissing and then blab it all over the school and/or town is something that makes me self-conscious as hell. And when you put Self-Conscious and Kissing in a jar and shake them up, what comes out is something nobody wants to taste twice. The good thing about the Franklin Museum is that it's in Philly—a whole train ride away—and it has a bunch of Planetarium shows, which are nice and dark. Dark enough to kill any self-consciousness that might ruin my first kiss with Sallie. I want that first kiss to be awesome, not awkward.

All I needed was Sallie to say yes.

She looked at me in the hall this afternoon, smiled, and said, "Sure."

So tomorrow I'll be making my move. I just hope I don't end up staring at condemned buildings and brick walls.

SALLIE

It was bothering me so much I had to Google it so it would stop bothering me. *"Why is he taking so long to kiss me?"* Actually, all I typed was "Why is he taking so long to" and Google figured out that the rest of it was "kiss me." And just to be on the safe side, Google also offered "propose," "commit," and "reply." Apparently, guys take a long time to do a lot of things. "Reply" got the most results, with just over 189,000,000. So I guess there are 189,000,000 girls (and guys) out there right now, waiting for some guy's answer. "Kiss me" got the least amount of results, with 14,500,000. (The completionists out there—this one's for you: "Commit" came in second, with 125,000,000, and "Propose" came in third, with 75,000,000.) It was comforting to know that there are 14,499,999 other people out there who are dealing with what I've been dealing with for the last three months: the funniest, sweetest, most gorgeous guy I've ever met wants to do everything with me—talk, walk in the park, FaceTime, watch spaghetti westerns—except kiss me.

I'd been nursing a hopeless crush on Ulysses Gates since last year when we were both in Mrs. Lorimar's English class. Uly— that's what everyone calls him (pronounced "Yoo-lee")—has a beauty that sort of sneaks up on you. The first time you see him, you think,

"Hmm, not bad." The second time you see him, you think, "Wow, not bad at all." The third time you see him you think, "Damn, why hasn't anyone else stumbled across this treasure?" And the fourth time you see him you don't think anything—you *know* that this is the guy you want to give co-star billing on your life's marquee. In other words, he has Idris Elba's dark-brown skin, Michael B. Jordan's full lips, Tupac's intense stare, and Taye Diggs's megawatt smile. And whenever he touches my arm or my hand I turn into a human generator, filled with electric charges and currents that zig-zag and zag-zig and zig-zig and zag-zag.

I don't believe in fate or kismet or whatever the hell, but it must've been at least fate-*flavoring* (you know, like the movie-theater popcorn that doesn't have butter but butter-*flavoring*) that put the two of us in that terrible play together. Because if it wasn't for that play, I don't think I'd be one date away from calling him my boyfriend right now. You should've seen him on that first night we clicked. He was so hot, standing there on the staircase, laughing at my dumb jokes, cranberry juice all over his white waiter's uniform. And that's another thing: most people look like pathetic bums with spilled cranberry juice (or any kind of juice) all over their clothes, but that night I was looking at the first boy who managed to make spilled cranberry juice work *for* him instead of against him: he looked great in white and red. Well, actually, white, red, and brown, if you include his skin.

We got closer and closer after the play, but never close enough to kiss. I tried to give him some signs that I was kiss-friendly—I put my head on his shoulder, I touched all the PG-rated areas of his body, and yesterday I even kissed him on the cheek; but either he suffered from street-sign color-blindness (where green lights and red lights and amber lights all look gray) or I sucked as a sign-giver.

Near the end of last month, after Uly and I had been "dating" for about two months, I came THISCLOSE to asking him why he hadn't kissed me yet, but I decided not to because the problem with asking for an answer is that, 90 percent of the time, you'll get an answer, and what if I didn't like the answer? What if his answer was "You're pretty but, um, your breath, like, really smells"?? What if his answer was "You're smart, but I like girls who are smarter"?? What if his answer was "You're funny, but I don't like girls who are funny"?? And, oh my God, what if his answer was "I'm into you, just not *that* into you"?? That last one is, hands down, the rabid pit bull of the bunch because every woman over 12 and under 112 has heard a variation of that from at least one guy (or girl) at some point in her life. And I really don't feel like hearing it again anytime soon.

But that was then.

And this is today.

And today is what I want to tell you about.

So Uly and I went to Franklin Institute, a museum in Philly. (It's sort of like a poor man's Epcot Center, but nobody wants to come out and say it.) He kept saying he wanted to check out the first Planetarium show at three-thirty and that was fine with me, but we needed to do something for the hour-and-change before three-thirty, so I suggested we check out the *Inside the Human Body* exhibit.

So we checked it out. And I have to admit: it's supremely bacon. It's this large-scale—like, *giant*—replica of the human body. It's so big that you can walk into it and up it and across it and whatever the hell. This thing actually has *stairs*. So Uly and I entered at the foot—like, *literally*, the foot—and we walked up the stairs, past the ankle, past the calf, past the knee, and so forth. And while you're moving your body through The Body you can hear sound effects that match whatever body part you're in—growling for the stomach, thumping for the heart, swishing liquid for the neck, and so forth. There's also a recording that tells you all these scientific facts about the particular body part you're moving past or walking across (if you choose to get off the steps).

The trouble—if you want to call it that—started when we got to the stomach. (And by the way, they conveniently suffered sculptural amnesia when it came to the groin area because there is no groin area—it just goes from the thigh straight to the stomach.)

So Uly and I get to the stomach and, all of a sudden, this little girl down in the calf has a stomach problem of her own and throws up all over everybody in the calf and everybody down in the ankle and everybody down in the foot. There are groans (mostly from the kid's parents). There are curses (mostly from the people in the ankle and foot). There are cries (mostly from the girl, and probably the other people stuck in the calf section with her). And there's an announcement that breaks through the growling and the drone of the scientific-facts recording to announce: "Everyone on the west end of the human body, may I have your attention please. Due to a minor accident on the lower level, we need to ask all of you to remain where you are until the issue has been resolved. We expect to continue moving you along in approximately five minutes. Thank you."

Because Uly and I got to the stomach before everyone else we're now the only ones in the stomach. We look at each other, raise our eyebrows, and smile. We've never been together in such a cramped space before and it's weird—the wonderful weird, not the weird weird.

Everything is quiet. Well, sort of quiet. While the scientific-facts recording has stopped, the gastric growling has been turned back on. Every so often we can hear echoes of controlled commotion coming from the calf.

After a moment, Uly says, "Ask me why we shouldn't get mad right now."

With a smile, I say, "Why shouldn't we get mad right now?"

He motions to the surrounding walls, which are draped with

beige and pink ropes and coils standing in for the large and small intestines, and he says, "Because we don't want to turn this into an upset stomach."

I grab my head, chuckle-groan, and say, "Oh my God, that was so lame!"

He smirks at me and says, "Oh, like you can do better!"

I say, "I can do much better."

He says, "Let's hear it."

I pull out the pack of strawberry Twizzlers he bought me earlier and I say, "Ask me why we shouldn't smack these walls with our candy."

He says, "Why shouldn't we smack these walls with our candy?"

I say, "Because we don't want to give this stomach a bellyache."

His eyes go wide and he says, "And *I* was lame??!! That was so corduroy I can see lines on your tongue!"

Laughing, I say, "No, but mine was clever! It worked on, like, two levels—candy really causes a stomachache, and I added smacking, which can also cause pain."

"Oh, like your jokes," he says.

With a mock frown, I say, "You know something? I can't stomach this anymore."

I turn around and head toward the stairs leading to the next level, but he quickly takes my arm and says, "No, don't go." He gently pulls me closer to him.

"You want me to stay?" I say.

He nods and says, "I want you to stay."

I say, "How much do you want me to stay?"

His smile fades. He looks into my eyes. Moves his face closer to mine. My heart starts beating louder than the sculptural one on the floor above us.

"This much," he says. He moves his lips to my lips.

And we kiss.

And his kiss feels like the first time I ever ate raspberry crème brûlée: I knew it was going to be good, but I didn't know it was going to be that good.

His lips feel like plush pillows flying across a lemon-lime sky, propelled by a July breeze.

We kiss for a long time that still doesn't feel long enough.

When his lips leave my lips, I murmur, "Um, okay, I guess I can stay."

He gives me that megawatt smile that could light up a hundred universes and kisses me again. This time I loop my arms around his neck and as I do it I can feel the back of my hand brush against one of the pink small-intestine coils that hang from the wall and it feels more slippery than I would've liked but I don't care. I'm kissing a boy who can make me feel like a walking generator. I'm kissing a boy who can turn a cranberry-juice spill into a fashion statement.

Uly and I probably would've kissed forever if the Human Body exhibit's announcer hadn't brought us back to the world by announcing "Everyone on the west end of the human body, may I have your attention, please: the issue on the lower level has been resolved and you can now resume your body tour. Thank you, and sorry for any inconvenience."

If that announcement didn't convince Uly and me to stop our kiss, the sound of the calf people's footsteps on the stairs as they made their way to our stomach did. So we stopped the kiss, took each other's hand—interlacing our fingers—and climbed up to the next level. And while we were up there in the heart all I could think about was the stomach. And while we were in the neck all I could think about was the stomach. And while we were in the head all I could think about was the stomach. As we navigated the rest of the exhibit Uly and I tried making small talk and even smaller jokes about the different body parts: we talked about how it would be so meta if the nauseous girl upchucked again while she was in the stomach area and we tried doing some pun stuff with the head—something to do with Brain Freeze and Head Rush, but our hearts weren't really in it. Every time we looked at each other you could sort of tell that all we wanted to do was get back to that kiss. I know that's all I wanted to do.

After the Human Body exhibit, we immediately left the museum. And when we got back on the PATCO train, we got back to that kiss. We picked a seat at the back of the train, and while my body rode the train, my lips rode the plush pillows again. Lemon-lime sky. July breeze. We kissed from Philly back to Jersey and when we got back to Jersey we went to Newton Lake Park and kissed some more. It was like we'd been on some kind of hunger strike for the last three months, but instead of No Food, it was No Kisses; and now that the strike had ended, we couldn't gorge fast enough or frequently enough. And the best part about a Kiss Binge is that you never get full or get indigestion. And while your heart burns, you don't get heartburn.

While we were sitting in the park, leaning against a tree, we briefly put our Kissing Marathon on pause and lazily stared at a lonely merry-go-round, keeping our fingers interlocked. After a moment, Uly sort of laughed.

I looked at him and smiled. "What?"

He said, "You know why I wanted to take you to the Planetarium? I was planning on kissing you there."

I said, "Really? The Planetarium?? Why?"

Tucking a strand of hair behind my ear, he said, "I thought it could be, you know, romantic—kissing under the night sky and stars and space . . ."

I said, "But it's so pitch-dark in there you can't even see what you're doing. You're liable to end up making out with Saturn; or even worse, the eighty-five-year-old woman sitting in front of you."

Uly said, "Whoa, I'm down with the whole cougar thing, but eighty-five? When you gotta go to the nursing home to pick up your date, you might've overdone it a little."

I laughed and snuggled closer to him. "So you like older women, huh?"

He said, "Only if they're forty-five, dress up in a business suit, spill cranberry juice all over me, and give me a dollar with a purple Post-it note attached."

I looked up at him and smiled.

And the Kissing Marathon continued.

As always, he walked me home and as he walked me home I couldn't help but think that we had passed two invisible signs. One that said: YOU ARE NOW LEAVING THE FRIEND ZONE and another one that said: WELCOME TO THE BOROUGH OF RELATIONSHIP. And it was exciting and scary. But mostly exciting. I've had boyfriends before. Actually, I haven't. I've had crushes on boys and some of them had crushes on me too and a couple of those crushes went from caterpillar to chrysalis—maybe we always ate lunch together or held hands in a crowded auditorium while watching some corduroy show or gave each other a quick kiss at our lockers—but none of them ever turned into a butterfly. This thing with Uly is the first one that's turned into a butterfly.

When we got to the door of my house, I turned around to face him. "So," I said.

"So," he said.

After a moment, I asked, "So, on a scale of one to four, how would you rate this date? Let's rate it *Good, Bad and Ugly* style."

He said, "Okay . . . I give it . . . Four Dead Handcuffed Prison Guards Out Of Four . . . How about you?"

I said, "Hmm . . . I give it . . . Four Handcuff-Breaking Trains Out Of Four . . ."

He kissed me one last time, then whispered, "Bye."

"Bye," I whispered.

"I'll call you tonight," he said.

I said, "Okay."

I watched him walk down the block and disappear around the corner.

I was so excited I could hardly move but I eventually managed to move enough to make it inside the house and into the living room where three people were sitting. It took a few blinks for me to remember that I knew these three people: one was my sister, one was my sister's boyfriend, and one was the sister of my sister's boyfriend.

Leona's boyfriend Wilk Watercutter—his full first name is Wilkins but everyone calls him Wilk—was sitting on the arm of the couch, counting flyers with a picture of my sister's face on them. His sister Ashley was hunched over the glass coffee table in front of the couch, sliding a thick screeching marker over a huge sheet of poster paper that looked more sheet than paper because it practically took up the entire table. Leona was sitting next to her, texting someone on her phone.

"Wow, look who still walks among us," my sister said, referring to me even though her eyes were on her phone screen.

"Who?" Ashley asked, looking up, her eyes glazed over and confused.

"Hey, Sallie," Wilk said, his eyes on the flyers.

"Hi, Sallie," Ashley said, moving her attention back to Leona's campaign poster.

"Hey, guys," I told them.

"Where ya been?" Leona asked me.

"Just hanging out with a friend," I told her.

She followed me into the kitchen.

"Where's Lady M?" I asked her. Lady M is what we call our stepmom, mainly because she's so bacon.

"Went to Staples to get me some more poster paper," Leona said.

Taking an apple out of the refrigerator, I said, "Wow, you're really going through with this, huh?"

"Going through with what?" she said.

"You know, running for president," I said.

She said, "Of course I am. I told you last week I was gonna kick off my campaign this week. We had, like, a two-hour conversation about it upstairs."

"We did?" I said, biting into the apple, trying to remember.

She said, "Yeah, we did." Narrowing her eyes, she said, "What's going on with you?"

I said, "Me? What do you mean?"

"You've been acting all dazy and foggy since Christmas. If you were cool enough, I'd think Oxy. But the strongest thing in your medicine chest is Clearasil, so who is he?"

Coyly smiling, I said, "What makes you think it's a 'he'? For all you know, maybe it's a 'she.'"

"Yeah, right. You wouldn't last two episodes on the Dyke Channel. You can barely drink from juice boxes that have a straw."

"Why you gotta be so mean?" I asked her. "And that's not a nice word."

She said, "Are you gonna tell me or what?"

I said, "It's on a Need To Know basis, as in I *need* to say *No* to you."

"Why the big secret?" she asked.

"Why the big nosy?" I asked.

She said, "Okay, but I'm gonna find out sooner or later. When you're living under the same roof, secrets last about as long as my ex-boyfriend."

"Oh I'm sure I can keep this secret longer than thirty seconds," I assured.

"Why you gotta be so mean?" she said.

I laughed and went back to munching my apple. Leona started talking again but, to be honest with you, I was just barely listening.

As I gazed out the window all I could hear was the Franklin Institute's growling stomach as Uly kissed me for the very first time.

"*. . . then she messed up that poster and we had to do another one . . .*"

As my teeth dug deeper into the apple all I could feel on my lips wasn't the apple but his full, soft, soft lips.

"*. . . wanted to use brown markers but I told her red would be better . . .*"

As I gazed out the window all I could see wasn't the window but his intense dark eyes beaming at me like I was the . . .

"*Sallie . . . . !*"

Like I was the only one in the . . .

"*Sallie . . . !!!*"

Like I was the only one in the wor—

"Sallie!!!!!"

I moved my eyes from the window to my sister, who was standing there, glaring at me.

"Hm?" I said.

She said, "Oh my God. Seriously?"

"What?"

"Were you tuning me out just now? Seriously?"

"Hm? Um, no. No."

"Seriously?" she said. "This guy has gone *that* viral inside your head?"

"Hm? No, no. I'm sorry. Okay, I'm listening now. What were you saying?"

Leona snapped, "You know what? Forget it. You don't really care."

She was about to storm out of the kitchen when I grabbed her arm and pulled her back.

"No, don't go," I said, pulling her back some more. "Seriously. I'm sorry, Lee. I was just—I had something on my mind. But I'm okay now. Seriously."

I pulled a chair out from the table with more fanfare than

a chair probably needs, placed it squarely in the middle of the kitchen, grandly sat down, and looked up at my sister, who was eyeing me skeptically.

"Seriously," I said. "The only one in my world right now is you, I swear. I'm here. You're here. We're here. And I'm listening. Speak."

And I was serious. My sister's kitchen confrontation made me realize just how much property Uly had been renting in my head over the last couple of months. It was like he and I had been on a two-month vacation on our own little island—an island paradise, really—and now it was time to get back to the work of life. I really didn't want to go back to work, but I knew our island wasn't going anywhere and that it would patiently wait for us to return whenever we were ready, and I knew I'd be ready again in about ten minutes. So the least I could do was work this five-minute shift and listen to my sister.

"Speak," I repeated to my sister, who was still giving me a skeptical stare-down. It was weird to see her standing so still. Leona usually seems to run on some kind of motor; she's almost constantly moving—pacing, tapping her foot, drumming her fingers, running her hands through her hair; when that motor stops, it's usually because somebody screwed up, badly. And this time I guess it was me.

"You're sure you're here now?" Leona said.

"I'm here," I assured.

"Okay." She started pacing the kitchen. The motor was on again. "I've been thinking about dumping Ashley as my campaign manager."

I said, "Why? What did she do?"

Leona said, "She's breaking my life. She keeps messing up my campaign posters. Look at this." For the first time I noticed that she'd been tightly grasping a long rolled-up tube. She unrolled it and showed me a campaign message written in red marker:

WONDERS OF THE WORLD:
1. Viagara Falls
2. Leona Walls

"Oh my God," I said.

Leona said, "See what I'm dealing with here? I got a campaign manager who reaches the age of sixteen and mistakes a beautiful famous Canadian waterfall for a boner pill, and can't even spell the boner pill right. She's breaking my life!"

I popped up from the chair and touched her arm. "Okay, calm down." I didn't want Ashley to hear from the living room.

Leona kept pacing. "The first fucking week and already my campaign is off the rails. Because of her! I have to constantly check after her to make sure she didn't screw anything up. Pretty soon I'm gonna be getting busier and busier with the campaign and I'm not gonna have time to spoon-feed her and wipe her chin with a bib and tuck her in! I don't have time for this! She's gotta go."

Touching her arm again, I said, "Okay, calm down. Have you tried talking to her? Maybe you could just tell her nicely that—"

"I don't have time for that!" my sister snapped. "I don't have time to tell a sixteen-year-old that the place where a bunch of water goes down isn't the same as a product that makes a bunch of dicks go up!"

"Would you keep your voice down!" I said, trying to keep my own voice down.

"Anybody who doesn't know that by now is somebody who shouldn't be my campaign manager!" She suddenly stopped pacing. "But here's the thing: see, if I fire her, then Wilk's gonna give me shit for letting his sister go. You know something? Fuck it. If he does, then I'll let *him* go." She went back to pacing.

I said, "Okay, nobody's letting anybody go. Your boyfriend is staying. And your boyfriend's sister is staying. All you have to do is just sit her down and nicely tell—"

"Could you be my campaign manager?" my sister suddenly asked me.

"Me?"

With hope in her eyes, Leona said, "Yes! You'd be so bacon: you're organized, you're calm, you know the difference between Niagara and Viagra. Come on, be my campaign manager."

With a flattered smile, I said, "Come on, Lee, I can't be your campaign manager."

"Why not?"

"I don't know anything about politics."

Leona said, "Me neither. Politics? What does that have to do with running for president? How else do you think that dumb asshole Elvin Petraglia got elected last year? He's been president for five months now and nothing's changed in this school. Come on, Sallie—be my campaign manager. Please?"

Mentally grasping at the air for an explanation, I said, "I-I wouldn't even know what to do. What would I do?"

Leona said, "You'd just manage my campaign, and me. You know how much of a psychotic bitch I can be when I'm stressed out. You can calm me down."

I said, "What about your boyfriend? He can do that too."

My sister rolled her eyes and gave the suggestion a sort of dismissive wave. "He's just the fan. But you're the air conditioner. You're the only one who knows how to *really* make me cool. You know how to make *things* cool." She put her hand on my arm. The motor had long stopped. "Come on, Sal—don't break my life. Be my campaign manager."

I softly told her, ". . . I'm gonna have to pass, Lee."

She groaned.

I quickly said, "Only because I got a lot on my mind . . ."

Uly's sun-melting smile swung across my mind on a cortical rope.

"I know how much this campaign means to you, and I don't want to be so distracted that I end up screwing you over. That makes sense, right?"

My sister moved her disappointed eyes from the floor and just stared at me.

I hate to see her sad, so I squeezed her arm and offered, "Okay, look, how about this. I won't be your campaign manager, but maybe I could, like, help you with slogans or something."

My sister seemed to pep up a bit. "Actually, I could use some help with that. That last one sucked ass."

"What?—the 'Coming Attraction' one? I kinda liked it, actually," I said.

"Yeah, but I need to do better if I want to get people's attention!" she said.

I thought for a moment. And another moment. And another moment. Then I thought of something. "Hey, what about this . . ."

I took out my phone and wrote this on my Samsung Notes app:

You Know She's Right,
So Be A Leonite!

When I showed it to her, she sort of gasped and looked at me with smiling eyes. She said, "Oh my God, Sal—that is so kick-ass."

"Really? You think so?"

"I *know* so!" she said. "Leonite!"

"Right," I said. "That could be the name for anyone who likes your message and decides to vote for you. Sort of like a Leona follower—a Leonite. You could even set up a Twitter page and make it into a hashtag or something."

"Hash Tag *Be A Leonite*!" she joyfully confirmed.

"Right," I confirmed.

"Leonite! I like that! I love that!! Oh Sal, you so rock my

life!" She kissed my face and ran out of the kitchen into the living room. I overheard her tell Wilk and Ashley, "Guys, we got a new slogan . . . !"

I turned to the counter and spotted my half-eaten apple, which had gone oxygenation-brown from accidental neglect. I tossed it in the garbage. The kitchen was so quiet now. I picked my phone back up. And I sent him a text: Miss you already.

After not even a minute, he texted back: Missed you when I said goodbye.

I smiled and looked back out the window.

My phone buzzed. This time, a long buzz. It was Dandee, my best friend.

Smiling, I picked up my phone and said, "Hey!"

In her usual deadpan voice, Dandee said, "You sound weird. Like you're too happy or something."

I couldn't wait to tell her about the stomach.

I couldn't wait to tell her about the Kiss.

I couldn't wait to tell her about the plush pillows and the lemon-lime sky.

I couldn't wait to tell her that it was now official: I had a boyfriend.

But instead I told her, "Dandee, I just ate the most amazing apple I've ever eaten in my life."

She said, "An apple? You got issues."

I laughed, and we talked about a bunch of stuff, but none of the stuff I really wanted to talk about.

Why didn't I tell my best friend that Uly and I are now official?

Was I afraid that telling her we're official would jinx us and make us unofficial?

I wish I knew.

| ULY

Okay, check it out: I'm starting to think staircases don't like me anymore. Ever since that one staircase showed me love that night my girlfriend and I first clicked, it's like all the staircases at my school held a meeting one day and decided that their new mission in life is to kick my ass. I already told you what happened last week when I tripped on that flyer and fell down the stairs and almost broke my damn back. Then yesterday I was going down the stairs on my way to History class when my hand slid through something slimy on the banister. I don't want to think too hard about what it was, but I swear I'd never washed my hands as many times as I did that morning.

Then there was today.

Things started out bacon as hell. Sallie and I fake-bathroom-pass'd our way out of Study Hall and met up at the top of the stairwell on the west side of the school, near the elevator. And we just hung out there, kissing, holding hands, and joking around. These "bathroom breaks" of ours are taking longer and longer and I know it's just a matter of time before our teachers legit shut us down, but we didn't care. After a while we got to talking about

the theme song to that old TV show *Diff'rent Strokes*. I don't know
how many of you know about it, but for those of you who don't, it's
about this rich white guy who adopts these two poor black boys—
they're brothers—from Harlem. It's not my favorite show, but Sallie
and I agree that it's good for a laugh or three. So anyway, we got to
talking about the part of the theme song that says the two brothers
are so poor that the only thing they have are jeans. Sallie and I got
to focusing on that last word.

She said, "I know the word is jeans, as in dungarees. But you
know what's cool? It could also be 'genes,' like g-e-n-e-s. Like,
those two brothers have nothing but their DNA, the biological
stuff from birth that'll always link them, even when they're apart
from each other. You know: they're brothers, through and through.
It's actually really beautiful, if you think about it."

With a cynical wince, I said, "Yeah, I kinda feel you on that,
but, real talk? I don't think a bunch of TV theme writers were
thinkin' about Biology when they wrote that song. And even if
they were, they probably knew the audience wouldn't. You know
how it is with TV: they gotta keep things dumbed down for the
masses. So when they needed a word that rhymed with 'means'
they probably thought about havin' nothing but pants, which led
to 'jeans,' and they stuck that in and probably never gave it a
second thought."

"Yeah," Sallie said; there was a slight sadness rocking her tone.
"You're probably right. But I really, really wish they picked that
word because of the double meaning behind it. I don't know. I guess
I just want to believe I live in a world that can be deep like that."

"Yeah, me too," I said. *But we don't* is what I wanted to add,
but I really wasn't up for being a Debbie Downer at that moment.

Sensing that we'd way outstayed our bathroom break, we took
each other's hand and started heading down the staircase.

Sallie said, "Jeans and genes—what's that called again? Homonyms?"

I said, "Nah, homonyms are when the words are spelled exactly the same. I think the other one is homophones, when the words are spelled different."

Sallie said, "Homophones!"

I said, "So does that mean words like, say, 'chair' and 'biscuit' are *hetero*phones?"

Sallie laughed. "Heterophones. Doesn't that sound like some cheesy telephone dating service?"

By now we were at the bottom of the stairs. I said, "Yeah. I can hear the commercial right now: 'If you're feeling lonely and straight—but mainly straight—just pick up that phone and call Hetero—'"

Suddenly the staircase door flew open and whacked me in the shoulder, knocking me way to the side and off my feet. As I went down, the corner of my eye caught what looked like two black girls clenching each other in a hostile hug. One had the other's head in a headlock, and the second girl's arms were wrapped around the first girl's waist. As I hit the stairwell's floor they hit the stairwell's steps and tumbled down them, never letting each other go, all the while spitting muffled curses at each other through clenched teeth.

"Oh my God . . . !" Sallie yelled. She knelt over me, her expression tight with shock and concern, and said, "Are you okay?"

Trying to ignore the sharp pain in my shoulder, I nodded, sat up, and motioned my head toward the two fighting girls. "I better get in this . . ."

Pulling me back, Sallie said, "No! Are you crazy? You wanna lose your head??"

Before I could say anything, Sallie—keeping her hold on me—yanked open the stairwell's door and called out, "HEY, WE NEED HELP! THERE'S A FIGHT IN THE STAIRWELL! FIGHT IN THE STAIRWELL!"

The two girls didn't seem to hear Sallie's screams. By now they were each trying to pick up and body-slam the other to oblivion. I recognized both girls—one is a senior and the other is a junior—but I don't know them well. I tried to move toward them again, but Sallie pulled me back.

The door swung open and a brown blazer and green tie flashed by. It was Mr. Austin. He whizzed past Sallie and me and pounced on the girls, grabbing the backs of both of their shirts. "Lakaya! Natasha!—stop it! That's enough!" he pleaded.

Then something happened that I still can't believe.

Lakaya and Natasha, their faces contorted with blind rage, started beating the shit out of Mr. Austin. Lakaya knocked him to the steps and started whacking his face with her fist while Natasha stomped him over and over again.

By now a crowd had gathered in the stairwell and it wasn't long before Mr. Melendez and Mr. O'Shea, the school's two security guards, dove in and pulled the two girls off Mr. Austin.

The cops ended up coming. And so did an ambulance. The girls were arrested and Mr. Austin was sent to the hospital. I'm telling you: it was drama without a comma, real talk. The news spread through the school that morning like a virus with rabies and mostly everybody's face was rocking the same shaken, dazed expression. The halls got more quiet than usual, and kids zombie-walked to their classes.

But here's the thing: The stuff I just told you? That was just today getting warmed up.

The real Punch-time was at lunchtime. No actual punches were thrown, but I saw and heard something in that cafeteria that felt like a blow to the belly, and it all but took my breath away. Maybe it wouldn't have been so bad if Sallie was with me, but she had to take a makeup Chem test and I had to eat lunch by my damn self. Well, I wasn't really by myself; I had my default peeps by my side—my best friend Marilyn Ramirez and a couple of my other homies, but it wasn't the same without Sallie.

"What was the fight about?" my boy Rahkeem asked us.

"Nobody knows," my other boy Cecil said.

"Probably some dumb shit," Marilyn said.

"I heard they fucked up Austin real bad," Rahkeem said.

Marilyn said, "Yeah, but right before lunch I heard Ms. McCormick say he's gonna be all right. He's gonna be in that hospital not even a minute. They mainly just had to stitch up his face."

"Damn, that's still bad," Rahkeem told Marilyn. "You soundin' like he had to go in for a teeth cleanin' or something. Getting your face stitched up is some hardcore shit."

Marilyn said, "I know that. I just meant—it's not like he's critical or anything."

"Yo, check it out," Cecil said, pointing at the front of the cafeteria. "Goddess alert."

I looked where he was pointing and saw Sallie's older sister Leona holding a microphone at the lectern where Mr. Rezigno the vice principal usually stands whenever he wants to make mid-lunch announcements.

Leona. A lot of people think she's really pretty, and I ain't gonna front: she is. But she's what I call Boring Beautiful; she's pretty in a predictable way: she's got the blond hair, the blue eyes, the high cheekbones, and the tall, statuesque figure—she's easily about 5'10" or 5'11". She could actually be a supermodel if she wanted to. But that Classic Beauty stuff has never really appealed to me. I like the kind of beauty that throws you a curveball, like Sallie's beauty. She's got the "classic" blond hair but then you see those chocolate-pudding eyes of hers and you're like, "Whoa, what's up with that?" And she's not tall but she opens her mouth and you hear the deep, hypnotic voice of an Amazon warrior. That's the kind of beauty I like. Quirky, curveball beauty. Beauty that makes you wonder. Leona is a head-turner, but Sallie is a mind-turner.

Holding the microphone, Leona glanced at Mr. Rezigno, who

nodded that it was okay for her to start speaking. He stepped a few feet away, giving her the floor. Leona turned to all of us, and said, "May I have your attention, please?"

She really didn't have to say that, because the minute she took the mic she'd had at least half of the cafeteria's attention—you could tell by how quiet different areas of the room quickly got.

But some students were still talking, so Leona said, a little more firmly, but with a smile, "Everybody—your attention, please . . ."

Once the still-chatting peeps saw who it was, they got silent in a hurry too.

Now the whole cafeteria was so quiet you probably could've heard a librarian in Calcutta clear her throat.

Leona's smile got a little wider and she told us, "Thank you. For those of you who don't know, I'm Leona Walls—"

A bunch of guys called out her name, sports-fan style.

"—and I'm running for student-body president," she continued.

A few more students—mostly guys—let out some gravel-voiced cheers: "YEAH! LEONA FOR PREZ!"

Smiling, Leona did the Lowering motion with her hand to get them to clamp the clamor, but you could tell it wouldn't have bothered her that much if they didn't. But they did, and she continued: "Thank you . . . I actually want to talk to all of you about something really important. By now, many of you have probably heard about what happened this morning. And I know a lot of you have been worried. So first, let me just say: Mr. Austin is going to be fine. The hospital got in touch with the school about an hour ago and said that his condition is stable and that he'll be out in just a few days."

We all clapped.

When the applause died down, Leona said, "Yeah, that's definitely great news. By the way—if Hank Keller is in here, Mr. Austin still wants the late work by this Friday."

The cafeteria laughed. And Hank Keller's buddies started pointing at and *Ooh*ing him.

Leona's smile faded and she continued: "Actually, I wanna talk about something that's not so funny. I wanna talk about *why* Mr. Austin—a teacher we all love—is lying in a hospital bed right now. Actually, he's lying in that hospital bed for the same reason sophomore Suzanne O'Mally was lying in a hospital bed back in December. He's lying in a hospital bed for the same reason junior Roger Van Buren was lying in a hospital bed last October. Mr. Austin, Suzanne O'Mally, Roger Van Buren: What do they all have in common? They were all brutally attacked by students who have no business being at this school. Mr. Austin's face was pounded so hard this morning his skin opened up. Suzanne O'Mally's face was slammed into a wall so hard last December that her nose was shattered in not one, not two, but three places; and she couldn't spend Christmas with her family because she was too busy getting prepped for a second surgery. Roger Van Buren got kicked in the mouth so hard he lost so many teeth that he had to get fitted for a set of dentures. This guy is sixteen years old and he has to go through the same routine his seventy-seven-year-old grandfather goes through whenever he eats a meal . . . So now that we all know what these three people who were attacked have in common, let's talk about what their *attackers* have in common. Mr. Austin was attacked by Natasha Mitchell and Lakaya Jones. Suzanne O'Mally was attacked by Freda Walker. And Roger Van Buren was attacked by Marcel Evans. So, what do these attackers have in common? Well, I'm gonna answer that by asking this question . . ."

She kind of cupped her hand around her ear and said, "Do you-all hear that sound? Listen really hard now. Do you-all hear it?"

Confused murmurs rattled through the cafeteria as mofos looked around, wondering what the hell she was talking about.

"You don't hear it, do you?" Leona said. "I guess it's because I'm the only one who does. What's the sound? It's the sound of a forty-thousand-ton gorilla stomping through the halls of this school, trying to tell us something that nobody wants to hear or talk about. Well, I hear it and I'm gonna talk about it . . . Natasha Mitchell. Lakaya Jones. Freda Walker. Marcel Evans. *None* of them—I repeat, *none*—of them live in this town our school is in. Natasha Mitchell lives in Woodlawn. So does Freda Walker. Marcel Evans lives in Oakville. So does Lakaya Jones. So if they live in Woodlawn *and* Oakville, what on God's green earth are they doing going to this school? I'll tell you why: because many years ago, back in the 1980s, some despicable genius decided that our fair town of Collingswood should start what's called a Send & Receive relationship with the towns of Woodlawn and Oakville. What does that mean? It means that, because Woodlawn and Oakville are too small and poor to have a high school of their own, they send their kids here to our high school. Now, some of you might be thinking 'Okay. So what's wrong with that?' Here's what's wrong with that: ever since our town started this Send/ Receive thing, this high school has been steadily going down in quality. Our national ratings have gone down, our graduation rates have gone down, and our state funds have gone down. Oh, but you know what's been going up? The number of kids getting hurt every year; the number of kids getting sent to the nurse with a nosebleed because some Woodlawn kid didn't like the way you looked at him; the number of girls getting cornered in the bathroom and all her hair cut off because a bunch of Oakville girls were jealous her hair was longer than theirs; the number of kids getting pushed down the staircase because some Woodlawn or Oakville kid just happened to be in a bad mood that morning and you just happened to be the one standing closest to them . . . But it wasn't always like this. Knight High School used to be one of the most respected schools in New Jersey. Y'know, a few weeks ago, I interviewed some retired teachers who taught here, like, forty years ago. And you know what they told me? When they were teaching here forty, fifty years ago, there was maybe one or two fights every couple of years. And they said *none* of those fights ever ended with someone being rushed to the hospital. That was how nice it was here at Knight High before they started letting in the Woodlawn and Oakville kids. And now that they're here, look where it's gotten us: life-threatening injuries every couple of months, and now even a teacher is getting attacked. A teacher?? Teachers are the gateway to our future. So when teachers start getting attacked, our future starts getting attacked. So the writing is on the wall, everybody. Are we gonna read it? Well, I know I am. And so I'm choosing this moment to announce to all of you what my main mission is gonna be if you make me school president this June: come September, I will start putting pressure on this school's administration to *stop* the Send/Receive policy and send all Woodlawn and Oakville kids *back* to Woodlawn and Oakville where they belong!"

And then I heard something that gave me the gut punch I told you about earlier.

Applause.

The cafeteria clapped. Not everyone in the cafeteria clapped—I knew because I looked around—but, damn, it sure sounded like the whole cafeteria. Mixed with the clapping were choruses of Boos that cascaded out from different pockets of the room. But the Boos didn't seem to bother Leona; it was like the clapping boosted her so much that the Boos didn't matter.

She yanked the mic out of its holder and did an arc from behind the lectern so that the only thing between her and us was the air. She said, "And you people in here from Woodlawn and Oakville—I'm not trying to be a hater, I swear. I know some of you are okay. But too many of you are *not* okay, and we're simply tired of being okay with that."

More applause exploded from the cafeteria. Again, not

everybody, but enough to make your intestines feel like they had contorted into enough twists to make a pretzel say, "Goddamn." At that moment the cafeteria no longer felt like the familiar, cozy, comfortable place I'd eaten in for the last almost two years. It now felt like some invisible layer had been peeled away to reveal a cafeteria that had been on another planet all along, and instead of a student sitting among schoolmates, I suddenly felt like an extraterrestrial sitting among terrestrials who were angry at me for invading them.

You see, I live in Oakville. And so do the peeps who were sitting next to me—Marilyn, Rahkeem, and Cecil; none of those three are ever at a loss for words, but at that moment I caught them being just as stunned as me.

When the applause died down again, Leona said into the mic, "Today Mr. Austin got rushed to the hospital. If we don't start speaking up and doing something, tomorrow it's going to be *you*." She pointed at a random person in the cafeteria. "And the day after that, it's gonna be *you*." She pointed at another random person. "And the day after that, it's gonna be *you*." Another random person. "Well, I'll be damned if—sorry for cursing, Mr. Rezigno, I'm just being honest here—I'll be damned if I'm gonna just sit back and let some district with a PC fetish break our life. If you make me school president I pledge to do everything in my power to turn this school back to what it was before: a safe place we're all proud to actually call our school!"

This time the applause was so loud it vibrated the floor.

And right when Leona started talking again, the applause instantly died down. It was like she had every mofo under a spell or some shit. She said, "You know what we need to do? We need to turn Knight back to Day! Let's turn Knight back to Day! Turn Knight back to Day! Turn Knight back to Day! Say it with me!"

Sections of the cafeteria started chanting "Turn Knight back to Day!" About five or six people even stood up.

"What the fuck?" a shocked Cecil mumbled, to everybody and nobody.

Leona held up her hand, instantly quieting down the crowd. Then she said, "Turn Knight back to what?"

"Day!" the cafeteria said.

She said, "Turn Knight back to what??"

"Day!!" the cafeteria called back, a little louder.

Leona said, "TURN KNIGHT BACK TO WHAT????"

"DAY!!!!" the cafeteria called back, way the hell louder than before.

Then Leona said, "Turn what back to Day?"

"Knight!" the cafeteria called back.

Leona: "Turn what back to Day??"

Cafeteria: "Knight!!"

Leona: "TURN WHAT BACK TO DAY????"

Cafeteria: "KNIGHT!!!!"

Smiling, Leona said, "That's right! And it's easy to do. But you know what you gotta do first? Vote for me this June!"

As if on cue, two people popped up from the crowd, each holding up a sign. I recognized them as football player Wilk Watercutter—I think he's Leona's boyfriend—and his sister Ashley. They both started walking back and forth in front of the crowd, showing us their signs, and both signs said the same thing: YOU KNOW SHE'S RIGHT (on one side), SO BE A LEONITE (on the other side).

Leona pointed at Wilk and Ashley, nodded, and told the crowd, "That's right. Be a Leonite and vote for me. That's all you have to do. Vote for me this June, and, I swear, we will turn Knight back to Day! I'm Leona Walls—thank you!!!"

As the thunder of applause rained on her, Leona triumphantly handed the mic back to Mr. Rezigno, waved to the crowd, and walked out of the cafeteria, followed by Wilk and his sister.

Pointing at the doors Leona and her crew just left through, Rahkeem said, "Damn, she practically ran outta here."

"Yeah, so her ass wouldn't get beat, that's why," Marilyn said.

Still looking confused, Cecil said to everybody and nobody, "What the fuck just happened?"

I spent the rest of the school day in a dazed, half-depressed funk. I kinda felt the way I feel when an acquaintance dies. In this case, it wasn't a somebody that died, but a something. I'm not exactly sure what it was. I just know it died today.

I wanted to reach out to Sallie, but I knew she was going to be busy all afternoon with back-to-back tests. I wanted to talk to her so badly. To see her and touch her. There was a rainy day going on inside me and I needed to touch sunshine. I know that sounds corduroy as hell but I'm just keeping it 100.

I didn't get to walk Sallie home after school because it's Tuesday, the day she has Chem tutoring, so I got to walk home with nothing but my bad thoughts keeping me company:

Two girls nearly killed each other today. Both girls put a teacher in the hospital. One girl managed to get half a cafeteria to make me feel like an alien in my own school. And that girl's sister is my girlfriend.

Please believe: that long walk home was longer than usual today.

By the time dinner rolled around, I felt a little better. I'd gotten a little textual healing from Sallie about an hour earlier when she sent me this text: Just wanted to check in with you. God, it feels like we haven't talked in forever. How are you? I miss you.

I texted back: I'm okay. How was the Chem test?

She texted back: OMG, terrible. I'm so screwed. I'll call you tonight!

Just as my mood was starting to brighten, I noticed that my sister Regina's mood seemed to be stuck at Dark. But then again, my sister mainly has two moods: Crappy and Slightly Less Crappy. If she was a weather station, the forecast would always be either "Rain all day" or "Cloudy with a chance of rain." I can count on half a hand the number of times Regina has laughed. And the last time she smiled was . . . Hmm. I think it was a Thursday. Don't ask me the year.

She wasn't always like this. I think it started when our mom died four years ago. Regina was only thirteen at the time but I think she felt like she had to prematurely become the Woman Of The House and be the Family Rock that Mom had been to me, her, and our dad. Sometimes when I look at her it's like her shoulders are sinking from some kind of burden—I don't know the burden's color or height or shape; all I know is its weight, and my guesstimate would be somewhere north of five thousand tons. But check it out: she'd rather die than admit that it's killing her shoulders. That's just the way she is.

As for our dad, he's good people. Works as a construction supervisor. Loves us not by telling us but by feeding us and clothing us and keeping a roof over our heads. And you know something? That's fine with me. I'd rather have someone do "I love you" than just coo "I love you." He's one of those assembled-right, unbroken brothers you never hear about on the news: a single father who does his job, pays his taxes, and takes care of his kids without a speck of baby-mama drama in sight. That's what's up. He's stayed solo since Mom died, and I think he's done that for two reasons: 1. He knows Regina would probably give him a lot of shit if he ever remarried, and, 2. To quote him—"Sisters today got more issues than *Newsweek*."

Sometimes I wish he and I were closer. I'm not saying we're strangers at a bus station up in here, but it seems like we tend to run out of things to talk about after ten minutes. I think part of the problem is that he's heavily into sports, and I'm not. I'm more a movies, TV, and music guy. Maybe it's my imagination, but sometimes when he looks at me I can see slight disappointment, like as if he was all excited when he found out his second child was going to be a boy, somebody he could play catch with and go to football games with and obsess over baseball stats with . . .

only to find out that his only son is more interested in NBC than NBA. He actually seems to click more with my sister, who can go back and forth with him about sports for forever & two days. If you ever stumble across our dinner table it's usually the Dad & Regina Show and I'm the occasional guest star, usually hunched over my phone, chiming in with a low-caliber comment every few minutes.

But tonight that vibe was in reverse. Dad and I were talking to each other while Regina just sat there at the table, off in her own world. She'd actually been more quiet than usual since dinner started. As she brought our plates to the table—whenever I offer to help her set the table, she refuses, insisting on doing it herself—I could see that her mood was more rainy than cloudy. And as Dad and I talked about an incident we'd heard on the news—this Philly guy, hours before his wedding, sent a text to the woman he was cheating with, telling her he couldn't see her anymore, but he sent the damn thing to his fiancée by mistake—Regina never said a word; she just picked at her food (the food *she'd* made for all of us) like she couldn't remember how to eat.

When her quiet started getting too loud, Dad looked at her and said, "You been really quiet tonight, Jeen. You good?"

Regina kind of slid her plate away and said, "I've just been thinking about this thing that happened at school today."

"What thing?" Dad asked.

Regina looked at me and said, "Were you in the cafeteria when that girl gave that speech?"

Suddenly I felt guilty. And I wasn't sure why. I mean, my ass wasn't the one who gave the damn speech. "Yeah, I was there," I told her.

She said, "Why didn't any of you say anything?"

Dad said, "Wait—speech? What speech?"

Regina turned away from me and looked at our dad. "This girl at school—Leona Walls—gave this racist speech during lunch and nobody shut her down."

Dad's eyebrows went up. "Real talk? What did she say?"

Regina said, "They said she was like, 'All you people from Oakville and Woodlawn need to go back there and leave our school alone, because y'all are the reason it's not safe here anymore.'"

Dad's eyebrows went higher. "She said that?? Who is this girl?"

"Leona Walls," Regina said.

"What grade is she in?" Dad asked.

"She's a junior," Regina said. "She's runnin' for school president and I guess that was her opening speech. I hear she gave it both lunch periods. She better be glad I was away at my club meeting for the hour." She turned to me again. "I can't believe none of y'all did anything."

I said, "What were we supposed to do?" I could hear my voice's octave switch from low to defensive. "Jump on her and make a citizen's arrest?"

"People actually clapped," Regina told our dad.

"Really?" he said.

"But not everybody," I said. "Just as many people boo'd. So not everybody was feelin' her."

"Yeah, but *some* people were feelin' her," Regina said. "In this day and age, if a racist speech can make just *two* people clap, we got a problem."

Dad said, "I feel what you sayin', honey, but maybe the girl wasn't trying to be racist."

With a bitter smile, Regina said, "I love when white people 'try' not to be racist. You ever notice they never try hard enough?"

Dad said, "I know, but check what I'm sayin': maybe it wasn't a race thing as much as it was just a region thing."

I quickly piped in with "That's what I was thinking. I mean, you got some white kids who live in Oakville and Woodlawn, too. And you got some black kids who live in Collingswood."

Regina said, "Oh, come on, I know y'all ain't takin' it there. Yeah, there are white kids from Oakville and Woodlawn, but everybody knows that *90 percent* of the kids from there are black and Latinx. And Collingswood? You can count on half a hand the number of black and Latinx kids who live there. See, I'm hip to her game. She's using the classic maneuver of every modern-day racist: code language. If there's a book out there called *How to Relax and Be Racist Without Sounding Too Much Like It*, Code Language is probably Chapter Four. Oakville and Woodlawn are just code words for 'Not White.'"

Dad said, "Maybe, but maybe not, honey. There's no sense ruinin' your dinner over a maybe. The only way to know if somebody's really racist is by bein' inside their head, and if we could do that, we'd be in a thirty-room mansion in Tahiti, not a two-bedroom apartment in South Jersey." He pointed at her plate. "Come on, honey—eat the nice dinner you made."

Regina looked at her plate for a long moment. Then she shoved it farther away from her and said, "It just makes me sick to know she got away with that today. Ahh, the joys of being a beautiful blond girl in America." She wiped her mouth and got up. "I'll check y'all later."

She left the table and went to her room.

Dad and I looked at each other, kind of shrugged, and went back to our grub.

But I was having a hard time swallowing. I wanted to believe everything my father said, but I had this nagging feeling that my sister's words shared way more DNA with the truth.

While I was doing my History homework Sallie called me. We talked about our classes and what we plan on doing this weekend, but Regina's words kept leaving their muddy footprints all over my mind and I guess some of the mud was starting to drip down on my voice because Sallie suddenly paused in the middle of our conversation and said, "Uly, what's wrong? You okay?"

"Huh?" I said.

"You sound like you're worried about something," she said.

Oh, I'm fine. I've just been spending all day wondering if I'm dating the sister of a racist, that's all . . . If you know how to add that to a bowl of conversation without making a person gag, I sure as hell could've used you tonight.

I wondered if she'd heard about what her sister did. Was she not talking about it because she didn't know about it? Or did she know about it, but just didn't want to talk about it?

I had to find out. So here was my answer to her question: "I'm okay . . . Did you hear about your sister's speech today?"

She said, "Actually, I did. I guess you heard it, huh?"

"Yeah."

She said, "Was it as bad as some people are saying?"

"Pretty much," I said.

She said, "I'm sure there's been a misunderstanding."

"Have you talked to her yet?" I said.

She said, "Not yet. She hasn't come back home yet. I sent her a couple of texts but she hasn't answered. Don't worry—I'll talk to her. I'm sure it was a misunderstanding."

"Okay," I said.

As Sallie and I continued talking, the mental echoes of my sister's words kept competing with our damn conversation. The echoes got so loud at one point I actually expected Sallie to pause and say, "Wait a minute, what's that sound?" But she didn't.

SALLIE

I hate telling people it's my birthday, but it's my birthday today. I guess I don't like telling people because I'm thinking *they're* thinking I want them to make a fuss over me, and I really don't like being the target of fuss—though I don't mind a little fuss-flavoring.

There's something else that's today. Valentine's Day. Yep, my birthday and Valentine's Day have the same date on our driver's licenses (well, I don't have my driver's license yet, but I think you get the gist of it). Some people think it's supremely bacon to have a birthday on Valentine's Day; I guess it's because it's the official day of love, and what better day to have a birthday on? But that's sort of the problem. At first I was happy to share a birthday with Valentine's Day, but when I started getting old enough to feel lonely and sad whenever I was romantically unattached, that's when I realized the birthday gods had done me a disservice by scheduling me for February 14th. For the first time, I realized that, for the rest of my life, my happiness on my birthday would always depend on my happiness in the Romance Department. It's not so bad if your birthday is February 23rd or May 11th or August 8th. Those aren't days when love is a giant float that you see everywhere you turn, so you can still be happy on those days even if you don't have a boyfriend.

But I so wasn't depressed today.

And it's all because of a boy I poured cranberry juice on three months ago.

His text was the first text I saw when I woke up this morning:

S = Special, A = Amazing, L = Lovely, L = Loveable, I = Intriguing, E = Excellent. Uly = Happy. Sallie = The reason. February 14 = Happy Birthday, Sallie :)

That gave me my first smile of the day. Then about thirty seconds later, he sent this text:

And something you're probably going to hear a lot today: Oh, and Happy Valentine's Day! ;)

And that gave me my second smile of the day.

My third smile was when his phone call came about ten minutes later. We couldn't talk long because we had to get ready for school, but we planned to meet at Newton Lake Park this evening at six. We would've made it earlier but I had to go to Wilk's house right after school for a surprise party for Leona to officially kick off her campaign. And then it was off to my house for a much quieter, smaller celebration of my birthday; it would be just Lady M and me, and maybe Leona if her campaign schedule allowed it.

And speaking of her campaign: I've been trying to get some heavy-duty ear time with her since yesterday about her speech—the speech that everybody's been going *crazy* about—but I haven't had a chance. By the time she got back home last night, I was asleep, and when I woke up this morning Wilk had already picked her up and driven her to school so they could get an early start on putting up more campaign posters. It's like her motor has shifted into high gear and I'm realizing my own motor needs to shift into high gear just to keep up with her.

When I got to school I noticed that its walls weren't so much walls as much as they were big square panes for my sister's campaign messaging, which was all over the place: you couldn't walk more than ten feet without seeing her posters. Most of the posters said *TURN KNIGHT BACK TO DAY—VOTE LEONA WALLS THIS JUNE!* On some of those posters was a drawing of Knight High School sitting under a moon on one half of the sheet and a drawing of Knight High School sitting under a sun-and-birds-filled sky on the other half. Other posters had the slogan I came up with—*YOU KNOW SHE'S RIGHT, SO BE A LEONITE!*

As I walked through the poster-plastered halls, I felt this weird mix of pride . . . and something else. I was proud of my sister for coming up with a second, stronger slogan all on her own: Knight Back To Day—that's brilliant. And I was proud of her for working so hard with this campaign.

But that Something Else feeling stopped me from completely enjoying the Pride feeling. I'm not really sure what that Something Else was; I'm just sure it was the opposite of whatever stuff Pride is made of. Part of the reason I was feeling this way—actually, *all* of the reason I was feeling this way—is because of the dirty looks some students were giving me as I walked through the halls. And I knew it was because of my sister's speech yesterday. God, I wished she'd gone over it with me before she gave it, and I wished I'd heard it while she was giving it. But I had to take that stupid Chem test. From what I could piece together from Dandee and some other people, it was bad. I mean, telling the school that a segment of them shouldn't go to the school? You can't make that pretty even if you're a world-class stylist.

Somebody else who probably didn't find it pretty was Uly. When I talked on the phone with him last night I could tell he was upset. There was something different in his voice whenever the subject came up, so I tried to stay away from the subject.

All I knew this morning was that I needed to find Leona so I could find out exactly what she'd said and why she'd said it.

I had to wait all the way till after Period G before there was a Leona sighting. I saw her in the Second Floor hall, near the foreign-language rooms, while we were moving between classes. I practically had to pounce because when her motor's going, she's so fast the only way you can get her is by being more fast.

"Leona!" I said, running up to her.

She stopped and smiled at me. "Hey."

I said, "Damn, the Loch Ness Monster is easier to get a hold of. You don't answer texts anymore?"

She shrugged and said, "I'm a busy girl, Sal. Places to blow, people to knee, things to glue."

When I didn't laugh, she said, "What's wrong?"

I said, "What did you *say* yesterday? People are breaking my balls about that speech, and I wasn't even there."

My sister gave a dismissive wave and said, "Don't let 'em get under your skin. Haters are gonna hate, no matter what you do."

"What exactly did you say?" I asked.

"What everybody needed to hear," she answered. "I just said this school needs to stop letting the Woodlawn and Oakville kids come here. Ever since they've been here, this school has been turning more and more into a war zone: fights every day, people getting rushed to the hospital. If they wanna do that, fine; just let them do that to the schools in *their* towns. I mean, shit—our town is a safe place; our town's *school* should be a safe place too."

"Leona For Prez!" a couple of passing boys shouted at Leona in a drive-by greeting as they ran to class.

Leona smiled and waved at them then looked back at me.

I looked at my watch; I knew it was getting closer and closer to the Period H bell. I had just under two minutes to ask just enough questions to make sure my sister wasn't a racist. It probably wasn't enough time, but I had to make it enough. I leaned a little closer to her and sort of whispered, "But Lee, when you say stuff like that, don't you know how that makes you look?"

She nodded. "Like a girl who wants to go to a safe school."

I sort of whispered, "Maybe to some people. But to a lot of people, it makes you look like . . . Most of the kids from Woodlawn and Oakville are black . . . so when you say all Woodlawn and Oakville kids should stop going here, it's like you're saying all the black kids should stop . . . you know . . ."

Leona smirked and said, "Oh my God, you too? That so wasn't the point of my speech."

I challenged, "So most of the kids from Woodlawn and Oakville aren't black?"

She said, "Of course they are, but there are black students here who live in our town too and I didn't say anything about *them* leaving. All I said was Woodlawn and Oakville—those towns have white kids too! But everybody wants to go around, pretending like I was standing up there yesterday with a burning cross and a white hood, yelling 'All you black people—get out!!!' But that's just a bunch of haters, trying to twist my words around 'cause the truth gives them allergies."

Period H sonically told us it was tired of us talking.

"I gotta go," Leona said.

I nodded and said, "Okay, I'll see you at Wil—" I caught myself. She wasn't supposed to know that I was going to be at her boyfriend Wilk's place for her surprise party.

"Huh?" she said, her eyes squinted in confusion.

"I'll see you later," I said, saving the moment.

She hurried to French class and I hurried to Latin class, but Latin was the last thing on my mind as I watched Mr. Zampora talk about the ablative case of "discidium." I knew my sister had been misunderstood, but how could I get everybody else in the school to know that? By the time the bell rang fifty-three minutes later, I still had no answer.

I actually welcomed the distraction of going over to Wilk's house for Leona's surprise party after school. It was an impressive turnout—about twenty-five people, most of them her friends, some of them friends we've co-friended.

And of course our stepmom Lady M was there. The M is for Madeline. Leona and I decided to call her Lady M because we respect her too much to call her Madeline and the first letter of her name is M, which of course is also the first letter of Mom, and since she's been so much like a mom to us—loving us like we're her own instead of the rentals we really are to her, and still hanging in there with us even after our dad died five years ago—we decided that there's no other name for her but Lady M. She's a great stepmother, but she also would've been a great regular, non-step mother: she's loving but not smothering; she's concerned but not nosy; she doesn't set a curfew for us, but if we come in at three in the morning with a cut on our arm she'll clean the cut, put a Band-Aid on it, say, "Are you okay?", and, depending on our answer, she won't say anything else about it ever again; she's in her forties but wears a nose ring; she works as a paralegal but plays guitar for local bands. She's an aunt-flavored mother, a.k.a. the best type of mother.

As we stood in Wilk's living room, waiting for Leona to come, Lady M came over to me and kissed me on the head. "Hey, birthday girl," she said, smiling, then her smile faded when she didn't see my smile. "What's wrong?"

"Nothing," I lied.

She said, "I hope you know—we haven't forgotten about you. As soon as this is over, Leona and I are taking you back home for *your* celebration. Just the three of us."

"I know," I said. "It's not that."

"What is it?" she asked.

Before I could tell her about the Leona/Oakville/Woodlawn misunderstanding, my phone vibrated. A text from Wilk: We just pulled up to the house. I'm about to bring her in. You know what to do.

I quickly stuffed the phone back into my pocket and told the crowd, "Everybody—shhh!"

The crowd quickly quieted down.

I loud-whispered to them, "They're here now. Everybody to the den."

I led everybody to the den, which is almost as big as the living room. Actually, everything in Wilk's house is as big as the living room, including the bathroom. The rumor is that his parents are so rich they could misplace $10,000 and not notice for at least a week. I can't believe they send him to public school, with all the money they have; they have to be either cheap or clueless.

Once everybody was assembled in the den, I closed the den's door, and just as I turned around to go down the steps and join everyone else, everyone else shouted "SURPRISE!!!!" at me.

I thought my heart was going to stop. "What?" I murmured.

A grinning Wilk burst out of a closet in a corner of the den and then he pointed at the closet on the other side of the room. That closet's door slowly opened.

And out walked Leona, holding a big square cake with a lit 16-shaped candle on top. She was smiling at me.

Everybody clapped.

My sister walked over and handed me the cake. "Happy Birthday, Sal."

As I took the cake everybody clapped again.

I normally don't like surprises, but some surprises are so good at being surprising that you just have to like them. And I really liked this one.

"Wow, I don't know what to say," I said when I finally thought of something to say. I looked at everyone and said, "So the whole time, the campaign party was—"

"—a party for you," Shannon, a mutual friend of Leona and me, completed my comment with a smiling nod.

I looked over at Lady M and said, "Was this you?"

Lady M shook her head. "Nope. It was all Leona. She planned the whole thing."

I turned my eyes back to my sister, who was still standing in front of me with a smile.

"Wow, Lee, thanks," I said.

Wilk said, "Hey, I just got a text from the cake—it said: **Are you-all gonna just stand around, looking at me or are you gonna eat me?**"

Leona told him, "No, that wasn't from the cake; that was from your ex. She meant it for the football team but sent it to you by mistake."

Lady M interrupted the chorus of laughter and "Oohs" to say, "Okay, on that note, I think it's time to eat the cake." She pointed at the long table at the center of the den and said, "You-all take a seat, I'll get the plates. Ashley, why don't you go grab the cake."

Wilk's sister trotted over to me to get the cake. "Happy Birthday, Sallie!"

"Thank you, Ashley."

"So how old are you?" she asked.

"It's right there on the cake, Ashley," my sister said, pointing at the candle.

"Oh, yeah! Well, Happy Birthday!" She took the cake and set it on the table.

Wilk announced, "All right, let's get this party started! Hey, Jace, let's hear it!"

Crouched next to a laptop and a bunch of wires and speakers in a corner of the den, Jace tapped a couple of keys on the keyboard and within seconds the room was booming with Drake's "Nice For What."

As everybody started dancing, Leona took my arm, leaned closer to me, and said, "Hey, let's go out to the living room. I wanna talk to you."

She led me out of the den and into the empty living room where the music, so loud just seconds earlier, now sounded muffled through the walls.

My sister unzipped her purse and took out a rectangular present that was wrapped in pretty red paper with a cute white bow. She handed it to me and said, "So this is for you. Happy Birthday."

"Oh, wow. Thanks, Lee."

I gently tore off the wrapping paper and found a black velvet case in my hands. I opened the lid, and saw a gold necklace nestled inside the red silk interior.

I put my hand to my mouth and said, "No way . . . No way . . . ! Lee! What did you do? You didn't have to do this . . . !"

My sister shrugged and said, "You didn't want a Sweet Sixteen, so I figured I'd do this. Your sixteenth birthday is supposed to be special; it's supposed to be the Oscars, not the Screen Actors Awards."

I lifted the necklace from its red silk cradle and watched it undrape itself to reveal a pendant made up of a number and a series of letters, forming this: #1 SISTER. The golden pendant sparkled under the living room's lights.

I could feel tears coming to my eyes. "Wow, Lee . . . This is so beautiful . . . How much was this?"

Leona said, "None Of Your Business dollars and Don't Be Rude cents."

I laughed.

She said, "Here, let me . . ." She took the necklace from me, stepped behind me, and gently draped it around my neck. Then she stood in front of me again and nodded, appraising me with approving eyes. Then she took out her phone and held it up for me so I could see my reflection on the phone's black screen. The screen made it look like I was standing in a dark room and the gold necklace was the only thing glowing in the dark. "Look how beautiful you are," she said.

I smiled and touched the pendant again.

Leona nodded and said, "That's what's you've always been to me. I know I never say it, but I'm always thinking it."

Trying to keep my tears back, I said, ". . . I appreciate that."

She touched my face then she put her hands on my shoulders and gripped them with a soft grip. "Sal, when you really get down to it—you and I: we're all we've got in this world. Mom is gone. Dad is gone. And as great as Lady M's been to us, she's not blood. You and I—we're blood. You're the only one in this world I *really* trust. I mean, stepmoms—they're cool, but they can go rotten any minute. And boyfriends—they're beautiful, but they can go asshole any second. But sisters—when you can't trust your own sister, life is just hell with a heartbeat, you know?"

I nodded. "I feel the same way."

She said, "Remember when Dad died?"

I nodded.

She said, "I never told you, but right after he died, for the first time in my life, I felt like I didn't wanna live anymore. Mom was long gone, and now our dad was gone and Lady M had only been in our lives for just a couple of years at the time and she was pretty much a stranger to me. I just felt so alone in the world. Crying every night. And whenever you heard me cry you'd come to my room and lie down with me and we'd cry together. You'd put your arms around me and say, 'It's gonna be okay.' And you'd fix me soup and tea, and your tea *never* had enough sugar in it, what was going on with that?"

I laughed as I wiped away a tear.

She said, "But I didn't say anything. The tea doesn't have to be sweet when the person giving it to you already is. You so got me through that first month, Sal; you got me through that first *year*. It felt so weird to have my own little sister take care of me, but you did. And I didn't feel alone anymore."

Trying to keep my voice from shaking, I said, "I sort of feel like an asshole now. After all this, the gift I gave you for your six-teenth birthday *sucked*."

My sister said, "Don't beat yourself up—everybody needs a fifty-dollar gift card to Chick-fil-A at least once in their life."

I nodded. "Okay, go ahead, rub it in, I deserve it."

She laughed, then said, "Well, if you're *really* in the market for a belated sixteenth birthday present for me . . . why don't you be my campaign manager?"

The awkward silence was very silent and very awkward. When I finally remembered my tongue, I said, ". . . Lee, we already talked about this . . ."

My sister's grip on my shoulders got grippier. "Sal, you *know* how much I want this. You know how much I wanna be presi-dent. And already I can tell this campaign is gonna be a bumpy ride. I need someone who can be strong enough to ride shotgun with me, no matter how big the bumps get. And I'm looking at her. Please, Sal. Be there for me . . . like you were when Dad died."

I stood there, thinking. Thinking about my sister. Thinking about me. Thinking about Uly. Thinking about the gold necklace around my neck. Thinking about the word—and number—that hung from the necklace. Thinking about my father. Thinking about my mother.

Leona said, "I think you were born to be one, actually. People *love* my Leonite slogan, and that was you!"

When I still didn't say anything, she said, "If you don't do it, that'll leave me with Ashley. Are you really gonna do that to me? The other day I asked her 'Which streetlight means Go?' and she had to Google it."

I laughed. But my sister didn't. She was too busy staring at me with pleading, almost helpless eyes.

"Please, Sal . . ." Her voice was practically a whisper now. "Be my campaign manager."

After a moment, I said, "Lee . . ."

She seemed to stand straighter as she waited for my answer.

I said, ". . . It'll be an honor to be your campaign manager. Yes, I'll do it."

Leona joy-screamed then hugged me tight, put my face between her hands, and gave me a kiss on the nose. "Thank you, Sal! Thank you so much! With you in the passenger seat I know I can ride this car straight to a June win!"

I sort of held up my hand and said, "But Lee—just promise me you won't fire Ashley. Let her stay on—maybe she could be manager's assistant or something?"

Leona said, "Okay, I can do that." She quickly took my hand. "Come on, let's tell—"

I sort of held up my hand again and said, "Wait, Lee. Here's the thing: if I'm gonna be your campaign manager, you're gonna have to Swipe Left on saying the kind of stuff you said yesterday—you know, about the Woodlawn and Oakville kids. You can't say stuff like—"

"Oh yeah, we'll have plenty of time to talk about that." She pointed toward the den. "Come on, let's tell everybody the good news!"

Holding hands, we ran back to the den. And we told everybody the good news. And everybody cheered and clapped. And I did a little dancing. And a little eating. And a lot of thinking about whether or not I'd just made the right decision. And a lot of thinking about Uly and how I couldn't wait for our date to start. The closer it got to six o'clock, the more I looked at my watch.

At five-thirty I drifted over to Lady M and told her I had to go meet a friend. I purposely saved this news for Lady M instead of Leona because I knew Leona would've given me shit about it.

Lady M looked a little surprised but, thanks to her aunt-flavoring, not that surprised. She said, "Oh, okay. We understand. Happy Birthday again, sweetie." She hugged me.

And just as I was about to turn away from her she said, "Oh, and Happy Valentine's Day."

I smiled, remembering what Uly had said that morning, and thanked her.

It was a little weird to walk out of my own party, but when you have a guy like Uly waiting for you, isn't it more weird to stay at the party?

Leaving my surprise birthday party to go to my date with Uly was like leaving Six Flags to go to Busch Gardens. This birthday of mine wasn't even over yet and already I knew it was going to go down in the Sallie Archives as the most epic one ever.

When I got to the park Uly was standing there with a smile on his face and a pizza box in his hands. He was wearing my favorite jacket—I love the design: it's black, red, and green in a zig-zag pattern. I think he might be the best-dressed guy I've ever gone out with.

When I leaned in to give him a kiss he thrust out his hand, motioning for me to back up.

"Whoa, whoa, easy, easy," he said, pointing at the pizza box.

"What's *in* there?" I said.

"You'll find out," he said, then leaned carefully over the box to kiss me. Then he said, "So how was the party? Was she surprised?"

"Actually, her surprise party turned out to be *my* surprise party."

"Huh?"

I said, "The whole thing was a surprise party for me. My sister's idea."

Uly raised his eyebrows and nodded an impressed nod. "That's what's up."

I unzipped my jacket and showed him the necklace my sister had given me, and he looked even more impressed.

I said, "She can really be bacon like that sometimes." I wanted to say more about why he could trust my sister and why her speech yesterday was misunderstood, but it didn't feel like the right time. What felt more like the right time was finding out what the hell was inside that pizza box, so I asked him again.

He smiled at me for a long moment, then he slowly lifted the box . . . revealing the name SALLIE in big block letters carved into the cardboard and inside each letter block were paintings of my favorite scenes from *The Good, the Bad and the Ugly*, and each letter of my name was bordered with Skittles, my favorite candy; so really, my name appeared twice inside the box: in block letters and in Skittle pieces.

". . . You like it?" he asked, almost like he wasn't sure.

"Do I like it? I *love* it!" I pointed at my gift. "How did you do all of this?"

"Marilyn hooked it up for me," he said.

"Wow, I didn't know she was *this* talented. Did she want any money or anything?"

"Nah, we're bros from way back. And actually, she owes *me* money, but she's always broke as hell so she uses her art to Add To Cart, if you can feel me on that one."

"This is beautiful," I said, sliding my finger through the movie images in each letter, being careful not to mess up the Skittles line-up.

"I tried to get all your favorite scenes in there. I wanted to include the one where the cannon knocks Tuco off his horse, but Marilyn ran out of space."

"No, this is perfect, as is."

He said, "I mean, it's not exactly a gold necklace with '#1 Sister' on it, but I tried . . ."

I play-punched him. "Shut up. It's from you and that makes it perfect."

He gave me a sarcasm-ish smile and said, "Bullshit. Come on, if I gave you a chewed-up pencil with a bow on it you wouldn't think that was perfect. You'd look at that pencil and be like, 'Oh.

Okay. No, I like it. Um, so, Uly, I've been meaning to tell you—maybe we should start seeing other people.'"

Laughing, I play-punched him again and said, "Shut up! I wouldn't say that."

After joking back and forth for a few minutes, he handed me the pizza box so he could take a picnic blanket out of his backpack. He spread the blanket on the grass and we sat down on it. He took a candle and candle holder out of his backpack; he put the candle in the candle holder, lit the candle and stood it on the edge of our picnic blanket.

And we fed each other Skittles by candlelight.

Of course the February-evening wind kept blowing out the candle and Uly had to keep relighting it, but it was the most romantic thing I'd ever experienced. And actually, aside from the wind, the weather really wasn't all that bad, for February—otherwise there's no way Uly and I could've worn thin jackets and sat in the middle of a park at night, eating Skittles without shivering.

After we were done with the Skittles—and Uly was done relighting the candle for the seventeenth time—he stood up and said, "And now, it's time for Part Two."

I squinted up at him. "Part two?"

With a smile, he nodded and reached down for my hand. "We're going on a little trip."

"Where?" I asked.

"You'll find out," he said.

About an hour later we were stepping onto the pedestrian path of the Ben Franklin Bridge at the Camden entrance. Holding hands, we started walking across the bridge. We weren't walking two minutes before Uly abruptly stopped. "Whoa," he said.

"What?" I said.

He said, "I think this bridge is trying to tell you something, Sallie."

"Huh?"

He pointed at the railing on our left; hanging from the blue rail was a purple Post-it note, flapping in the wind. He took the note off the rail and said, "Look at this—it has your name on it . . . '*Dear Sallie*—'"

I looked at the purple square and he was right: *Dear Sallie*— was written on it.

"What the hell?" I said with a confused chuckle.

Looking just as confused, he said, "Maybe they're talking to another Sallie. But most Sallys have the 'y' at the end, not 'ie.' I guess we'll just have to keep walkin' and see what else it has to say . . ."

Smiling the smile of someone realizing they're about to play a romantic game, I nodded and walked along with him.

After a couple of minutes, he stopped and pointed to the right. "Wait, I think the bridge has something else to say . . ."

Hanging from the blue beam was another purple Post-it. He took it off and showed it to me. "*When I kissed you . . .*" he read. Then he looked at me and asked, "You think there's more?"

My smile got wider as we walked a few more yards. Then Uly stopped and pointed to the railing on the left. Another purple Post-it: ". . . *inside that empty stomach . . .*" he read. Then he looked at me and said, "Okay, now I *know* it's for you."

My heart started beating faster as we walked a few more yards. Uly stopped again and pointed to our right. Another purple Post-it hanging from the beam, flapping in the wind. "*. . . you filled up my heart . . .*" he read.

My body switched to human-generator mode as we walked the next few yards.

The next purple Post-it read: *I . . .*

The next one read: *. . . love . . .*

As we walked toward the next one, I was so excited my whole face started heating up.

We got to the next purple square, this one flapping from the blue beam: *. . . you.*

My hand was overflowing with all the love squares as we reached the midpoint of the bridge, where the final purple Post-it hung, flapping in the night air, the Philly skyline right above it.

This time Uly let me take the note off the rail. It read: *Happy Valentine's Day, Sallie—Love, Uly*

Tears filled my eyes.

Uly reached into his backpack, its strap slung across his chest, and took out a long-stemmed purple rose. And handed it to me.

I brought the rose to my nose. It smelled just like a red rose and I wondered how he got it to look purple but still smell red, but I was too speechless to ask. I looked up at my boyfriend. He was smiling at me, but this smile was different from all the other smiles he'd given me; this smile wasn't diluted; it was purely purebred: it wasn't mixed with other stuff like doubt or stress about homework or worries about what to say next. It was just my boyfriend smiling at me and only me.

When I finally remembered I had a tongue, I said, "Uly . . . I love you too."

And the Philly skyline watched us as we kissed.

When our lips unlocked, a bolt of guilt suddenly zapped my insides. I'd forgotten to give Uly *his* Valentine's Day gift! My mind mauled me with an image of a card sitting on top of a box with a chocolate mini-drum (he'd once told me that was his favorite instrument) sitting inside it, all of it sitting on the nightstand next to my bed. My plan had been to pick it up when I got back home from Leona's surprise party but since her surprise party ended up being my surprise party there was no reason to go back home and because I didn't want to be late for my date with Uly I rushed out of Wilk's place and completely forgot about the present.

The way I explained it to Uly was even more convoluted than the way I just explained it to you; you were spared my hyperventilation and half-sobs and seven hundred sorrys; but he understood.

"It's okay," he said.

"I just can't believe I— "

"—Sallie, I said it's okay. Calm down." He gently put his hands on the sides of my face like he was trying to squeeze me back to serenity. "It's cool, okay? You can just give it to me tomorrow."

That calmed me down. I finally got my breath back and nodded.

He said, "And anyway, you already gave me a Valentine's Day gift, back in November."

"What do you mean?"

He took out his wallet and plucked out a slightly dog-eared purple Post-it note and, with a grin, he showed it to me. I recognized my loop-heavy cursive handwriting right away: *The Good, the Bad and the Ugly?* the note read.

"The one that started it all," Uly said.

Giggling, I said, "I can't believe you actually kept that!"

His face turned serious, and he said, "I always will."

That made me kiss him again.

We wanted to walk the other half of the bridge, ending at the Philly side, but we both had a lot of homework to do, so we knew we had to head back home.

As we rode the PATCO back to Collingswood, our fingers interlocked, I decided to bring up the thing I really didn't want to bring up but knew I had to.

"So I spoke to my sister about that speech she gave yesterday and it was just like I said: the whole thing was a misunderstanding."

He looked hopeful. "Really?"

I nodded and said, "Absolutely. She told me she wasn't trying to say that all the black kids should leave Knight High. She was really just focusing on the Oakville and Woodlawn kids, and not all of them are black; some of them are white too. I mean, all she really wants is for our school to be safe. She really didn't mean any harm."

After a moment, Uly said, "Okay."

Even though he said "Okay" the look on his face didn't seem to say okay, so I added, "I mean, I told her she has to be careful how she says things, you know? Because people can take it the wrong way."

"Exactly," Uly said.

The unconvinced look on his face told me I had some more convincing to do. So I added, "Oh, and I meant to tell you—at the party she told me she wants me to be her campaign manager."

His eyebrows went up. "Oh . . . Really?"

I nodded. "Yeah. I think that's a good sign, you know? It shows that maybe she wants me to, like, help her not repeat the same mistake she made yesterday. So don't worry. I'll be there to make sure she does this whole thing right."

Uly nodded. "Bacon." He looked more convinced now.

But I knew I still wasn't finished. There was something else I had to say. Already I could feel my face getting warmer with shame.

I said, "And Uly . . . I probably should've told you this yesterday . . . but, um, on behalf of my sister, I'm sorry if her speech offended you."

Uly nodded and said, "I appreciate that."

He gave my hand a light squeeze and he gave my lips a light kiss.

I smiled at him, then I turned my smile to all the Passion Post-its from the bridge. Somewhere along the way they had gotten scrambled, so I carefully put them back in order.

ULY

I'm so glad Ben Franklin didn't betray a brother tonight. I didn't say anything to Sallie, but I was nervous as hell as I walked with her across his bridge. Check it out: in the afternoon, right after school, I went to the Ben Franklin Bridge to strategically place some Post-it love notes I'd written her for Valentine's Day so that I could bring her there later to see them. As I put the Post-its on the beams and railings, I had this bad feeling that the wind was going to knock them away by the time I came back with Sallie, so I Scotch-taped each Post-it for extra reinforcement. You know how it is with Post-its: their adhesive is mad wimpy. Post-its are basically the paper version of fair-weather friends: they'll stick with you while shit is mellow, but the minute shit hits the fan, they're more gone than Vaughn and out of there like Vladimir. Even with the Scotch tape in place, I was still afraid that the wind would be too strong for all the Post-its to hang in there and that a couple of them would get blown away, making my entire love message sound like something from Cookie Monster: *Dear Sallie, when kissed inside stomach, you filled life, love you, Happy*, and Sallie would be like, "What the hell?" But to my relieved surprise, all the Post-its were on point.

So a deluxe shout-out to Ben Franklin and Scotch tape: wherever you are, thank you for not making a brother look bad.

I know that message I wrote her was kind of corduroy, but a girl like Sallie can legit pull out the poet in you. I think every guy has an inner Walt Whitman. Even the most hardcore, most gangsta brother out there—you show him the right girl and I'll show you a guy putting a long-stemmed rose inside her favorite book while putting a bow on top of a box of chocolates while practicing a speech peppered with words like "hither" and "whither" and "yonder" and phrases like "let me count the ways" and "till we part." Maybe that's why those chocolates are called *Whitman's* Samplers?

When I got back home tonight I tried doing my homework but I was still in a Sallie fog, seeing her dark eyes on every page of the Algebra 2 textbook.

What kind of snapped me out of it was my sister, who kept pacing back and forth in front of the living room couch where I was sitting. She usually does that when she has some heavy shit on her mind. Finally I looked up and said, "What's up with the one-woman march?"

She looked at me and said, "Wanna do a CakeTalk?"

I could tell she wanted me to say yes so I nodded, closed my book, and got up.

We went to the kitchen and I gathered the pan, big bowl, and stirring spoon while Regina collected the eggs, butter, flour, vanilla extract, etc.

The CakeTalk is something she and I usually do on Tuesday nights, but sometimes we do it on other nights when something— it could be anything from a funny piece of scandalous gossip to a serious personal problem—is weighing on us too hard to wait till Tuesday. I guess you could say the CakeTalk really started when she and I were little and our mom used to talk to us about our day while she baked an after-dinner cake; Mom would do all the baking while Regina and I mostly watched but also handed her things as she needed them, all to the sound of classic Philly soul

(the O'Jays, Spinners, Harold Melvin & the Blue Notes, etc.)—
my mother's favorite music, which played on a CD boom box she
kept in a corner of the counter. When Mom got sick, Regina and
I continued the CakeTalk, mainly to fix her something that would
cheer her up enough to make her forget that she was confined to
a bed; but it also gave us a chance to be each other's therapist and
unload our feelings about the mom situation. After our mother
passed, Regina and I kept the CakeTalk going: mothers might go
away, but not problems, if you can feel me on that. So the Cake-
Talk is still in business, right down to the Philly soul music.

As Lou Rawls crooned "See You When I Git There" from my
sister's phone, which sat in a corner of the kitchen counter, she
cracked the eggs into the big bowl I held out for her.

After cracking the second egg, she finally spoke. "Lemme
ask you something. Leona Walls's campaign slogan—where you
stayin' on that?"

I said, "You mean the *You Know She's Right So Be A Leonite*
one?"

Regina said, "No, that other shit—*Turn Knight Back To Day.*"

I actually knew she was talking about that one the whole
time. I said, "Real talk? I'm not down with it."

Cracking the next egg, she said, "Yeah, me neither. But check
it out: when I went to Mr. Woolery today to complain, he was
all like, 'I don't see what's racist about it. The way I see it, she's
just using a play on words. The name of our school and the dark
time of day—Knight, night—and how she wants to symbolically
turn the darkness back to the opposite: brightness and hope.' And
so then I was like, 'Well, the way *I* see it is, she's trying to say
night is black and day is white, and let's turn this school white
like it was way back in the day, before it let in the Oakville and
Woodlawn kids, who are mostly black, and who she said should
be kicked out of this school in her speech the other day.' So then
he was like, 'Regina, I think you're reading too much into this.

I can't make a girl take down her campaign posters over some subtext that might not even be there. I can only go by what I see, and the poster plainly says Knight to Day, not Black to White.' And so we start goin' back and forth like that and after a while, I was just like, 'Fuck it' and left. I mean, I didn't actually say, 'Fuck it' to him; I didn't wanna get my ass suspended, but you know what I mean."

"Yeah," I said.

She cracked the last egg into the bowl and I started stirring the yolk into the flour and sugar and stuff while she swept a big block of butter up and down a cake pan.

Just to stay real here: I wanted to ask Sallie about that Knight To Day campaign slogan and why her sister had thought of something like that. But I didn't because I thought maybe I was overthinking it and being paranoid, mistaking charm for harm. Sometimes a baseball bat just wants to play baseball and not beat somebody's brains out.

But when I heard Regina's complaint tonight it was kind of a relief to know I wasn't the only one who saw a fly in the milk Leona was making the school drink.

". . . have no idea how pissed off I was." My sister's voice snapped me out of my daze. "He couldn't see that she's just usin' code words to pretty up her racism." She turned on the oven, setting the temp to 450, then said, "This is the *second* bullet this girl has dodged, and I'm tired of it. I mean, check it: if none of the other stuff happened and all she said was that slogan, I'd be down with the whole she-didn't-mean-it-that-way darkness-to-hope interp. But she *also* threw shade at not only the Oakville kids but the Woodlawn kids too. My whole thing is this: if you see a fish in the living room—no problem; if you see a fish in the bedroom—a little strange, but no problem; but if you see a fish in the *bathroom* too, it's time to say, 'Something fishy is going on.' And something fishy is definitely going on with this girl. I mean, we're all watchin' a bigotry beanstalk getting taller and taller right in front of us, and nobody's sayin' a damn thing. What's up with that? Just 'cause she's pretty? Well, fuck that. All this silence is startin' to hurt my ears. It's time to bring the noise. It's time to shut a bitch down."

I kind of mumbled, "Yeah, I hear you." I was wondering if this was a good time to tell her that I was madly in love with the sister of this bigotry-beanstalker, but as fired up as Regina was at that moment, you can best believe I kept my mouth shut—at the rate she was going, she was liable to bake me before the cake.

She glanced at my bowl. "Is it ready?"

I looked down at the batter I'd created. "Yeah."

She pointed at the cake pan on the stove and said, "Okay, pour that shit."

As I poured the batter into the pan, she said, "So I made a big decision today. And I want you to tell me what you think. And I want you to be straight with me. You know how I roll: Keep It Real Or Keep It Killed."

I nodded. "I gotcha."

She opened the oven door. I slid the pan in and she closed it. Then I looked at her, waiting.

She said, "I've decided to run for president."

That was great news, right? So why did my stomach suddenly feel the way it does when I'm on a rollercoaster that's dropping thousands of feet? As my intestinal insides went down, my eyebrows went up and I said, "On the real?"

She nodded and said, "I gave notice to Mr. Dranger this afternoon. I'm officially In now . . . You think I made a mistake?"

Hoping she didn't hear the flopping in my stomach, I said, "No. Hell no. If anybody can bring the noise right, it's you. You're gonna be large and in charge."

My sister gave me one of her rare smiles. "Real talk? You think so?"

"Hell yeah," I said.

She said, "The only thing that's kinda fuckin' with my head is, I don't know all that much about politics. But when it comes to recognizing a racist, all you really need is a brain, not a campaign."

"That's what I'm sayin'," I said.

Then she gave me this weird look. For a long time. She finally said, "So, check it: I was wonderin' if you could do me a favor— like, a big one. But before I ask, I need to know something."

That made my heartbeat switch to Olympics sprinter mode, but I played it off like everything was bacon. I nodded and said, "What's up?"

She said, "Do you agree with me that Leona Walls is runnin' a racist campaign?"

I nodded. "I agree."

She said, "Then I was wonderin' if you'd help me—you know, with my campaign. Be my . . . whatchamacallit. What do they call that?—the person who keeps the campaign organized and running smoothly? Campaign director?"

"Campaign manager?" I said.

"Yeah that's it. Could you be my campaign manager?" she asked.

There was now an orchestra playing inside me and "No! No! No!" was the only song it knew, but I ignored it and told her, "Okay."

"For real? You don't look like you're sure or something."

"No, I'm sure," I said. "I'm down with it. Your campaign manager—I can do that."

I forgot all about my discomfort when I saw Regina's smile. This time it was her all-cylinders, full-throttle smile—the one that lights up her whole face and makes you think you're related to an angel: it's a smile she breaks out about as often as your family takes out the good china or takes the plastic off the couch—only on the most special of occasions—but when you see it, you always know it was worth the wait.

"Thank you," she said.

I shrugged and said, "No prob."

Since the cake was already in the oven, we had to do the Waiting thing now. And as we always do during this phase of CakeTalk, we both leaned against the counter, took out our phones, and started tapping away.

After a while, Regina said, "Love you, lil bro."

I said, "Love you, big sis."

We didn't say anything else until it was time to take the cake out.

ULY

I had my first dream about Sallie this morning. It was beautiful in a mad bizarre way. I was standing on a corner, waiting for a bus at night in some Vegas-type city (neon-lit casino signs were all over the place). When the bus came, I got on and saw Sallie sitting there behind the wheel. For some reason she was dressed like an old-school locomotive driver: visored cap and overalls.

"Sallie?" I said, happy and confused.

She didn't respond. She just stared at me, closed the double doors, and continued driving. I sat in the first seat right across from her and I watched as she steered the bus. I guess I was waiting for her to recognize me and smile or something, but she kept her stare straight ahead. Then, after a few minutes, she turned to me, grinned, and pressed a gigantic red square button on her dashboard—it was a button I hadn't noticed before; when she pressed it, it turned green and it blinked with the word WINGS.

I shook my head and said, "Bullshit."

Still grinning, she looked at me and nodded.

And suddenly I heard this metallic thump, like something was popping out from both sides of the damn bus.

And the bus started rising, sailing above the highway railing that, just seconds before, had been to the left and right.

I shouted out something but I can't remember exactly what it was. Sallie laughed as she steered the bus higher and higher into the sky. When the bus was in licking distance of the moon she let go of the wheel, walked over to me, and sat on my lap. I think I said something like, "Wait, what about the bus?" but Sallie ignored the question; she just smiled at me, took off her cap, put it on my head, and gave me this long kiss. As we made out, a part of me wondered when the bus was going to realize it had no driver and drop our asses to a fiery death, but a horrendous crash from the sky didn't seem worth interrupting a make-out session for, so I kept the kiss going; and the bus didn't seem to be in much of a dropping mood anyway—it was on some weird kind of autopilot, even though it wasn't a plane. In the middle of the make-out, I suddenly remembered that a bunch of passengers were watching us, so I tore my lips away from Sallie's and whispered to her, "Maybe we shouldn't do this here, in front of everybody." Sallie whispered, "There's nobody here" and she pointed behind me; when I turned around I saw that the entire bus, which had been at least half full when I'd gotten on, was now empty. With a smile that some corduroy-ass romance novel might describe as "naughty," Sallie moved her forehead to mine and whispered, "So, do you want to bake the salad, or should I?" Before I could ask her what she meant, she kissed me again, and just as our tongues were about to touch I heard a voice—that didn't belong to Sallie—call my name.

"Uly!"

It was a familiar voice.

"Uly!"

A female voice.

"ULY!!"

It sounded like it was coming from outside the flying bus.

"ULY!!!!!"

It was my sister.

Waking me the hell up.

My eyes opened to the anticlimactic sight of the living room and my sister standing over my sofa bed with a fistful of magic markers just inches above my face.

"What?" I murmured.

She said, "I need you up and out. We got some defacin' to do."

It took my groggy mind a few seconds to connect her comment to the markers in her hand but before I could even congratulate myself I noticed that there was someone standing behind her: sophomore Narmeen Saad, my sister's best friend. A stunned blink of my eye was all the time it took for me to go from sleepy to self-conscious. I *hate* when Regina brings her friends to the apartment while I'm still in bed.

Tightening the blanket around me, I told my sister, "Damn, Jeen. Can't a brotha get outta bed first before you turn the living room into a tourist attraction? Whassup, Narmeen."

Narmeen just nodded. She doesn't talk much. I noticed she was holding a small ladder, but I was too pissed off to ask about it.

When I looked at my watch and saw 5:30 I got even more pissed. I told my sister, "I don't get up for another thirty minutes. What's up with this early shit?"

Regina said, "We're gonna give Miss Leona's campaign posters a little magic-marker makeover. But we gotta do it before everybody gets there so we're done before anybody can point a gun. Come on—up and out!"

With my eyes I said, "Just let me sleep for twenty more minutes."

With her mouth she said, "Did you agree to be my campaign manager last night or not?"

I said, "Well, yeah, but . . . messin' up somebody's posters? I ain't sure I wanna live there."

Regina said, "Oh, what?—you wanna live in a place full of signs tellin' us we're not wanted there? 'Cause that sure as hell ain't where I'm stayin'."

I said, "I feel you on that. It's just—isn't there something else we can do?"

She nodded. "Oh yeah, there are about thirty things we can do." She raised the fistful of markers higher. "This just happens to be the first one. Are you down or not?"

After a moment, I nodded. "I'm down."

She pulled my arm. "Then I need you *up* and out. Come on, campaign manager!" She thrust the markers into my hand.

When we got to Knight it was so empty you could actually hear echoes in the hallways.

We started with the Freshman Hallway on the first floor, stopping under one of Leona's TURN KNIGHT BACK TO DAY posters. With her foot Narmeen slid the ladder over to my sister, who mounted it, and uncapped a magic marker. I'm sure you've heard of plastic surgery. Well, my sister gave Leona's poster some paper surgery, inserting an *L* between the *B* and *A* in BACK and making the *O* in TO and the *D* in DAY bigger so that they looked like one word instead of two. When the magic-marker makeover was done, this is what the poster said:

TURN KNIGHT BLACK TODAY

Then she moved her marker to a corner of the poster and wrote, in cursive, VOTE REGINA GATES and circled it.

I knew it was wrong but the shit felt so right.

"Damn, Jeen," I told her. "That's cold-blooded."

"Honey, I'm just gettin' warmed up," my sister said. She jabbed two markers down at me. "Here, I need you to do the second floor."

As I stared at the markers that orchestra inside me piped up again but the music was hard to enjoy because it was playing three songs at the same damn time: "Don't Do It," "What Will Sallie Think?" and "But You Promised Your Sister You'd Have Her

Back." As the three songs click-clacked back and forth inside my head I nodded and grabbed the markers.

Regina said, "That's what's up. And don't forget to write 'Vote Regina Gates.' Narmeen's gonna hang down here with me."

As I performed paper surgery on all of Leona's second-floor posters I tried to give my conscience some Tylenol by rubber-stamping my brain with the message *Relax, You're Just Trying To Change The World*. But here's the problem with that: when you hold that message in front of the mirror, it looks like this message: *You're Hurting Your Girlfriend's Sister . . . And Maybe Your Girlfriend Too.*

SALLIE

Three minutes into school this morning, Leona and I saw that all her TURN KNIGHT BACK TO DAY posters had been defaced.

Five minutes into school this morning, I saw that the posters had been defaced by Regina Gates.

Regina Gates.

Also Known As: Uly's older sister.

Uly.

Also Known As: my boyfriend.

Regina Gates.

My boyfriend's sister.

She's running for president.

Against Leona Walls.

Leona Walls.

Also Known As: my sister.

Six minutes into school this morning, I felt like throwing up.

Seven minutes into school this morning, I wondered exactly when Uly's sister made the decision to run against my sister.

Seven-and-a-half minutes into school this morning, I wondered why Uly hadn't told me his sister wanted to run against my sister.

Seven-and-three-quarter-minutes into school this morning, I

figured he had a good reason for not telling me, but I wondered what it was.

Eight minutes into school this morning, I took out my phone to text Uly.

Eight minutes and two seconds into school this morning, I had to put away my phone and calm down my sister, who was going from poster to poster, screaming, "I can't believe she did this!!"

Twelve minutes into school this morning, we saw that the posters on the second floor were defaced too.

Fifteen minutes into school this morning, we saw that the third floor had a lot in common with the second floor and first floor.

Twenty minutes into school this morning, I realized I was three minutes late for English, but, being my sister's campaign manager, I felt I couldn't desert my post, so I walked shotgun with her as she stormed toward Mr. Dranger's office.

Leona barged into the office, practically stomped toward Mr. Dranger's desk, and showed him a defaced poster she'd torn from the wall. Glaring at him, she said, "Did you see this?!"

With his oversize polka-dot mug suspended in coffee interruptus between his desk and his mouth, he squinted at the revised words on Leona's poster then leaned back in his chair and said, "I guess I just did." He didn't seem as agitated as I thought he'd be. Actually, he didn't seem agitated at all.

"'*Turn Knight Black Today*'?" my sister said, quoting the poster. "She's disqualified now, right?"

"Absolutely not," Mr. Dranger said.

My sister's eyes went way wide and she held her defaced poster higher. "You're still letting her run after what she did to all my posters??"

"Absolutely," Mr. Dranger said, still leaning back in his chair, now cradling the back of his head with his hands.

My sister's eyes went even wider and she said, "How can you let her stay?? This is *school property* she defaced!"

Mr. Dranger said, "Uh, actually, it's *your* property she defaced."

Leona said, "But it was hanging here in the school, so doesn't that make it the school's property too??"

"Did the school pay for it?" Mr. Dranger asked.

Leona said, "Well, no, but—"

"Who paid for it?" he asked.

Leona said, "Well, I did, but—"

"So that makes it your property," he said. "The school just lent you some wall space so you could temporarily hang it up. Think about it: if you go to a club and hang your coat on one of their coatracks and somebody rips up your coat, was it the *club's* property that was destroyed, or yours?"

My sister was stumped to silence. And she wasn't the only one.

She broke the silence with a crumple of the poster and said, "It's so not fair that she gets away with this."

Still leaning back in his chair, Mr. Dranger shrugged and said, "Welcome to democracy. It's a muzzle-free zone. Everybody has a say."

Pointing at her half-crumpled poster, my sister told him, "But she's saying this whole school should be black!"

Mr. Dranger shrugged and said, "Well, some could say your original poster implied that this whole school should be white."

The space between my eyebrows got more crumpled than my sister's poster. I asked him, "What do you mean?"

He gave me that look people give you when they're pretty sure you're an idiot but not 100 percent sure. "Knight and Day. Night equals dark, black. Day equals light, white." He looked back at my sister and said, "Maybe you didn't mean it that way, but some students of color thought you did." He pointed at the crumpled poster in her hands. "Well, now you know how they felt."

With a sarcastic smile, my sister said, "Oh my God, that is so . . ." I'm not sure what else she was going to say, but whatever it was, I guess she decided it wasn't worth saying. So instead she said, "So what're you saying—if I put up some more of these posters, and she defaces them again, you're gonna let her keep getting away with it?"

"That's exactly what I'm saying," Mr. Dranger said. "If you don't want her to directly say this whole school should be black, then don't indirectly say this whole school should be white. Other than that, I don't know what else to tell you."

I nodded, looked at my sister, and told her, "Maybe you should just stick with the Leonite one."

Leona snapped, "Whatever" and stormed out of the office.

I looked back at our advisor and said, "Uh, thank you, Mr. Dranger."

When I caught up to Leona in the hall she said, "That hack asshole. He probably gets a hundred grand a year. To do what? Sit on his fat ass and drink coffee from a dirty mug and give bullshit advice."

I said, "I think he was just trying to—"

"And you're supposed to be my campaign manager. Why didn't you back me up?" she snapped.

I couldn't believe my ears. "I *did* back you up. I'm, like, ten minutes late to class right now from backing you up. And I think he's right." I pointed at her dead poster. "She never would've done this if *you* hadn't done *that*." I pointed above at one of the few KNIGHT TO DAY posters that Uly's sister hadn't gotten to.

"Whatever," my sister said as she disappeared down a staircase, leaving me alone in the hallway with nothing to keep me company but a bunch of thoughts that thoughtlessly tormented me: *Why is my sister mad at me? Why didn't I know that her Knight To Day slogan is racist? Is Uly mad at me for not knowing? Does he think I was the one who came up with the slogan? Is Mr. Bauer going to be mad at me for being eleven minutes late? Were we supposed to read up to page thirty-seven or forty-seven in* Handmaid's Tale *last night? Is he going to be in one of his sadistic moods today and randomly call on people and ask plot-related questions? Why am I still standing in this hallway?*

I eventually stopped standing in the hallway and went to class, and over the next few minutes and hours, discovered the following three things:

1. Mr. Bauer was sort of mad at me but also sort of wasn't.

2. Uly wasn't mad at me at all. We sat together at lunch and I told him I had nothing to do with my sister's Knight To Day slogan, and he understood. I also wanted to say, "Sorry for not realizing it was racist," but I didn't want to Debbie-Downerize our nice lunch, so I didn't say it. I really should've said it, though. I think.

3. There's now a third candidate running for president. His name is John Smith and he's a junior, just like my sister and Uly's sister. I don't know much about him, other than that he seems nice and he's a football player. Actually, he *was* a football player, but last summer he got in a car accident that left him blind. So of course he doesn't play football anymore. (I didn't want his blindness to be the first thing I mentioned about him, like as if the only note-worthy thing about him is that he's blind. I don't think blind people like that. If I was blind, I know I wouldn't like that.)

When I got home I saw Ashley and her boyfriend Skip lying on the floor, gluing glitter to one of my sister's *LEONITE* campaign posters, but they seemed to be gluing lips more than glitter.

"Hey guys," I said.

"Hey Sallie," Ashley said, coming up for breath from her make-outing. "Hey, did you hear? John Smith is running."

"Yeah, I heard," I said. Then I sort of looked around the room and said, "Where is she?"

Ashley gave me a confused look. "She? John Smith is a he."

I said, "No, I meant—my sister. Where is she?"

"Oh, she's upstairs with my brother." She went back to gluing lips more than glitter.

As I walked to Leona's bedroom Wilk walked out of it, closing the door behind him.

"Hey," I greeted as I walked past him.

But he wouldn't let me walk past. He was sort of blocking the door.

"What?" I said.

"It's not a good time," he said.

I said, "What do you mean it's not a good time?"

"She needs to be alone right now," he said. "She's getting ready for tomorrow's Speechathon and she doesn't need any distractions."

I said, "Okay, first of all, I'm not a distraction, I'm her sister. And second of all, how about getting the fuck out of my way so I can go inside and talk to her?"

He stared at me for a moment, then he grinned and said, "You know, if she'd taken my advice, you wouldn't be her campaign manager. You should never send a girl to do a man's job."

I said, "Well, when you see a man, you can offer him the job. But for right now, I'm the one punching in. That's a hint, by the way."

He pointed at her door and said, "She's really upset right now. And whenever she's upset, I'm upset. You know what She's Upset plus I'm Upset equals? An *ex*-campaign manager."

I said, "Well, you know what She's Upset plus I'm Upset plus I Told Her You Upset Me equals? An ex-*boyfriend*. Now, get out my way."

He said, "All I'm asking, Sallie, is that you do your job so my girlfriend can see a win this June."

I said, "And all I'm asking, Wilk, is that you get away from this door so you can see tomorrow."

He stared at me for another moment then he moved away from the door, *finally*.

I really don't know what got into him tonight. He and my sister have been dating for about a year and for the most part, he and I have gotten along, but sometimes he treats her like her name is Wilk's Property instead of Leona Walls and it really pisses me off.

When I walked into my sister's bedroom she was pacing like pacing was going to be banned after tonight.

I leaned against her dresser and said, "What's wrong? You worried about John Smith?"

She gave the thought a dismissive wave and said, "I could beat him with my eyes closed."

I sort of cringed and said, "That's probably not the best choice of words."

She stopped pacing and shot me an irritated glare. "What, everybody's supposed to forget what a big, bullying, stuck-up asshole he was before he was blind? Two years of beating up freshmen and yanking down girls' skirts, and we're all supposed to Clear History just 'cause he was lucky enough to go through a windshield and slam his head against a brick wall one fine summer day when he was texting instead of watching the road? I don't think so."

I said, "Okay, calm down."

She started pacing again.

I said, "So what is it?"

"Regina Gates!—who else!" she blared. "She ruined all my Knight To Day posters and now I can't put any more up, all 'cause of her race-card victim bullshit! But that's okay. She wants to break my life, but I'm not gonna let her. I never liked her anyway. Always walking around with that smug look on her face, like her shit smells like strawberry shortcake. I can't *wait* for her to go down, and the only face she'll be looking up at is mine. She just messed with the wrong white girl. I'm gonna be president this June, and I will destroy anybody who tries to get in the way, whether it's Regina or John Smith or anybody else who adds their name to the running."

I said, "It'll just be those two. Today was the deadline."

She nodded and said, "Then the skeletal remains of two people will be at the school entrance, come June."

I said, "Okay, well, on that happy note, why don't we go over your speech for tomorrow. Have you written it yet? Let me take a—"

"No, no," she snapped, "I don't write down my speeches. I like to speak as it comes to me. It's more fresh that way. If I write it, I'll have to read from it, and that'll make me sound too mechanical and rehearsed. I want everybody to feel like I'm having a conversation with them right in my living room or something."

I could feel my throat getting dry as a vision of my boyfriend's offended face crash-landed in my head. I gulped away the dryness and asked my sister, "You sure that's a good idea, after what happened the last time?"

Leona threw another irritated look at me.

"I just don't want you to get misunderstood again," I explained.

My sister stopped pacing; she picked up one of the hairbrushes from her bureau and started brushing her hair in the bureau's mirror. "Look, I know what I'm doing," she told me. "You're my campaign manager, not my babysitter. You handle the campaign, I'll handle my speeches."

I looked at my watch and thought about my best friend. I really needed to talk to her. When you have Sister stuff and Boyfriend stuff on your mind, the best person to talk to isn't always your sister or boyfriend. So I told Leona, "Well, I'm gonna head over to Dandee's now."

My sister put down her brush and looked at me like I'd just confessed a mass murder. "You're leaving?"

I said, "Yeah. Why?"

She said, "The Speechathon is tomorrow and you're leaving??"

I half-threw up my hands and said, "I don't know what you want me to do, Lee. I offered to help you with your speech but you Swiped Left on that. I don't know what else I'm supposed to—"

"You know what? Just go," she said, and went back to brushing her hair.

I moved toward her. "Look, if you want me to stay, I can st—"

"I said go!" she snapped. "Have a dandy time at Dandee's."

She kept brushing her hair in the mirror. I kept standing there, waiting to see if she was going to move her eyes from mirror to me, but she didn't; that's when I knew she really wanted me to go. So I went.

Dandee lives on the other side of town, and since Collingswood is a fairly small town, I didn't have too far to go.

When she opened the door—she's always the one who opens the door at her house—she said, "You look weird. Something's wrong."

I nodded and said, "Your eyes are working."

As always she led me to her basement bedroom. She actually has a regular non-basement bedroom on the second floor but she's been running a computer-repair business since she was fourteen and she persuaded her parents to bedroom-ify the basement for her so she can dream and American-Dream in the same space.

I could actually fill up an entire journal on Dandee. She's the closest thing to a superhero I've ever known, right down to her full name: Dandelion Majestyk. That's the actual name that appears on her birth certificate. She showed me once. I've always been secretly jealous of her name. Not that I hate my name, but, come on: Sallie Walls? It's so bland and beige you can practically taste the vanilla. Sallie Walls knits lace place mats. Sallie Walls bakes lattice-topped apple pies and uses them to welcome new people to the neighborhood. But Dandelion Majestyk? Shit. Dandelion Majestyk runs up walls and cartwheels from rooftop to rooftop in the middle of the night and can make stubbly faced hard-bitten criminals tearfully confess with just a lift of her left eyebrow and she stalks through the countryside in shiny black leather boots in constant lookout for a chance to preserve truth, justice, and the American Way.

Okay, maybe she doesn't do all of that, but I swear, if she ever told me she did, I wouldn't need too much convincing to be convinced.

Even though I've known her for three years, there's still a cloak of mystery she keeps around herself; the cloak has gotten thinner the longer I've known her, but the cloak is still there. She only wears black clothes, but whenever I ask her why, she just shrugs and says, "Why not?" And on every black shirt she wears—and when I say every, I mean absolutely nothing less than every—there's this message:

UNSCRAMBLE:
ielv

It could be either "live," "evil," "veil," or "vile," but every time I ask her, she just says, "I can't believe you even have to ask" like it's the most obvious thing ever.

And I've never seen her parents. I've seen pictures of them in the living room, but I've never seen them face to face. Oh, I've *heard* them—sometimes they'll call out things to her from upstairs ("Dandee, don't forget to give that form to Mr. Woolery!" or "Dandee, there's ice cream in the freezer!" or "Dandee, I sewed up that hole on your pants—they're in your closet!"), but by the time I come back up to the living room, they're gone. It's actually really creepy when you think about it; that's why I don't think too much about it. Dandee says both of her parents are agoraphobic—they avoid people and the outdoors; whenever the school needs to have a conference with them, they do it either by Skype or by sending Dandee's aunt as an understudy. So I guess it's possible they really are agoraphobic; but I wonder if something else might be going on. My sister thinks her parents are sunlight-hating Satan worshippers who are using their only daughter as a decoy—you know, to *lure* me in and make me comfortable enough to let my guard down so they can swoop down and slice me open as a sacrifice to Lucifer. "You better stop going over there," Leona is always telling me. "One of these days you won't come back."

But I keep going over there, because—to quote Dandee—Why not? I guess I see her not only as my best friend but also as sort of an Amusement Park with a pulse. She's mystery and intrigue and suspense all rolled up into a sixteen-year-old girl. With her, you get vanishing, voice-only parents and a basement bedroom and black clothes and coded scrambled messages. And admission is completely free. Who wouldn't keep coming?

And there's one more thing about her that I probably shouldn't tell you, but I'll tell you anyway. About a year ago, she told me she blackmailed Mr. Baumgartner—one of the Tech guys at our school—into giving her a code that will allow her access to the computer account of pretty much every teacher at Knight High. So if she wants to know what websites Mr. Lebrock visits during his spare time, she can know it. If she's curious about what dating sites Ms. Spadaro visits during her lunch breaks, she's not curious for long. Dandee won't tell me exactly what "dirt" she has on Mr. Baumgartner, and, to be honest with you, I'm sort of afraid to know. I'm afraid it might make me lose respect for him or her or him *and* her. Especially after she wrote this short story last semester for our creative writing class where this sixteen-year-old girl named Diana dyes her hair red and puts in green contacts and pretends to be eighteen years old and sets up an OkCupid account for the sole purpose of meeting up with her school's Technology Director, who's also on the site; he meets up with her and they have sex and it's only after the sex that she reveals to him that she's a sophomore at his school and that she will tell everybody everything if he doesn't give her two of the computers from the computer lab. I *pray to God* that it was only a story and not a memory.

And that's not all. She also has a habit of secretly recording people—usually students—with her phone if she catches them doing or saying something they probably shouldn't be doing or saying. And then she stores all the recorded videos' links on one of her computers in a file called BeigeMail. Why BeigeMail? She said, "I only use it against the person if they screw me over—like, steal my rabbit or borrow money from me and not pay it back or bump into me without saying excuse me. Blackmail is when *you're* doing the Screwing Over. But with BeigeMail, you're the victim."

If you think Dandee's BeigeMail thing doesn't work, think again. Just ask Shannon Filarski. Shannon once called Dandee a "zombie freak" in front of the whole class and everybody laughed. Well, it just so happened that Dandee had recorded Shannon picking her nose in the back of the library about six months earlier and now she had a reason to use the footage. So she sent the link to Shannon's boyfriend, who got grossed out and promptly broke up with Shannon because shallowness. So now it's Shannon who looks like a zombie as she wanders around the school, wishing she'd never called Dandee a zombie.

So I never know what Dandee is going to tell me when I visit her. But on this particular night, it was me who had something to tell her.

"So what's wrong?" she asked as I sat down. She handed me a can of lime Red Bull and sat on top of a broken computer monitor, looking intently up at me. Dandee doesn't have a lot of friends at school—a lot of kids, especially girls, have told me they think she's too weird: her intense, unblinking stare, her almost robotic voice, and her black clothes are just too much for them. But if they only knew what a great listener and an even greater advice-giver she is, they'd know they've been swimming past a buried treasure.

"So, I have to tell you something," I said. "You're the first person I'm telling."

She said, "Okay." She took a sip of her lime Red Bull and waited.

With a smile, I said, "Uly Gates and I . . . We're a Thing now."

Rubbing the excess drink from her mouth, she said, "I sort of figured that. But I wasn't sure. I mean, you two seem to always be together at lunch and in the hallways. But I just figured you two were working on a project or something. So you and him are really a Thing, huh?"

I nodded. "Really a Thing." I could feel my face getting warm with the good-blush. It felt so great to say it out loud.

She said, "You have a thing for black guys."

That took me by surprise. "Really? I don't think I do."

"You do," she said. "All the guys you've been attracted to are black."

"That's not true," I said.

She said, "LaKeith Williams—black. Dwayne Barkley—black. Kenya McCormick—black."

"What about Raj—he's not black," I said.

"Indian—close enough. You definitely have a thing for dark skin."

I said, "Really? I never saw it that way. I just saw all of them as these cute, funny, smart guys whose skin just happened to be darker than mine. But I wouldn't say it's, like, a preference or anything. I mean, if you go to a vending machine and you always pick Pepsi or Dr Pepper, it doesn't mean you'd never drink Sprite or Sierra Mist. You just happen to have more of a taste for Pepsi or Dr Pepper most of the time."

"I hate soda," Dandee said, in sort of a daze. I'm not really sure what her point was, but maybe her point didn't matter because right then she looked up, smiled at me, tapped my knee, and said, "So give me some deets. What's he like? How's the kissing? How's the . . . everything?"

I spent the next ten minutes telling her everything about the Everything: how Uly is the Real Deal, how I never thought Luck liked me so much that it would let me have a Variety Pack boyfriend: romantic, funny, cute, nice, edgy, stylish, loves *The Good, the Bad and the Ugly*—all in the same package.

When I was done, Dandee—who'd been hanging on my every word—sat back and got rid of her smile. She said, "You know something? I just realized I'm offended. I really hate you right now."

My mouth fell open. "What? Why? What did I do?"

She said, "You've been dating this guy since November and you're just now telling me?"

I reached out and took her hand. "Please don't hate me, Dandee. It's just, I didn't wanna say anything till I was really sure. Too many times I've told you I've met The One, only to not have him be The One, and it's embarrassing. And I just didn't wanna be embarrassed again." I made my eyes go beggar. "Forgive me?"

She said, "No. Actually, yes."

"Thank you."

We raised our Red Bull cans and clinked them together in a toast, then sipped.

When she was done sipping she said, "But something's wrong, isn't it?"

I nodded.

She said, "Don't tell me. I wanna guess."

I said, "Okay."

She said, "Your sister is running for president."

I nodded. "Keep going."

She said, "You're her campaign manager."

I nodded. "Keep going."

She said, "Regina Gates is also running for president."

I nodded. "Keep going."

She said, "Uly is Regina's brother."

I nodded. "Keep going."

She said, "Which means you're the campaign manager of your sister and the girlfriend of the brother of your sister's opposition. Which basically means you've been touching tongues with someone from the enemy camp."

I thumbs-upped her, then I said, "How screwed am I?"

She said, "It sounds worse than it is."

I relief-sighed. "Really?"

"No, actually, you're pretty screwed."

"Damn." I looked at her. "On a scale of One To Ten: How screwed?"

She said, "I'd give it a Nine."

"Wow, that's bad," I said.

She said, "Well, it's a Soft Nine."

"What the hell is that?" I asked.

She said, "Well, you're screwed, but not that badly. It's the sort of thing that's only a problem if you let it be one."

I said, "How do I do that?—or how do I *not* do that? I mean, I don't wanna stop being my sister's campaign manager but I also don't wanna stop being Uly's girlfriend. But his sister and my sister . . . Isn't that a . . . What do they call that? A something of interest?"

"Conflict Of Interest," Dandee said.

"Conflict Of Interest! Isn't it a conflict of interest?"

Dandee shrugged and said, "Only if you're conflicted about finding both of 'em interesting. Your sister already knows you're dating him, right?"

It was time to hang my head in shame. "I haven't told her yet," I mumbled.

Dandee's eyes almost never go wide, but tonight they did.

"You haven't told her yet? The screwometer just went from Nine to Ten."

"No!" I pleaded.

"Why haven't you told her?" she asked.

I sort of shrugged and said, "I guess for the same reason I didn't tell you . . . Does that really put me at a Ten?"

She said, "Most definitely. But here's how you can get it back to a Nine."

"I want the *soft* Nine," I said.

Dandee held up her hand and said, "Well that's what I'm about to tell you—how to get it back to a soft Nine. It's actually pretty simple: just tell your sister you're dating him. But you have to do it now. The earlier you do it, the less unpleasant it'll be later. And another plus about telling her is that you'll be putting the bowling ball back in *her* lane: when you tell her you're swapping spit with the enemy camp, she'll either fire you as campaign manager or she'll swallow her disgust and keep you on. Either way, the decision-making burden is all on *her* shoulders. See what I'm saying?"

I nodded. "I see." I thought for a moment, then said, "I'm gonna tell her."

Dandee said, "Bacon." She stood up and headed toward the forest of computers at the back of the room. "So let me tell you about Mr. Morrison. You have *got* to see his OkCupid profile." Tapping on the keyboard, she said, "You won't believe what he wants his dates to wear when they meet him . . ."

ULY

Tomorrow's the big Speechathon so tonight I helped Regina with her this-is-what-I'm-all-about speech. She mainly needed me to proofread—you know, make sure no sentences were colliding and no commas were hiding. Her speech was pretty tight, but she had some trouble wrapping it up. She wanted to end with a slogan, but coming up with a bacon one was hard as hell.

Clutching her dog-eared speech as she paced the living room, Regina said, "What about 'Don't Vote For Nina, Don't Vote For Tina, Vote For Regina'?"

Pacing right along with her, I kind of winced and shook my head. "Who the hell are Nina and Tina? They ain't runnin'. I don't even think there's anybody at our school *named* Nina and Tina."

My sister said, "Yeah. Damn." She punched her paper. "See, the problem is Regina doesn't rhyme with shit!"

Watching us from the couch, Narmeen piped up with, "Maybe you could do something with your *last* name."

Regina and I gave each other a why-didn't-we-think-of-that glance and quickly started mentally Word Searching for things that rhyme with Gates.

My sister said, "What about 'So Put Down Your Plates And Vote For Gates'?"

I shrugged and said, "I'm feelin' it, but not all the way."

Regina turned to Narmeen. "What do you think?"

Narmeen gave us the Thumbs Down.

Regina asked her, "What's wrong with it?"

Narmeen said, "Makes it sound like everybody's a greedy pig that wants to do nothing but eat."

My sister gave a defeated groan.

I said, "Wait, how about 'Lower The Crime Rates And Vote For Gates'?"

Regina grimaced and said, "Crime rates? It's a school, not Chicago."

I told her, "I bet our girl likes it." We both turned to Narmeen. I said, "Narmeen, what do you think? 'Lower The Crime Rates And Vote For Gates'?"

Narmeen gave me the Thumbs Down.

"Damn," I said. Then I told my sister, "You know something? Forget the rhyming. Let's just go back to your first name. Maybe we can do something nice without a rhyme."

Regina and I paced while Narmeen skeptically watched.

My sister said, "What about 'Open Your Eyes And—"

"You can't use that," I interrupted.

"Why not?" she shot back.

I said, "Smith is blind, remember?"

"Oh yeah," Regina said.

We both continued pacing and thinking.

Then I stopped and snapped my fingers. "I got it!! How about: 'Join The Regina Regime'?"

My sister stopped pacing. I could see her eyes slowly draining out the doubt. "Join The Regina Regime . . . Join The Regina Regime," she repeated. She looked at me and said, "You know, the more I think about it, the more I like it . . . Join The Regina Regime . . ."

I said, "Let's check with our girl."

My sister and I both turned to Narmeen.

Regina told her, "You know how I roll: Keep It Real Or Keep It Killed . . . 'Join The Regina Regime.' What do you think?"

After a moment, Narmeen gave my sister a salute.

Armed with Narmeen's yes bless, Regina and I cheered and did a Triple F.

"Now I got a slogan!" Regina said as she quickly scribbled the words along the bottom of her paper.

Then my sister recited her entire speech for Narmeen and me. When she was done, I gave her a couple of notes—mainly about saying certain words more clearly and taking some pauses in a few spots—but other than that, her delivery was tight and quite right. I think she's a natural-born speaker.

After Narmeen left, Regina whooshed off to her room to practice her speech some more and I plunked down on the couch to try to do homework. But, as usual, Sallie rented most of my mind time. I wondered whether she knew I was one of the people who ruined her sister's posters. When I was hanging with her earlier she didn't look like she knew, but some girls are so good at hiding what they know that a shovel isn't enough to dig it out; sometimes you need a damn *drill* to hit that shit. And I'm still trying to figure out if Sallie is one of those girls.

". . . What do you think?"

My sister's voice shook me out of my thoughts.

I looked up at her. She was holding up a light green blouse and a royal-blue one.

"Which one should I wear tomorrow?" she asked me.

I pointed at the blue one. "That's what's up. It pops more." I pointed at the green one. "With that one, they'll fall asleep." I pointed again at the blue one. "But with that one, ain't nobody fallin' asleep."

My sister nodded. "Yeah, I was kinda thinkin' that too. Thanks, bro!"

She smiled at me and whooshed back into her room.

It's been nice seeing my sister smile more than once a week. Her campaign is only two days old but already she seems more happy and, I don't know, more connected to *life* than she's been in the last two years. She was especially cheerful tonight after scoring a major hit with her TURN KNIGHT BLACK TODAY jam because it made Leona take down all her KNIGHT TO DAY posters, and Sallie told me she won't be putting any more of them up.

So while the Regina situation had me elated, the Sallie situation had me deflated, if you can feel me on that. I felt like I'd been operating on Sneak Mode all day. I no longer felt like a resident of Real City, and once you leave that particular town, you're more lost than Jack Frost in July.

I knew what I had to do. So I picked up the phone and did it.

"Hey, U," Sallie said when she picked up.

"Hey, Sallie," I said. "Are you home?"

She said, "No, I'm at Dandee's. What's up?"

I said, "Tell her I'll give her ten bucks if she admits it's 'veil.'"

Laughing, Sallie said, "Okay, hold on." I could hear her telling her friend what I said. Then Sallie got back on the phone and said, between giggles, "She said to give you the Finger. I can text you a picture of her giving it to you, if you want."

"No, I'm good." Now that the Stalling portion of the program was over, I switched to Showtime. "So listen, I just wanted to tell you . . . last night, my sister asked me to be her campaign manager, and I agreed."

There was a pause at the other end, then Sallie said, "Oh, okay."

I was about to ask "Are you cool with that?" but her permission wasn't my mission. I just wanted her to know. So I said, "I just wanted you to hear it from me and not somebody else."

Sallie said, "Of course. Thank you . . . How's it going so far?"

I said, "A little too early to tell, but I'll keep you posted."

"Yeah, same here," she said.

Now there was silence at both ends. I was silent because I thought maybe she had more to say, but now that I think about it, she was probably silent because she was thinking the same way.

When the silence started getting muscles, I said, "Well, I better get back to this homework."

She said, "Okay. I love you."

"I love you too," I said.

After hanging up, I felt better, and my concentration reported for duty again, at least enough for me to finish all my homework.

On nights when my homework load is light and the shit on my mind is heavy, I head over to my girl Marilyn's place, just down the street.

It's too bad Life doesn't give us two legs, two arms, two feet, and one instruction manual called *When Your Best Friend Goes from He to She (Or She to He)*. Having a trans best friend wasn't exactly a beach walk at first. I think I would've seen my best friend as a girl more quickly if Marilyn had gone more *full throttle* with her He to She change, but she really didn't. All she did was put on lipstick, color her nails, and wear eyeliner. There was no voice change. And even though her hair changed from straight to curly, she kept it just as short as it had been in the pre-Marilyn days. And she continued wearing the same clothes worn pre-Marilyn: sweatshirts, jeans, plaid shirts, and shit like that. Where the hell were the dresses, skirts, long hair?? When I confessed all that to Marilyn I could tell she was kind of offended (and I don't blame her; it was an asshole thing to say), but she kept the Cool on and sat my ass down and patiently explained to me that her identity isn't an Outside thing but an Inside thing. She said it wasn't about breasts and dresses; it was about her heart and mind, and she said she's always felt and thought like a girl. "I could put on a suit of armor and have a sword in one hand and a shield in the other," she explained, "and I'll still feel like a girl inside. It doesn't matter what you put *on*. It's all about what's been put *in*." We talked for a long time that day and I was glad we had the conversation because when it was over my eyes were more Open about her situation than they'd been before.

And even with my new knowledge I had some trouble accepting—*really* accepting—that Marilyn is still the same person I flew kites and had water-gun fights and talked about girls with; gender was the only thing different, at least for me. My uninformed ass had me thinking that our whole relationship had to change and that we'd have to start talking about mascara, crocheting, and Lifetime movies—shit I know nothing about. But Marilyn still wanted to play violent videogames and talk about girls. And she kept all the pre-Marilyn posters of bikini-clad women on her wall and was still thirsty for the same girls she'd always been thirsty for. I'd always thought that boy-to-girl trans people were sexually attracted to boys and that girl-to-boy trans people were sexually attracted to girls, but that's not always the way it works. The first few months were kind of hard. When I'd visit with her in her room the conversation would wander to a girl I was attracted to and just as I was about to go into specifics I'd stop, remembering that I was now talking to a girl and not a boy. And Marilyn would always say, "Bro, what's the matter with you? It's *me*. Gimme the deets." And I'd eventually give all the details, and the more I did it, the less strange it got, and pretty soon it was like I was talking to my old friend again. Because I was.

Something that depressed the hell out of me was the way a lot of our mutual peeps jumped ship the minute Marilyn came out last year. Our posse used to be bigger: besides the current crew of Marilyn, me, Rahkeem, and Cecil, there used to be Omar, Teddy K, Luis, and Lamont, but after Marilyn became Marilyn, they became Gone. It was really depressing when they started warning me with shit like, "Yo, you better watch out—any minute now he's gonna start puttin' the moves on you." When I told them she liked girls (not that it would've mattered to me if she liked boys) they still weren't interested in jumping back on the ship. Teddy K told me, "So wait a minute. He becomes a girl but still wants to fuck girls? If you wanna fuck girls, why not just stay a boy? I don't even know what we're dealin' with here anymore. I mean, is he a straight boy or a gay girl, or a gay boy pretendin' to be a gay girl?" I said, "How about—she's our friend." He said, "Yo, she's *your* friend now. Shit, my life is confusin' enough; I ain't tryin' to add more cups. I'm outta here like Vladimir, bro. Peace." And off he walked.

Even though the remaining crew members—Cecil and Rahkeem—chose to stay on the ship, you can tell they want to keep at least five feet between them and Marilyn at all times. They don't seem to be as comfortable talking to her like they used to be. And one time when Marilyn invited them over to her place to play the new Black Ops game they both looked at each other and gave her some weak-ass excuse that even a deaf newborn in Nigeria would've known was bullshit. The look on Marilyn's face damn near broke the hell out of my heart.

As Marilyn and I played GTA V tonight—as usual, she sat in her "money chair" (its backer is shaped like a dollar sign, her favorite symbol) while I sat in a regular chair—she said, "So I hear that Narmeen girl is workin' on your sister's campaign. *Damn*, I love me some Indian girls. When are you gonna hook me up with her?"

I said, "When she stops liking guys, so it might be a while."

She said, "That's just like you to bust my buzz. Don't you think she's fine as hell?"

I shrugged and said, "I guess she's pretty. But those dead eyes of hers shut down the party. She always looks like she's thinkin' to herself, 'Damn, I should've chopped those bodies into forty pieces instead of twenty this morning.'"

Marilyn laughed. "Oh shit. That's cold-blooded. But you know something? I wouldn't even mind that. I bet serial-killer pussy is the best."

Laughing, I said, "I know you didn't just say that."

She said, "Yo, think about it—you already know she's pas-sionate. And second of all, if she can aim an Uzi, you *know* she can tame a floozy." She pointed at herself.

I chuckled and said, "Only you would say some sick shit like that."

She said, "So what's the latest and greatest with Sallie The White Girl?"

I said, "Why do you always say that? Why can't she just be Sallie? 'Sallie The White Girl' makes it sound like she should have a Registered Trademark after her name."

Firing at a passing car's windshield, Marilyn said, "I still can't believe you went Vanilla. White girls are boring as fuck."

"Not this one," I said. "Didn't I tell you how funny she is?"

Firing at another windshield, Marilyn said, "I can't believe your sister asked you to be campaign manager, knowin' you're smashin' Leona's little sis."

I said, "Well . . . uh . . . I kinda . . . haven't told Regina yet."

Marilyn dropped her controller and turned around in her chair to gape at me. "Black man, is you serious?? Your sister doesn't know you're smashin' a white girl??"

I said, "I'm not smashin' her. I already told you we haven't got to that point yet. We're taking things slow . . . And I guess I haven't told Regina yet 'cause . . . Well, you know how she is about the whole interracial thing. I mean, even back when I was dating an Asian girl, she gave me some shit about it. But not as much shit as I know she'll give me about Sallie. So I guess I've just been tryin' to put off that drama for as long as I can."

Marilyn said, "Well, if you *keep* puttin' off that Drama it's gonna turn into Horror when you finally tell her and her head starts spinnin' around. Then it'll turn into Sci-Fi when she knocks you all the way up to Mars. Then that shit'll turn into a Musical when we're all standin' at your grave, hummin' 'Taps' in your memory. Dude, it's time to spill. You gotta 'fess up and tell her, UG. The goddamn *Speechathon* is tomorrow!"

"I know, I know," I said. "I was actually gonna tell her tonight, but I didn't want to blow her flow and get her all distracted. Her mind needs to be focused and free of locusts for that speech tomorrow. But I'll tell her after the speech, real talk. I'll tell her."

Marilyn nodded and said, "That's what's up."

After a while I said to my friend, "But check it out: I guess another reason I haven't told her yet is, she might not want me to be her campaign manager anymore. And I really wanna help her with this campaign."

Marilyn looked at me and said, "You mean to tell me, if it's between Sallie The White Girl and some stupid-ass school election, you're pickin' the school election?? Bullshit. Everybody knows: when it's Politics versus Pussy, Pussy always wins. The End."

I rolled my eyes. "Who said that—Lincoln?"

"I'm pretty sure it was Jefferson," she said.

SALLIE

Uly and I, holding hands, sat together in the audience while his sister, John Smith, and my sister sat together, not holding hands, up there on the stage. The Speechathon was about to start. The crowd quieted as Mr. Dranger approached the microphone, and I have to admit that I was a little nervous. Actually, I was a lot nervous. As you know, Leona hadn't written a speech and she wouldn't tell me what she was going to say, so I didn't know whether her mouth was just minutes away from releasing words or nuclear weapons.

Before speaking, Mr. Dranger gave the auditorium a left-to-right once-over with that small smile of his that's not so much smug as it is smug-flavored, as if he and the universe are sharing some inside joke about the secret to life and he's proud of his promise not to share it with the rest of us. He gave the microphone two taps—sending two sonic burps our way—to test for amplification, and now that the test was passed, he spoke to us:

"So good morning, and welcome to our third annual Speechathon. For those of you who either don't know or may have forgotten, the purpose of the Speechathon is simply to give our candidates for school president a chance to formally introduce themselves to all of you and let you know why they're running for the highest, most honored position at this school. The Speechathon also marks the official start of the election season, which will go from now till this June, when you will actually vote for our new school president."

A couple of guys in the audience—it sounded like it came from the Seniors section up front—shouted "LEONA FOR PREZ!" triggering a thin cascade of claps throughout the auditorium.

Mr. Dranger said, "Okay, let's settle down."

The auditorium got quiet again.

I could see Leona go from smile to serious again.

Mr. Dranger continued: "This is something we all need to take very seriously." He pointed behind him. "Three of your schoolmates are sitting up here right now because they think they have what it takes to be your new leader. And I hope to heaven they're right because being a leader is something that should *never* be played around with . . . Leadership. A skill claimed by so many but possessed by so few. It's a skill that, as school council advisor for the last ten years, I've been steadfastly trying to cultivate in all my students, because it's a skill that's so badly needed in our world. That's why, as some of you know, I dismantled this school's old election system four years ago. Prior to that, this school's elections were much like many other schools' elections: they were done on a class-by-class basis. Ninth graders voted for ninth grade president. Tenth graders voted for tenth grade president. And so on. But I noticed something very troubling under that system. The class presidents didn't give it their All. It was just a title to them. Nothing more. Half the time kids either didn't even know or had forgotten who their class president was. So, with the administration's blessing, I decided to fix that broken system and made all subsequent elections *school-body*-based instead of class-based. Instead of being president of just one class, the elected candidate would be president of the *entire school*. Because when you're the leader of just two hundred, there's always that temptation to sleep on the job; but when you're a leader of eight hundred and fifty, you're more likely to stay wide awake and do the job to the best of your ability. In other words, you're more likely to be a true leader. What did they say in that Spider-Man movie?—'With great power, comes . . . ?'"

"Great responsibility," the auditorium said. Uly and I didn't say anything. We don't like the Spider-Man movies.

Mr. Dranger smiled and nodded. "That's it. When you're the leader of bigger numbers, the responsibility gets bigger too. And I wanted this school's presidential candidates to get a real taste of what it's like to be an actual Leader, so that by the time they graduate and go out into that world, they'll have the necessary tools to be what everybody out there so badly needs." He paused for a moment, then continued. "Now, before I bring up each of our three candidates, I just want to say that I was, frankly, a bit disappointed that there was such a small number of students who came forward and requested to run this year. I'm not sure if it was because of the GPA requirement or because you were just shy or because you thought it was just for eleventh graders. So let me just say, to all of you, and I hope you'll keep this in mind for next year: if you think you have what it takes to be president, then run. As simple as that. It doesn't matter if you're a freshman or sophomore or junior. And yes, there's a minimum GPA requirement of 3.0, but that's not set in stone by any means. You could have a GPA of 2.1: if you have the right amount of passion, we'll let you in. So please keep that in mind. Remember, I want to see a bigger candidate turnout next year." He looked at his watch then looked back up at the audience. "So, without further ado, let me give the floor to our candidates. Just to give you a quick overview of how it works: I'll briefly introduce each candidate, in alphabetical order, and each one will have up to five minutes to tell you what they're all about. I implore each of you to give your utmost attention and respect to each candidate, and refrain from calling out comments during each speech."

He cleared his throat, took a white index card out of his

inside blazer pocket, and, looking at it, told us, "Our first candidate is an eleventh grader from the town of Oakville. She entered Knight High two years ago and has been building quite an impressive academic and extracurricular record of achievement. Among other things, she's the head of the Dark Voices club and the Assistant Managing Director of the Treasury for the Black Box Theater. Let us all welcome our first candidate— Regina Bernadette Gates!"

As the auditorium clapped, Uly's sister stood up and walked over to the microphone, taking the place of Mr. Dranger, who sat in a chair in a corner of the stage.

Uly's sister is gorgeous. She's tall, with almond-shaped eyes and prominent cheekbones and dark-brown skin, and her hair is in long thin braided ropes. And she has this smoky, sultry jazz-singerish voice. And she moves and walks like someone who's been in command ever since she went from womb to world. Sometimes I wish I could *be* her. But since that would mean I'd be dating my own brother, I better rephrase that: I wish I could be *someone like* her. Just overflowing with so much confidence that it spills out of me and forms a lake called Lake Confidence where parts of it freeze and form glaciers called Pillars Of Confidence. She's way more confident than I could ever be.

Uly's sister also happens to scare the shit out of me. I've never told Uly or anybody else, but I always find myself intimidated by her. I've eaten lunch with him and his sister a few times and each time lunch felt like thirty hours instead of thirty minutes. For one thing, she's serious as all hell. And when I say serious, I mean *serious*. Drill sergeants with a million Botox injections to their name smile more than her. And she has this way of looking at you that makes you want to apologize for something, even though you did nothing wrong.

Before Regina even opened her mouth behind that microphone this morning she did something that shocked me. She looked out at the crowd . . . and smiled.

Then she started talking.

"Truthanasia—that's where I live. And in my mission to Keep It Real with you, I want to start by saying this: last year if you had told me I'd be up here running for president, I would've said, 'Sorry, I think you got me mixed up with somebody else.' Even as recently as last month, I had no plans whatsoever to run for president. But a few days ago something happened. One of the candidates up here gave a speech that basically said that most of the black and Latinx students in this school should stop coming here. Then, a few days later, this same candidate put up campaign posters that implied that this school should go back to being all-white, the way it was many years ago. Well, a Racial Insult doesn't have to wear a name-etag for me to recognize it, and so here I am. Why am I running for president? To tell you that, I gotta tell you this . . . Imagine, for a minute, that Mother Nature is a racist. But instead of white or black, the only color she loves is orange. According to her, all the other colors in the world should just go away forever—black, white, green, yellow, red, gray, purple. But not orange. Now, because she's a firm believer in Orange Supremacy, she sets out to redesign the world. And now, instead of blue, the sky is orange. And now, instead of green, grass is orange. Trees are orange. All the oceans, rivers, and lakes are orange. Elephants are orange. Bears are orange. All your dogs are orange. Zebras are now orange with light orange stripes. Apple juice is orange. Grape juice: orange. Vanilla shakes: orange. Strawberry ice cream: orange. Leather jackets: only available in orange. Wedding dresses: orange, and so are the diamond rings that go with them. Baseball caps are orange, no matter what the team is. The streetlight for Go is orange, and the streetlight for Stop is orange. Olympic gold medals are orange, Olympic silver medals are orange, and Olympic bronze medals are orange. That famous album by Prince is called *Orange Rain*. That cinnamon chewing gum is now Big Orange. That bus that takes you from Philly to Boston is now the Orangehound. That mysterious gap in space is the Orange Hole. When you're singing sad music, you're singing the oranges. In Vegas people play Orangejack. That last-minute plane you catch at night is the Orange-Eye. Will Smith and Tommy Lee Jones are the Men In Orange. Dorothy and the Scarecrow go down the Orange Brick Road. Spider-Man's toughest enemy is the Orange Lantern. The wolf scares Little Orange Riding Hood. Because, you see, every person and everything in the world now is orange . . . Raise your hand if you're tired of me saying 'orange.'"

So many hands went up that I couldn't even see Regina anymore. When the hands went back down I saw her again.

She continued. "And that was just two minutes of pretending. Imagine living your whole life in a world like that." She was quiet for a moment. Then she spoke again. "And that's my problem with posters like *Turn Knight Back To Day*. It's like living in an orange world. And when you're living in an orange world, dying is the one thing you can't wait to do. Being in a world with different colors makes you feel alive. Alive is how I wanna feel. And I'm guessing you do too. And that's why I'm running for president. So if you wanna be on the Alive team, then join the Regina Regime. Thank you."

There was so much applause in that auditorium that the claps sounded like thunderclaps. As I watched Uly's sister return to her seat on the stage I couldn't believe this stone-faced girl had just given a speech that put me close to tears. My hands started hurting and I looked down at them and saw why: they were creating some thunderclaps of their own. I looked up from my thunderclapping hands and saw my non-clapping sister staring at me. She looked hurt. So I quickly made my clapping go from thunder to firecracker to regular clap to nothing. And waited for the next speaker.

ULY

My sister rocked the block with her speech and I wasn't surprised; when she recited it for me last night I legit knew it was going to kill. The only thing that *did* surprise me was that she'd actually memorized the whole thing in one night. When she sat back down she wasn't smiling, but I could tell she was happy with what she'd just done, as she should've been.

Mr. Dranger, with his long-winded ass, was back behind the mic. He said, "Thank you, Regina . . . Our second candidate is also an eleventh grader, and he grew up right here in Collingswood. He joined Knight High as a freshman and he quickly made a name for himself on the football field, helping the school defeat Washington High, Cuthbert High, and Lambert High, among many others. He was named MVP two years in a row and consistently earned the respect of his coaches and teammates. Unfortunately, a life-changing injury last summer disrupted his plan to be on the field again this year. But, to slightly alter what an astute person once said: 'You can never keep a brave man down.' And that's why he's about to stand up right now and come to this microphone. Let us all welcome our second candidate—John William Smith!"

The whole auditorium erupted with applause and some of Smith's old football peeps stood up and fist-jabbed the air with chants of "JS FOR PREZ, JS FOR PREZ!"

Smith, wearing a football jersey over his shirt and tie, stood up and his girlfriend—head cheerleader Sherry Shipley—appeared from backstage to take his arm and lead him to the mic. Once he was there, she waited a few feet behind him so she'd be ready when he was done.

When the audience put a lid on the applause, Smith pushed his dark glasses farther up his nose and started talking. "Good morning, Knight High. I want to be your president so I can help make this school be a place that you're proud to call your own. School doesn't have to be a place that you hate getting up and going to when that alarm clock sounds in the morning. It's supposed to be a place where you build your future. And I plan to make this a comfortable place where you can use the tools you'll need to build that future. One of those tools is always being positive, no matter what happens to you. I'm living proof of that. Some people have asked me if I'm angry or bitter about being blind. But I'm not. My theory is that everything happens for a reason. I feel that, when life gives you lemons, you should make lemonade. And that's why I'm running for president. Thank you."

We all clapped as Smith's girlfriend took his arm, kissed him, and guided him back to his seat on the stage.

Mr. Dranger seemed to be in a daze when he got back to the mic, like his ass was surprised to be back there so soon. He quickly clipped his smile back on and said, "Thank you, John. I guess we can all file that under Short and Sweet . . . And now, next is our third and final candidate, also an eleventh grader and also born and raised right here in Collingswood. She joined Knight High as a freshman and has built quite a distinguished record here, ranging from making the High Honors list for three years in a row to serving as soccer team captain to being co-manager of the Yearbook Committee. Let us all welcome—though she already kind of got an early start last week—our third and final candidate: Leona Priscilla Walls!"

As the applause and whistles and calls of "LEONA FOR PREZ!" ripped through the auditorium, Sallie's sister—in a red dress and matching boots—damn near bounced her way over to the mic. She yanked it out of its holder and got out from behind the lectern—the same way she'd done in the cafeteria.

Sallie squeezed my hand for some reason. Before I could give the squeeze more mind time, her sister started speaking and right away the crowd put a lid on the applause.

"First of all," Leona said, "much love to Mr. Dranger for getting us all out of Period C this morning. I *so* wasn't ready for that vocab quiz."

The auditorium laughed and clapped.

Gripping the mic, Leona moved closer to her two opponents. "And second of all, how about another hand for my two candidates here."

The auditorium clapped for Smith and my sister.

Leona pointed at Smith and told the audience, "How many people can go through what he's gone through and still run for president?"

Then she pointed at my sister. "And Regina . . ." She turned to the audience. "How lit was that speech?"

The auditorium clapped again.

Leona turned to Regina and said, "You so rocked my life with that speech. I just gotta touch you."

Still gripping the mic, Leona moved closer to my sister and was about to touch her, then stopped and said, "Can I touch you? I mean, I don't wanna just do it without—Can I touch you?"

My sister just stared at her.

"I don't have cooties or anything, I swear," Leona assured my sister. "No cooties." She turned back to the audience. "My ex can back me up on that." She visored her eyes with her hand, squinted at the crowd, and said, "Where's Trevor Nelson? Trevor—where are you?"

A hand shot up from the pool of seniors at the front.

"There he is," Leona said. "Trevor, do you have cooties?"

Trevor said, "Yeah, but you didn't give 'em to me, so no worries."

The auditorium laughed.

Leona turned back to my sister and said, "See? But seriously—can I touch you?"

Regina looked at Leona for a long time. The silence in that auditorium was suddenly so thick you couldn't have cut that shit with the bloodthirstiest of chain saws.

My sister slowly nodded.

Leona reached down and touched Regina's shoulder. Then she said, "Ahh, yes."

Sallie looked at me. Her face was a canvas of confusion and tucked in the canvas's corner were the artist's initials: WTF.

My sister was staring at Leona's hand like it had more in common with a cadaver.

Leona took her hand away and told the audience, "And isn't she beautiful? I've always wanted to say that."

The auditorium clapped.

Still pointing at my sister, Leona told the audience, "I love those braids. I so wish I could pull off a look like that." She pointed at her own hair. "But it wouldn't work with me."

Some people in the audience laughed.

Leona said, "Braids on her and she looks like a goddess. Braids on me and I look like an escaped mental patient screaming in the middle of the street about the end of the world."

The auditorium laughed.

Leona and her mic walked back over to the middle of the stage. "It's the same with guys and shaved heads. A black guy with a shaved head looks cool, but a white guy with a shaved head looks either racist or sickly. Why is that?"

The auditorium laughed.

Leona pointed at someone in the audience and said, "Look at Ron Campinello over there, sliding down in his seat and putting on a baseball cap. It's too late, Ron—we all know you got a shaved head under there. Quick, somebody—give him Sensitivity training or a teaspoon of Robitussin."

The auditorium laughed some more.

When the crowd got quiet, she said, "Now I know what some of you are thinking. I shouldn't be saying things like that about black people's hair. White people should *never* talk about black people's hair, right? It's a territory with too many landmines, right? And each landmine has the same thing written on top: *You Might Offend Them.* Well, I don't agree with that. You know why? Because I was just being honest. Honest. That's all I've been since I started this campaign. Everything I've said has come from an honest place. I think we owe it to black people to be honest with them . . . I'm gonna tell you about something that happened to me a couple of summers ago. I was at camp and one night my roommates and I were really bored, so we asked one of the camp counselors to take us to the movies. We ended up seeing a Tyler Perry movie—I forget the name of it, but it was the only movie playing in town. So, when it was over, the camp counselor asked us what we thought of it. Now, two of my roommates were white and one was black and the camp counselor was black too. My two white roommates went on and on about how great the movie was—it was *so* funny and unique and way more witty than they expected. And when the camp counselor got to me and asked me what I thought of it, I looked her right in the eye and said, 'I thought it sucked. I thought it was an insult to the audience's intelligence. I didn't laugh once.' Now you should've seen how my white roommates reacted. They acted all scandalized, like I'd committed *sacrilege* or something—you know, how *dare* I say something negative about something black-people-related. But the black camp counselor and the black roommate? Not offended at all. The camp counselor shrugged and said, 'Well, you can't like every movie.' And the black roommate actually agreed with me and said, 'Yeah he's really overrated.' You see? I said something that was supposed to be so offensive to black people, but the only people who got offended were white people. Why weren't the two black people offended? Because they knew I was being honest with them. Honesty is the best gift you can give somebody. You know what *would've* offended the two of them? If I'd said, 'Oh my God, what a funny, unique, witty movie!' when I really didn't mean it. People want the truth, and black people are no different. And the truth was all I was giving you last week when I said that this school got worse after the Woodlawn and Oakville kids started coming here. And I stand by that statement, and will always stand by it. It would be offensive if I stood up here and said, 'Oh my God, this school is so much safer now that the Woodlawn and Oakville kids are here.' It would be offensive if I stood up here and said, 'Oh my God, this school was such a danger zone back when it was all-white.' It would be offensive if I stood up here and said, 'All the white kids are happy and comfortable going to school with all the Woodlawn and Oakville kids.' It would be offensive because I'd be lying to you. And I'm not in the lying business. I'm in the gift-giving business. And honesty is the gift I wanna give you. And that's why I'm running for president."

She started walking toward us, stepping so close to the edge of the stage that another step would've sent her ass plummeting into the crowd.

She said, "So if you wanna see the light, be a Leonite. If you wanna give Dishonesty a fight, be a Leonite. If you wanna kick Deception with all your might, be a Leonite! If you think this plan is tight, be a Leonite!! IF YOU THINK I'M RIGHT, BE A LEONITE!!!!!"

She held up the microphone and let it go, literally dropping the mic, then she shot both of her hands into the air.

The mic drop had sent an ear-splitting sonic boom into the audience but mofos were too busy—clapping, standing up, and chanting "Leonite!"—to recoil from the pain.

I didn't stand up but I still clapped because I didn't want to hurt Sallie's feelings, but inside I was disgusted. And I didn't clap too long because I didn't want to hurt my sister's feelings. She already looked hurt enough, if you can feel me on that.

ULY

My original plan was to tell Regina after the Speechathon when we got home. But she was withdrawn as hell for the rest of that day—the applause Leona had gotten seemed to still be echoing in her head—so I decided to give her some space and wait till today.

As we did a rare Saturday CakeTalk this afternoon—she wanted to go over some campaign strategies for next week—I figured it was either now or sever.

After I stirred the yolk and stuff into dough, I handed the bowl to her, and as she was pouring it into the cake pan, I said, "So Jeen, check it out: I got something to tell you."

Still pouring, she said, "What's up?"

I said, "Sallie and I are dating."

My sister paused the pouring, but it really didn't matter at that point, since most of it was already in the pan. She looked at me for a moment, then looked away and poured out the little that was left.

She stayed quiet as I opened the oven door. She carefully shoved the cake inside. I closed the door.

When she straightened she looked at me and said, "How long?"

For a second my dumb ass actually thought she was referring to the damn cake. Then my common sense came back and I said, "A couple of months."

She leaned against the counter, folded her arms, and stared at the oven door. The only sound was the Spinners playing on my sister's phone.

When the passing seconds started feeling like passing seasons, I said, "For real? You're gonna just shut down on a brother?"

She said, "What do you want me to say?"

I said, "Before you throw shade—do I have to remind you what someone who bore a strikin' resemblance to your ass said yesterday? Different colors make the world feel alive. That was you, right? Or do I have her mixed up with somebody else?"

After a few moments, my sister said, "I ain't trippin'. I'm cool with it. Just as long as you keep the Boyfriend clothes separate from the Campaign Manager clothes."

I nodded, put my hand over my heart, and said, "My word is bond."

She said, "'Cause I'm tellin' you right now, the minute those clothes get mixed together and fuck up my campaign, we're gonna have a problem up in here."

I nodded and said, "I promise: the Boyfriend clothes will always stay in one machine and the Campaign Manager clothes will always stay in the other machine."

We both stared at each other for a moment.

Then I raised my fist to offer a bond bump. "So we good?" I said.

She didn't say anything. Just stared at me. Then she nodded, bumped her fist to mine, and said, "Like 'Boyz N The Hood.'"

SALLIE

Sometimes when the weather is nice Leona and I take the row-boat out of the garage and head over to Newton Lake for a little R & R: the first *R* being Row and the second *R* being what you're used to the second *R* being. The way it's supposed to work is this way: I row for about fifteen minutes while she relaxes in the back, then she rows for about fifteen minutes while I relax in the back. But the way it usually works is this way: I row for twenty-five minutes while she relaxes in the back, then she rows for five minutes while I sit in the back, fuming about why she let me do all the rowing.

As I rowed the boat this afternoon I knew I was going to do 95 percent of the rowing again, but this time it didn't bother me, because it was Saturday, because February was continuing its streak of acting more April than February, and because I was in love.

I turned around to look at my sister, who was in the back, lying on her back, with her phone lying on her belly, the reas-suring sounds of T. Swift oozing out of her phone's Spotify. She seemed to be in an even better mood than me today. Even though she was in a boat, I could tell she was flying high about her well-received speech yesterday, which was more well-received than I thought it was going to be.

I'm still trying to figure out what I thought of the speech. If she'd shown it to me ahead of time I definitely would've suggested some changes, but one thing I'm glad about is that the speech made people understand her more.

But the speech's actual message is what my system is having a hard time fully digesting. Sort of like when somebody hands you a plate of food that looks perfect on the plate: it's well-cut and neatly arranged, but hours after you've eaten it you can feel it disagreeing with your insides and refusing to lie down peacefully.

My sister had no problem lying down peacefully in the back of the boat this afternoon. She looked so at peace that I felt like I could tell her anything at that moment. So I decided that this was the right moment to tell her what I should've told her a long time ago.

I let go of the oars, letting natural buoyancy do some of the work for a change, and swiveled myself around to face Leona, who was still lying on her back in the back.

"You awake, Lee?" I asked. It was hard to see her eyes through her sunglasses.

"Yeah," she told the sky.

I said, "I need to tell you something."

"Okay," she told the sky.

I said, "Uly Gates and I—we're a Thing."

My sister kept staring toward the sky. Then she said, "She finally confesses. That must've been the worst-kept secret since Georgina Bush came out last year."

FYI: Georgina's last name isn't Bush.

My sister rolled her head from sky to sister and stared at me through her sunglasses. "Why him?" she asked.

"Why not him?" I asked.

She rolled her head back to the sky. "I don't know, I just think you could do better," she said.

I said, "Maybe, but that would just be going backward, since he's already the best."

She didn't say anything.

I thought maybe she wanted me to say something else, so I sort of sat forward and said, "Just so you know: I won't let my Thing with him get in the way of being your campaign manager. I made you a promise and I'm gonna help you as much as I can."

The reflection of the sky and clouds slid off my sister's sunglasses as she rolled her head back to me, and now I saw me, in double, staring back at me. "I hope so," she said, then turned her head back to the sky.

The boat's natural buoyancy felt like it wanted another break, so I swiveled back around, took the oars, and continued rowing us.

ULY

When your girlfriend pulls a knife on you, it's usually bad news, but when Sallie did it today the news was pretty damn good.

We were in Philly's Rittenhouse Park—one of the most bacon places to spend a Sunday afternoon, if any of you ever happen to be in the area—and we were sitting on the grass, leaning against a tree, chilling and feeling. A couple of days ago we both decided to Go Public. Not as in bullhorns and rooftops; I just mean we've decided to no longer confine our kissing and hand-holding to staircases, Planetariums, and walk-in stomachs. Everything will now be out in the open.

We started by giving the 411 about our one-on-one to our sisters yesterday.

And I guess that's why Sallie and I were in such a good mood today. Dropping our We-mix on our sisters was something we were mad nervous about, but we both survived. As you already know, Regina didn't shove me in the oven, and Sallie was happy to report that Leona didn't throw her overboard. The way we see it, our sisters were the highest hurdle; and now that we've jumped it, we're ready for the World Championships.

As we leaned against the tree this afternoon, our fingers interlaced, Sallie said, "So I was thinking . . . We should make a promise to each other, that we'll never let the campaign-manager stuff interfere with our Thing."

I nodded and said, "I'm down with that. What do we do?—a pinky swear?"

She said, "Actually, I have something else in mind."

She dug into her backpack and pulled out a kitchen knife.

My heart started beating fast, but it was the *bad*-fast, not the good-fast.

She held out the knife, then looked at me and quietly said, "Give me your hand."

I stared at her and tried to think of the best way to tell my girlfriend that Sunday hand-holding and a knife go together about as well as her sister and my sister.

But then she burst out laughing and said, "Just kidding."

She twisted around and started carving something into the tree trunk.

As she carved, I relaxed again, chuckled, and said, "You have no idea how close a brother was to not just endin' the honeymoon, but sendin' a honey *to* the moon."

Giggling some more, she finished her carving, which turned out to be the letter *U*.

With a grin, she handed the knife to me. By instinct, I knew what to do: I carved *& S* into the tree trunk.

Looking at the *U & S*, Sallie nodded, then said, "But you know what I like better?"

She took the knife from me and carved *US* into the tree trunk, a few inches under the original carvings.

Pointing at the newly carved *US*, she said, "I like that better. That way, there's nothing between us—no symbols, no punctuation. And it also spells 'us.' I mean, I know it's kinda corduroy, but it's something I've always wanted to do."

Sliding my finger through the carving's curves, I nodded and said, "I'm a fan."

"Me too," she said and smiled at me.

We interlaced fingers again and kissed. For a long time.

We would've stayed at that tree longer, but it started to rain—really hard—so we got up and ran toward the train station, never letting each other's hand go.

PART

2

March

A golden-haired angel
watches over him.
—Angel Eyes,
*The Good, the Bad
and the Ugly*

SALLIE

As Wilk drove Leona and me home yesterday afternoon my sister twisted around to look at me from the front seat and said, "I need you to get me on the Knightly News tomorrow morning."

The Knightly News is Knight High's daily television news show and it's broadcast to all the classrooms during the first five to ten minutes of the first period.

I said, "I can get you on, but I don't know if it can be done by tomorrow morning. They pre-schedule things, like, three days in advance."

My sister shrugged and said, "Just squeeze me in. It's not like I'm some loser freshman with Sun Chip crumbs on her mouth. I'm running for fucking president. You tell 'em it's for me, they'll Swipe Right."

I said, "Okay." Then I said, "Why?"

"Why what?" my sister said.

I said, "Why do you wanna go on there and why the big rush?"

Looking at me in the rearview mirror, Wilk said, "You ask more questions than 6ABC. Can't you just do it?"

I snapped, "No, I can't 'just do it.'"

He said, "Really? Hmm, the last I heard, you're the campaign manager."

I snapped, "That's right. I'm the Campaign Manager. Not the Robot Who Just Blindly Takes Orders Without Making Sure They Won't Make My Sister Look Bad."

He said, "Campaign Manager plus Bad Attitude equals Somebody Who Shouldn't Be My Girlfriend's Campaign Manager."

I said, "Yeah, and Fuck plus You equals Fuck You."

My sister said, "This sexual tension between you two really needs to be dealt with. Do we need to pull over so I can step outside and let you two play Bury The Bone?"

I snorted and said, "That'll be the day. You'll be able to have a heatstroke in Antarctica before that happens."

Grinning, Wilk said, "Yeah, I'm a little too pale for her taste. Mother Nature didn't leave me in the oven long enough."

I narrowed my eyes, leaned toward him, and said, "What did you just say?"

My sister said, "Okay, everybody needs to just calm down here."

The car was suddenly quiet.

Leona looked at her boyfriend and said, "Are you calm?"

Wilk said, "Yeah."

Leona looked at me and said, "Are you calm?"

"No," I said.

"Well you need to *get* calm, 'cause I need you to get me on tomorrow morning. Now are you gonna do it or not?"

I said, "Of course I'm gonna do it. I just need to know why."

Leona didn't say anything for a moment. Then she said, "Let's just say I need to make an important announcement."

That made me go from nervous to really nervous. "About what?" I asked.

My sister twisted around in her seat again to look at me; she smiled, her eyes slightly narrow. "If I didn't know you better, I'd think you're saying you don't trust me."

"I'm not saying that," I said. "It's just—everybody's going to be watching you, Lee. The slightest wrong move, the slightest wrong phrase, the slightest wrong *word* could cost you this whole election."

She twisted back around to face the front. "I know what I'm doing. And if you do too, then I'll be in front of the camera tomorrow morning."

So when we got home I emailed Ms. Rothstein, the drama teacher, because she's tight with Ms. Mitchell, the advisor for Knight TV, and because I'm tight with Ms. Rothstein, Ms. Rothstein got Ms. Mitchell to agree to squeeze my sister into the tight timeframe.

Then I called Uly, to tell him about my sister's planned announcement. But when he picked up the phone I decided not to tell him; we'd promised each other we wouldn't let our sisters' campaigns spill into our relationship. But as we talked, I went back to wanting to tell him. So I told him. But as you've probably figured out, there really wasn't much to tell, except for this:

"So Uly, just so you know, my sister's planning on making some big announcement on the Knightly News tomorrow morning. She won't tell me what it is, but I figured I'd let you know so you're not . . . you know, taken by surprise or whatever the hell."

He said, "Real talk? Okay, thanks. I wonder what it is . . ."

I couldn't change the subject fast enough. And even though we started talking about a non-Leona subject, the Leona subject stayed on my mind. And I found myself thinking that maybe I'd just done a bad thing. To my sister.

I'm her campaign manager.

And I'd just told her opponent's campaign manager what her next step would be.

Was that betrayal or just betrayal-flavoring?

I told myself I was just trying to be an honest girlfriend.

But why does being an honest girlfriend mean I have to also be a dishonest campaign manager?

The more I thought about it, the more I couldn't stop thinking about it, and for the first time ever, I found myself distracted while my boyfriend was talking to me.

During first period this morning Mr. Lacey fired up the projector for the Knightly News. As always, there was sophomore Coral Bleeker—she has one of those faces that the phrase "cute-as-a-button" was invented for—smiling to the camera. But not as always, there was my sister sitting in the chair next to her.

"Good morning, Knight High," Coral began. "Today is Tuesday March sixth. Just fifty-seven days to the last day of school. Before I give you the latest in school news, I have a special guest with me today, as you can see. She's Leona Walls, one of the three candidates for school president next year, and she has an important announcement for all of you." She made the handing-something-invisible motion to my sister and said, "Floor is yours."

Leona smiled at Coral and said, "Thank you so much, Coral. And can I just tell you how gorgeous I think you are? I mean, I don't swing that way, but if I did, you'd be the first to know."

Coral said, "Oh. Well, that's good to know. I think."

My sister told her, "And after the segment you've gotta tell me where you got those earrings."

"Sure thing," Coral assured.

My sister now turned her smile to the camera. "So hello, Knight High. So by now, some of you have probably heard about something called Diverseaty . . ."

The word "Diverseaty" appeared at the top of the screen.

My sister continued: "For those of you who don't know, it's this program that the school wants to put into motion next month. The way it'll work is: the cafeteria will now have assigned seating. That's right, everybody will need to sit in alphabetical order, according to their last name. Why? To encourage people of different backgrounds to eat together and talk to each other and get to know each other. Well, here's my problem with that: nobody should ever be *forced* to sit next to someone they don't know. I just think that's wrong. For a lot of us, lunchtime is the only time we get to relax and unwind after a crappy morning of classes and before an even crappier afternoon of even more classes. We're tense all day—why do we have to be tense during lunch too? I don't wanna have to sit at the lunch table, racking my brains to think of something to talk about with somebody whose only thing in common with me is that our last names come right after each other in some stupid alphabet. I wanna sit and eat and laugh with my friends. We *all* should be able to do that if we want to. The last time I checked, we live in a free country. We're just a fifteen-minute train ride from the place where that was decided. We live in a free society, and if you elect me president, it'll be my mission to make sure this school stays just as free. So those of you who agree with me about stopping Diverseaty: I urge you to sign a text petition that I started this morning. It's real simple. All you gotta do is text 'No' to 69797."

The word "No" and the number "69797" appeared at the top of the screen, just below the word "Diverseaty."

"Again, that's text 'No' to 69797. That's actually Ms. Mitchell's work phone—she's the one in charge of Knight TV. We wanted a neutral party to oversee all the texts. Now, all we need is just one hundred of you to say no. It's my understanding that it'll carry enough weight for the administration to reconsider the plan. I can't promise that they'll change their mind, but at least it'll make them have a meeting to reconsider. People, I'm telling you: this kinda thing can work. Just a few months ago, a kid at Lambert High started a petition to allow a certain controversial book into their library; one hundred kids signed it and the next month, that book was in their library. See what I'm saying? Your voice is more powerful than you know. Use it today, to stop Diverseaty: text 'No' to 69797. Diverseaty—could that name be more corduroy, by the way? I feel stupid whenever I say it. Well, I guess that's it for now."

My sister smiled at Coral and said, "Thank you again for letting me hijack your show."

Coral said, "No problem."

My sister turned her smile back to the camera and said, "And thank *you*. And remember: if you think I'm right, be a Leonite."

As some of my classmates started taking out their phones, I sat there, feeling something that I've been feeling a lot whenever my sister gives a speech to the school: the feeling that she didn't mean any harm, but some people might've just been harmed. She's like a well-intentioned soldier holding an M16 as he strolls down a residential street but the weapon accidentally discharges and now a dozen innocent civilians are lying on the street, dead. But he didn't mean to shoot anybody.

That's what my sister is like, more and more each day. And now, once again, I have to clean up the mess.

ULY

When my sister saw Leona's Say No To Diversity speech yesterday, she was pissed the hell off. Before Leona could even get "Bye" all the way out of her mouth, Regina had already fired off a text to me: Get me on the Knightly News for tomorrow morning!!!!!!!!!!!!!!!!!!!!!!!!!!!!!!! There are twenty-eight ways to tell a sister ain't fucking around, and they're all exclamation points.

But there was only one problem: I don't know anything about how to get somebody's ass on Knight TV. All those Knight TV mofos are stuck-up as hell—like they're on planet Too Cool For School and you're on planet Waste Of Space Who Might As Well Just Die Right Now.

But I know how my sister gets when she really wants something so I went to the only person I knew who had a Knight TV connection.

"Sallie," I said on the phone between classes, "a brother's in a jam here. Regina wants me to get her on the Knightly News for tomorrow; how do I hook that up?"

She told me and it turned out not to be as hard as I thought. All I had to do was hit up Ms. Rothstein—she's the one who directed that raggedy play Sallie and I were in—who then hit up Ms. Mitchell, who runs Knight TV. And before lunch, I had the whole thing hooked up, with Sallie's help, of course.

And so this morning, the anchorgirl Coral Bleeker loaned the spotlight to my sister, who looked into the camera and said, "Good morning, everyone. As you know, yesterday Leona Walls told you about a text petition to shut down the diverse-seating plan that's scheduled for next month. I know that some of you have already texted in your No. Those of you who haven't: I urge you not to. And here's why. When I first came to this school two years ago, I really didn't know a lot of people. I was a freshman from Oakville and, as you know, kids from Oakville go to Oakville Middle School, not Collingswood Middle. So by the time the Oakville kids get here, all the Collingswood kids have gotten to know each other, but Oakville kids feel like they're starting over in a new town. Probably 'cause they are. It can be really lonely. *Very* lonely. That's how I felt that first year. My brother Uly hadn't started here yet and the few friends I had from Oakville didn't eat lunch during my half of the hour. So I spent a lot of lunches sitting alone, most of the time with nobody else at the table. I'm sure all of you have gone through that at least once—maybe it's that crazy Tuesday when all your friends have lab during your half of the lunch hour and now you're stuck in the caf, alone. Well, that Crazy Tuesday for you happens on Monday, Wednesday, Thursday, Friday, *and* Tuesday for them. And I know it's fun to hang with your friends during lunch, but what about the kids who don't have friends? What about the kids who go from ninth to twelfth, always sitting by their self?—either 'cause they're shy or gay or Indian or trans or bullied or abused at home? And yeah, I know we're livin' in a free society, but for some people, freedom always seems to cost about fifty dollars more than what they have in the bank. Shutting down diverse seating: that's the first step toward an orange world. Sometimes the only way to get blue, brown, black, green, red, gray, yellow, and white to join orange in the box is tellin' orange,

'Yo, if you can't move over and share your space, then maybe it's time you move out and *go* to space.' You feel me? So I'm here to tell you that there's *another* text petition—one I started this morning. It's that same number Leona gave you yesterday—69797, but this time you text 'Yes.' Yes to diversity-seating. Again, text 'Yes' to 69797. If one hundred of you do that, it can shut down what she's trying to start up. Text 'Yes' to 69797. Thank you."

The word "Yes" and the number "69797" appeared on the screen. And just like yesterday, it stayed there for the rest of Coral Bleeker's news cruise.

My sister killed it again. But I'm starting to wonder if maybe it was more injury than kill.

JULY

The shit turned out to be an injury. After school today Mr. Dranger told Regina and me that Leona's petition got more Nos than Regina's Yesses. (He wouldn't tell us the exact numbers—which was mad annoying.) And just when we thought the news couldn't get more raggedy, Dranger twisted the knife and damn near eviscerated: he said the school decided not to go through with Diverseaty.

"It actually wasn't because of the petitions," Mr. Dranger explained. "The administration claims the cancellation was already in the works, even before Leona started the petition. Apparently, there had been a lot of complaints from parents." He shrugged, then looked at my sister. "But my hat goes off to you for at least trying and giving the *people* a chance to make up their mind. You fought with the best weapon—democracy."

My sister nodded and mumbled, "Thank you," then she walked out of his office.

I felt really bad for her. I know how much she wants to knock out Leona—politically, not physically (though you probably wouldn't have to twist her arm too much for that second one)—and here it is the next round and *she's* the one pulling herself up from the canvas again. At least it feels that way. The first time was the Speechathon when Leona got more applause than she did. And this second time was the Diverseaty fail. My sister needs to win a round, but I don't know what boxing gloves to switch her to or what gym to transfer her to.

At dinner tonight Regina's sadness was still holding her face captive. But this time I don't think it was because of the two knock-outs she'd recently suffered. It was because of the two new additions to our table:

Sallie

Uncle KJ

Yes, for the first time, Sallie not only visited my place but also broke bread with us. That alone made Regina miserable, but Murphy's Law must've put my sister on blast tonight because there was Uncle KJ too.

Okay, check it out: Uncle KJ is my father's brother and it's no secret in our family that he's always been thirsty for white women. Uncle KJ loves the hell out of white women—and *only* white women—and that comes straight from the headquarters of Real City. Our father took Regina and me to his house a couple of times and all his walls are plastered with miles and miles of white actresses as far as the eye can see: from old-school (Cybill Shepherd, Anjelica Huston, Susan Sullivan, Meryl Streep, even Sophia Loren) to New Jack (Scarlett Johansson, Jennifer Lawrence, Anne Hathaway, Gal Gadot).

And check out what added to tonight's awkwardness: Uncle KJ seemed to be thirsty for Sallie too. He looked at her more than the mashed potatoes. And he kept asking her shit about her life: where she grew up, what places she likes to travel to, her favorite TV shows.

And don't let him get liquored up. Once that liquor hits his system, his ass gets *real* raggedy. Just as he was starting his second bottle, he told Sallie, "You know what your eyes remind me of? Chocolate M&M'S. Like as if you were eatin' a bag of M&M'S one day and two of the chocolate ones jumped right outta the bag and into your eyes and stayed stuck there."

Sallie kind of laughed and said, "Oh. Thank you. I don't think I've ever heard that before. Actually, I'm pretty sure I've never heard that before." To Sallie's credit, she was chill about the whole Uncle KJ thing. She seemed to find him more humorous than harmful.

My uncle took another sip from the bottle and asked her, "How'd you get your eyes to be so brown with that blond hair?"

My father looked at his brother and said, "Damn, KJ, it ain't like God handed her some crayons, pointed at her eyes, and said, 'Do what you want. I'm goin' to the movies.' Why don't you just leave the girl alone and let her enjoy her dinner?"

Sallie told my father, "It's okay, Mr. Gates." She turned back to Uncle KJ and said, "I'm half Italian." She touched her hair. "Now, this is from my father—he was a WASP." She pointed at her eyes. "These are from my mother—she was Italian. What's weird is that my sister's eyes are blue. She's always saying how she lucked out by getting our dad's WASP looks and our mom's Italian personality, instead of the other way around. Now that I think about it, it's probably not a nice thing to say, but that's my sister."

"It sure is," Regina bitterly said, her eyes on her plate.

My sister's comment kind of brought the room down. Tension was now officially at the table; I could all but see it tucking a napkin into its shirt, preparing to ask somebody to pass the bread.

Sallie must've had the same vision because she pointed at the food and said, "Regina, everything is so delicious. I didn't know you were such a great cook."

"Thank you," my sister said, still not looking up.

More silence. I guess Tension liked my sister's food too because its ass didn't seem in a hurry to go anywhere.

A vibrating sound broke the silence. Sallie took her phone

out, looked at the screen, and told us, "Oh, that's my stepmom. I'm afraid I have to get going. I told her to pick me up downstairs so she can take me over to this art store in Cherry Hill." She stood up.

"You're an artist?" Uncle KJ asked with interest.

Sallie said, "No, I have to get more supplies for my sister's campaign."

As soon as the words left her mouth I could tell she wished she'd put a lock on it. She gave Regina an awkward glance then shook my father's and Uncle KJ's hands.

"It was so nice to meet you two," she said.

"It was so nice to meet *you*," my uncle said, hand-sandwiching her hand. It was kind of disgusting.

Then my girlfriend looked at my sister and said, "And Regina, I'll see you tomorrow."

Regina nodded, never looking up from her plate.

As I walked Sallie downstairs to the lobby she said, "Okay, is it just me, or does your sister hate my guts?"

I said, "That might be a little strong. I mean, she hates you, don't get me wrong. But maybe not your guts too."

"Oh, I feel so much better now," she said.

When we got to the bottom of the steps, she asked me, "Is it because I'm managing my sister's campaign, or is it because I'm dating you?"

"Probably both," I said.

She said, "I don't know what to do. I mean, am I supposed to just stop being my sister's sister?"

I said, "Don't even trip on it. Just give her some time."

Sallie smiled at me and tugged on my arm. "Come on, I wanna introduce you to Lady M."

I kind of pushed back from her pull, stopping her.

"What?" she said.

I said, "Uh, maybe we should kiss goodbye right here instead of out there. I mean, is your stepmom . . . How should I say this? Uh, is your stepmom swirl-friendly?"

With a small smile, Sallie said, "What the hell is that?"

I said, "Is she okay with watchin' love in black-and-white?"

She said, "I've never asked her, but I'm sure she is. I told you—she's the Coolest Stepmother In The World. And she saw that movie *Get Out* and really liked it."

I said, "That don't mean shit. I really liked *Jaws*, but I still hate sharks."

Sallie reached up and pulled my forehead down to hers. "Well, you're not a shark—you're cuter. Now shut up and let me show my stepmom exactly how cute."

She pulled me toward the lobby doors. But after just two steps, she stopped us, looked at me, and said, "Actually, you're right about kissing goodbye right here. Not because my stepmom's a bigot but because she's my stepmom. Come on, let's do it."

We kissed goodbye.

Then we ran outside to her stepmother's waiting car.

Lady M rolled down the window and smiled out at me. She's pretty, somewhere in her forties, with short spiked red hair.

Putting her hand on my shoulder, Sallie said, "So Lady M, here he is."

"What a handsome young man," Lady M said.

Shaking her hand, I said, "Nice to meet you, Ms.—" I was suddenly stumped. I looked at Sallie and said, "Is it Walls?"

Lady M said, "Actually, Davenport, but don't worry, you can just call me Lady M."

My eyebrows went up. "Oh yeah? I get 'Lady M' privileges too? I'm honored."

Lady M laughed. Then she told Sallie, "You should invite him over for dinner sometime."

Sallie looked at me and said, "Definitely. We'll have to do that."

Her eyes seemed to be telling me, "I asked to come to your house. Why haven't you asked to come to my house yet?"

I tried to get my eyes to tell her, "Because of your sister."

I'm not sure if my eyes were loud enough for her to hear.

Before Sallie got into the car, we instinctively moved toward each other to kiss, but then we remembered that there was a SITA (Stepmom In The Area) situation, so we said our Goodbyes, and I watched the car drive off.

When I returned to the dinner table Uncle KJ gave me a slow clap and said, "I gotta hand it to you, nephew—you got ahold of some delicious, *fresh* Vanilla. The best kind."

My father looked at him and said, "Nigga, stop frontin'. With you, even when the vanilla's been on the shelf for two months and it's in dry, rotten clumps, you still can't wait to gobble up that shit."

Uncle KJ said, "Okay, maybe. But I prefer it fresh."

"You prefer it vanilla," my father said.

"Okay, maybe." Uncle KJ looked at me. "But let's get back to this Sallie girl. I can't believe how prett—"

"Is everybody done here?" Regina said, standing up. She looked miserable.

We told her yes.

She started gathering our plates.

"Let me help you, honey," Dad said.

"No, I got it. I'm fine," Regina said.

We quietly watched as she quickly stacked the dishes and took them back into the kitchen. After a moment, we heard the water running.

Uncle KJ turned to Dad and said, "You gotta do something about her, Z. Before it's too late."

Dad said, "What do you mean 'do something about her'?"

My uncle said, "She's about to turn into One Of Them. Already I can see the signs."

"What signs? What're you talkin' about?" Dad asked.

Uncle KJ said, "She's got all the symptoms of BQS."

"BQS?" my dad said.

Uncle KJ nodded. "Black Queen Syndrome."

My dad sighed and said, "Aw, man, not that again."

Uncle KJ nodded and said, "You don't like to admit it, but her mom had it too. The Black Queen Syndrome. 'I'm a Black Queen. I don't need no man. I can do everything by myself. Don't try to help me 'cause you'll just slow me down.' That's why I stopped fuckin' with black women. Haven't dated one since P. Diddy was just Puffy. And never will again. They're beautiful but their attitudes are stank as hell. You know how you can tell you're dating a beautiful, strong, educated black woman? 'Cause she'll tell you every five minutes. 'I'm a beautiful, strong, educated black woman. Are the five minutes up yet?, because I wanna say it again. I'm a beautiful, strong, educated black woman.' I can't *stand* that black queen bullshit." He pointed at the empty chair where my sister had been sitting. "She's turnin' into one of 'em. If you don't watch it, one day you're gonna wake up and she's gonna *be* one of 'em."

My dad said, "Hell, I'd *rather* her be a black queen. Queens rule, and when you rule, that means you won't marry a fool. Notice there's no wedding ring on your finger."

Uncle KJ said, "Nigga, don't change the subject. You know I'm droppin' some Einstein here. Sisters are so full of themselves it's a miracle they still have room for food." He pointed at me. "I don't blame our boy for pickin' a white girl."

I told him, "That's not why I'm dating her, Uncle KJ. And there are plenty of white girls who are stuck-up too."

"Amen," my father said.

Uncle KJ went on and on and eventually I had to take out my phone, put in my earbuds, and tune him out until he finally left.

A few hours later, as I was doing my homework, my sister walked into the living room. "You got a minute?" she asked me.

I nodded, closed my book, and said, "What's up?"

She sat at the opposite end of the couch, on the arm. She said, "So I've been doin' some thinking. That seating petition thing has me down, but not out, and I just got this idea. And I need you to let me know if it's more flop than pop."

I nodded. "I'm listenin'."

She said, "Even though I couldn't save that petition, I still wanna reach out to the peeps who feel marginalized every day at our school. So I've been thinking about startin' a kinda informal service station in a corner of one of the hallways, where kids who feel left out can come and hang, and talk to us and ask for advice and whatnot—you know, kids who are black or Latinx or gay or trans or bullied. Kinda like a gas station, but instead of fillin' up on gas, they're fillin' up on guidance. What do you think? If you think it's wack, just tell a sister."

I said, "No, I think it pops."

Her eyebrows went up. "Real talk?"

I said, "Hell yeah. I'm down."

She said, "I just need to come up with a name for it. What could we call it? Something to do with different peeps comin' together. Could we call it 'Different . . . ' um . . . 'Different' what?"

I thought for a moment, then said, "How about Rainbow Relief?"

My sister's eye caught a sparkle and she smiled her plastic-off-the-couch, good-china smile. Nodding, she said, "That's what's up! Rainbow Relief! That shit pops!"

We fist-bumped each other.

Then she plucked out her phone. "I better write it down before my ass forgets."

After she put her phone away, she looked up at me. "So lemme ask you something," she said.

"What's up?"

She said, "You really think we can trust her?"

"Who?" I said, even though I knew damn well who she was talking about.

My sister smirked and said, "Who do you think? How do we know she won't leak our campaign plans over to the other camp?"

I said, "Would you stop sweatin' her. I keep tellin' you—Sallie's chill."

My sister said, "M'hm." The cynic's favorite lyric. Then she asked, "How did her stepmom take it when she saw you two together tonight?"

I said, "She was cool with it. She's swirl-friendly." I grinned and said, "She could teach you a few things."

Regina said, "Honey, she could have her PhD in Swirl: I'll never be down with it."

"So you're sayin' if a hot white guy—who has all the shit you look for in a guy—stepped to you and asked you out, you'd tell him to keep steppin'?"

"Yep," she said.

"Bullshit."

"It's happened before. A white guy asked me out last year. You know Harlan McKenna?"

I said, "Yeah, he's cool."

Regina nodded. "And smart and funny and hot. But one day when we were in Study Hall he said he liked that show *Mad Men*, and that's when I knew I couldn't trust him."

I said, "What's wrong with *Mad Men*? What's it about?"

She said, "It takes place in the 1960s when the world was all racist and sexist, and white men ran everything. A lot of white guys love that show, and it makes me wonder *why* they love it: Is it just because it's a good show? Or is it because the show fulfills this secret fantasy they have to live back in those times when everybody bowed down to them? My money's on that second one."

"You don't know that," I said.

She said, "I know enough about white men to know that. And even if I'm wrong, it doesn't matter, 'cause that's the fucked-up shit already runnin' through my head even when the cool white guys step to me." She shrugged. "If you can't trust, Swirl is a bust. Feel me?"

I said, "Damn. Don't you think that's kinda sad?"

She said, "It is what it is." She got up. "I'll check you later. Goodnight."

She went to her room, and I continued doing my homework.

After a while my phone buzzed.

I took it out and looked at the screen. It was a text from Sallie.

Who are you?

Smiling, I texted back: Sallie's boyfriend

Then I texted: Who are you?

She texted back: Uly's girlfriend

Corduroy, I know. But you had to be there.

SALLIE

For the last couple of days, I've been sitting with Uly, his sister, and their friends in the Rainbow Relief corner. Our teachers have given us permission to sit there during the second half of our lunch hour instead of sitting in our usual Enrichment room. The Rainbow Relief corner is something Uly's sister started a couple of weeks ago to help underrepresented kids feel more represented. Can I be honest with you? I so wish my sister had thought of it first. It's such a bacon idea. The setup is pretty simple: there's a table with some chairs around it, and it's all in front of a wall decorated with a rainbow-designed sheet painted by Uly's friend Marilyn, and the table has a rainbow sheet on it too, and the chairs are painted rainbow. It's really quite beautiful.

What's not so beautiful is the way I feel whenever I sit there. I feel like maybe I'm a traitor to my sister. She even told me the other day, "Give me one good reason why I shouldn't think you're a traitor for sitting at that table every day." I told her, "I'm not sitting there as your campaign manager, I'm sitting there as Uly's girlfriend. Just like when I'm making calls for you to get on the Knightly News, I'm not making those calls as Uly's girlfriend, I'm making them as your campaign manager."

My sister told me, "I don't even know what the fuck you're talking about!"

I explained, "Just because I'm your campaign manager doesn't mean I can't live!" She rolled her eyes and walked away. Actually, stormed away.

Life at the Rainbow Relief table isn't always so great either. Uly's sister always keeps at least two chairs between her and me. And whenever we're stuck being the only two people at the table, she barely glances in my direction and she looks the way you might look when you're dining with the Grim Reaper, only more miserable. But she doesn't look that way when other people are there. And you should see the way her entire mood changes when her friends—mostly black girls—come to the table. She's suddenly all smiles, all laughs, all talk . . . sides of her I've never seen before. As I watch her easily interacting with her friends I find myself feeling jealous of their easy interactions. I find myself wishing I knew the secret knock that would make her unlock her heart and let me in the way I know she would if I was a black girl dating her brother. Sometimes I hear her and her pals talking about things that make me feel like a Greek person sitting in the middle of France. Weaves? New growth? Hot combs? 40s? Old E's? Naps in the kitchen? DL? Purple drank? But I wouldn't dare ask them to translate.

As for Regina's friends, sometimes I think they hate me more than Regina does. I can tell by the way they look at me that they're not fans. Sometimes when I'm talking to Uly I'll overhear one of them say, "What's her ass doing here?" And even though I don't see them pointing at me, I can hear them pointing at me. And some of them are so bold they don't even wait for my back to be turned. They say it right to my face, as soon as they walk up to the table. "What's her ass doing here?" Someone from the table usually answers with "She's chill." When Uly is there, it's Uly. When Uly's not there, it's Marilyn. And when she's not there, it's Narmeen. But I can tell the asker never believes the answerer.

And it's not always Regina and her friends who make me feel like a Greek in France. Sometimes it's Regina . . . and my boyfriend. Sometimes, when they get good news, they do this thing called the Triple F—it's a complicated way of giving each other Five: first they low-five each other, then they high-five each other, then they high-back-hand-five each other, then they do this flutter thing with their fingers, then they do a fist bump, all with the same hands. Uly says it's called Triple F because Five, Flutter, Fist bump. It looks really bacon, but every time I see them do it, I get sort of depressed. I wish I could do a Triple F with my sister, but we'd look so *white* doing it: we'd probably get lost somewhere between the high-five and the flutter; we'd have to keep starting over again; the whole thing would look awful.

Not that Rainbow Relief has been all doom and doom. I've gotten to know kids I probably never would've gotten to know without Rainbow Relief. I've learned things about not only African-American culture, but also Indian culture, Latinx culture, East Asian culture. And I've found out there are a lot more troubled kids at my school than I thought. Kids whose fathers walked out. Kids whose mothers walked out. Kids whose fathers and mothers try to kick each other out. Kids whose fathers and mothers just plain try to kick each other. Kids who've thought about suicide. Kids who want to Come Out but can't, either because of family, religion, or themselves, or all of the above.

I never thought one of the best things to happen to me could be exactly the same as one of the worst things to happen to me, but it's possible, and its name is Rainbow Relief.

Today, before Rainbow Relief, I tried to go for the Secret Knock with Regina by bringing some ice cream cups to our lunch table. The cafeteria sells a different ice cream flavor each day, and today was chocolate chip. So I bought five cups—one for me, one for Regina, one for Uly, one for Marilyn, and one for Narmeen.

They all thanked me—Regina included—and peeled off the lids.

But Regina didn't. Her cup stayed unopened.

"What's the matter?" I asked her.

She said, "I don't like chocolate chip ice cream."

I said, "Why not?"

She said, "You really wanna know?"

I said, "Sure."

She said, "People chew up the chocolate chips, but gently suck the vanilla part. That's the way it's designed."

She gave me this long, hard look. It was the longest she'd ever looked at me.

Suddenly I had no appetite. Suddenly I was shocked. Suddenly I was angry.

I said, "You can't be serious."

Still hitting me with that hard look, she said, "I'm more serious than you could ever know, honey."

Sensing that something was off, Uly said, "What? What happened?"

I said to Regina, "So now I can't even eat ice cream without being a racist, huh?"

She shrugged and said, "You said it, not me."

Marilyn said, "Racist? Ice cream? What's going on??"

I pointed at the unopened cup and told Regina, "It's ice cream. It's ice cream!! Ice cream has to be controversial now?? Ice cream has to be a political issue now???"

Regina told me, "I didn't expect you to understand."

I told her, "Oh, I understand all right. I will *not* let you make me feel guilty about ice cream too."

With a small smile, Regina said, "Guilty? Where did that come from?"

I told her, "I'm gonna tell you something. Okay, yeah, the chocolate chips get chewed up and the vanilla part gets gently whatever the hell. But you know what? It all ends up getting swallowed anyway. So maybe the best thing we can do is just try to, I don't know, taste good together before nobody can taste *any-thing* anymore."

I gathered my bookbag and the ice cream cup, stood up, and told Uly, "I'll see you later." And I stormed off.

As I stormed off, I could overhear Regina saying, "I guess I hit a nerve." There was an undercurrent of satisfaction in her tone, like she won.

As I stormed out of the cafeteria I was angry at myself for getting so angry at her. And I was also angry at myself for giving her the satisfaction of knowing she'd hit a nerve with me.

As I stormed up the stairs to my locker, I suddenly stopped. The spoon and ice cream cup were still in my hand. I decided to try something. I moved to a corner of the staircase, took off the cup's lid again, spooned out a nice clump, and put it in my mouth. And ate it. And, for the first time ever, I didn't enjoy it. I realized my teeth really were chewing up the chocolate chips while going easier on the vanilla part, and I tried to get my teeth to go easier on the chocolate chips but then stopped when I realized how ridiculous it was. You shouldn't have to tell yourself, *"I'm a good, decent, compassionate person even though my teeth are acting really intolerant right now"* while you're eating fucking ice cream. But that's what I was doing in that stair-case this afternoon. And that's when I knew I'd never be able to enjoy chocolate chip ice cream—my favorite ice cream of all—again.

If you don't mind a little unsolicited advice from me: if there's a food out there that you really, really enjoy—eat it under the bed or something. *Don't* eat it around people. Because, mark my words, sooner or later, someone someday somewhere will say something that will forever ruin it for you. For me, that day was today. And that someone was my boyfriend's sister.

As I headed to my locker, I made a slight detour to the waste-basket. And tossed my mostly uneaten ice cream cup into it.

As I climbed up the stairs to the library, a voice behind me called out, "Sallie, wait up." It was a familiar, beautiful voice.

I turned around and saw Uly.

Giving me a confused smile, he stepped closer and put his hand on my arm. "What happened? You bolted out of the caf before a brother could ask What's Up. You okay?"

I nodded and forced a smile. "I'm fine," I said.

He skeptically smirked and said, "No you're not. Come on, something's up. What's wrong?"

I wanted to say, "Your sister forever ruined my favorite flavor of ice cream," but no one has ever said that sentence before in the history of people, and I didn't want to be the first one, so I said, "Nothing. Seriously. I'm fine." I kissed him. "Everything's fine."

He looked at me for a long time, then he put his hands on my shoulders and gave me that Franklin Institute Stomach smile that makes me forget what planet I'm on. He whispered, "I'm crazy about you. You know that, right?"

Smiling, I nodded.

After a moment, he said, "I know this is gonna sound kinda corduroy, but I wrote a poem for you the other day. I've never written a poem for anybody in my life."

My heart started beating faster. "Really?" I said. "For me? Where is it? Show it to me."

He pointed at his head. "It's up here, actually. I haven't written it down or anything."

"Then say it to me," I quickly said.

His eyes did a self-conscious shift from my eyes to the wall and he said, "I don't know. It's not as bacon as I want it to be. I mean, it sure as hell ain't gonna put Robert Frost out of business."

"Fuck Robert Frost," I said. "I wanna hear your poem."

His eyes went back to my eyes. "Real talk?"

My heart beating even faster, I nodded.

Slowly sliding his fingers through my hair, he said, "Okay, it goes like . . .

> *Next to you the sun feels cold*
> *In your hand a lump of coal looks gold*
> *You can beat Charm in a race*
> *You can make Hate slow its pace*
> *When you talk, my ears hear a song*
> *When you laugh, my—*

"ULY, YOUR SISTER NEEDS YOU TO COME TO TECH!" boomed a different voice, cutting him off.

It was LaShonda Carmichaels, one of Regina's friends/campaign workers.

"Right now?" Uly asked her.

LaShonda put her hand on her hip. "No, next year," she sarcasm'd. "Of course right now!"

Uly looked at me, then looked back at LaShonda and told her, "Now's not a good time."

LaShonda said, "Now's an even *worse* time for Mr. Hedges 'cause he's leaving for the week in just fifteen minutes and he needs to know which blueprint she wants him to use for her campaign website design. I told her to go with Number Three, but she doesn't trust my ass; she says she needs you to help her decide. They're all down there right now, waiting for you!"

Uly said, "Well, I . . ." He turned to me. "Uh, maybe . . ."

The silence was awkward and awful.

I told him, "Just go. It's okay."

"Really?" he said.

I force-smiled my third smile of the afternoon and nodded.

"I'm sorry," he said.

"It's okay," I said.

"To Be Continued," he assured me.

Still force-smiling, I said, "Of course."

"I love you," he whispered.

"I love you too," I whispered.

He gently squeezed my hand, then ran down the steps to join LaShonda, and off they went downstairs to rejoin Regina.

With tears stinging my eyes, I turned around and continued my climb upstairs to the library.

SALLIE

As I sat at the Rainbow Relief station this afternoon, holding hands with Uly and listening to Marilyn give Logan Cho some advice on Coming Out, a strange thing happened. Three boys in white-stocking masks and white T-shirts stopped at our table, unzipped their bookbags, took out what looked like one of those super-soaker things, and opened fire on us. But what came out wasn't water. What came out was something thicker than water. It was white, and it made a slushy sound as it shot out of the barrel. On a reflex, I jumped on top of Uly and pressed him to the floor as the white stuff started flying. Screams and curses rang out as the white stuff zapped Marilyn, Logan, Narmeen, and three of her friends. Then the white-stuff shooters sprayed the entire rainbow wall behind us and the entire rainbow table in front of us.

Then I heard one of them say, "Just figured Rainbow Relief needed a little *White* Relief."

Then I heard another one laugh and say, "Yeah, it's a better color now."

Then I heard their running footsteps.

Still keeping Uly pressed down, I looked up and saw the three white shirts disappearing around the corner of the hallway. On the backs of their shirts were the words THE DAY BACKERS.

Meanwhile Uly popped up and looked around in an angry daze. Seeing his sprayed friends, he yelled, "What the fuck!" Then he looked at the crowd of kids who'd gathered. "Did y'all see who did this?! Where'd they go?!"

It turned out that the white stuff was foam.

It turned out that the three kids who did it are Jason Sellers, Sheldon Cavanaugh, and Walter Brawley.

It turned out that the three of them did it because they belong to this newly formed group called the Day Backers.

It turned out that this newly formed group was formed by Wilk Watercutter.

My sister's boyfriend.

After school we—Leona, Regina, John Smith, his girlfriend Sherry, Uly, and I—went to Mr. Dranger's office so he could give us some instructions about tomorrow's debate, the first and only one between the three candidates.

We all sat down in the chairs around Mr. Dranger's desk, but Regina didn't sit down. I'd never seen her look so angry before. If her eyes could've shot daggers Mr. Dranger's office would've looked like a Trojan War battlefield.

Regina told Mr. Dranger, "Before we start talking about tomorrow's debate, we need to talk about *today's* debacle." She pointed at my sister and said, "Miss Thang needs to go."

My sister's mouth fell open. "What??"

Mr. Dranger also looked confused. "I don't understand."

Regina said, "My Rainbow Relief station was attacked today!"

Mr. Dranger nodded and said, "I know, and the three boys responsible are suspended."

"But don't you know why they did it?!" Regina said. "They did it because they're part of this club that *her* boyfriend"—she pointed at my sister—"started, called the Day Backers. And you know why they started it?! Because of that backwoods redneck campaign slogan that *she*"—she pointed

again at my sister—"came up with last month: 'Turn Knight
Back To Day.'"

Leona said, "I can't even believe you're bringing that up again.
I took those posters down the same week, because of *you*."

Regina said, "Well, you might've taken them down, but
your boyfriend's brain still has them up!" She turned back to our
advisor. "Mr. Dranger—straight up and down, she needs to go."

"I'm not going anywhere," Leona said.

Regina told Mr. Dranger, "There never would've been an
attack today if it wasn't for her."

Mr. Dranger asked my sister, "Leona, is this true, about your
boyfriend?"

Leona defended, "Well, yeah, he started the group to give
me some support, but he didn't know anything about that attack
today. He didn't know they were gonna do that!"

"How do you know he didn't know?!" Regina asked my sister.

"How do you know he *did* know?!" my sister shot back.

Regina whipped her eyes back to Mr. Dranger and said, "All
I know is, she's gotta go. This whole process stopped being pure
the minute her boyfriend started that club 'cause of her racist campaign slogan."

Smiling, my sister stood up and quietly told Regina, "You
know, Regina, if this is about you being afraid to face me in the
debate tomorrow, why don't you just come out and say it, instead
of playing the race card like this?"

My heart thumped faster as Regina walked over to my sister
and got so close to her that their noses were almost touching.
For the first time, I noticed that they were both the exact same
height.

Regina said, "Honey, I could wipe the floor, ceiling, *and* staircase with you in that debate." Still eye to eye with my sister, she
added, "Matter of fact—Mr. Dranger, why don't you let her stay
for the debate tomorrow, then drop her the day after. Already I

can tell the floor, ceiling, and staircase are looking mighty dusty right now."

I felt helpless. As one of the campaign managers, I felt like I should've said or done something at that moment, but I didn't know what to say or do. I looked at my boyfriend, who looked just as helpless.

With a small smile, Mr. Dranger looked over at the third candidate. "So John—still glad you decided to run with two women?"

John said, "Uh, yeah."

Mr. Dranger looked back at Leona and Regina, who were still eye-to-eyeing each other. "Okay, girls, that's enough. Have a seat, both of you."

My sister and Uly's sister reluctantly tore themselves away from each other. Leona sat down. Then Regina sat down.

Then Mr. Dranger sat forward and said, "So, this is what's going to happen. Nobody's getting dropped. Regina, I'm sorry about what happened to Rainbow Relief today, but Leona can't put a leash on her boyfriend or the members of her boyfriend's club. She wasn't directly involved with what happened today, so I can't penalize her. We all need to move past this now. So, before I start going over the debate, I need to confirm . . . Regina: Are you good now?"

"Yes," she said. She suddenly seemed way calm, as if she hadn't even been angry just two minutes ago.

Mr. Dranger looked at my sister. "And Leona: Are you good now?"

"Yes, sir," she said with a grin.

"Great," our advisor said. "So let's go over this debate . . ."

I sort of tuned out as he went over the instructions, so I'm afraid I don't have any details to give you.

But I do have some details to give you about what I was doing while I was tuning out. I did some Nexting (when you text with someone sitting right next to you) with Uly.

Me: Hi

Him: Hi

Me: Don't I know you from somewhere?

Him: Hmm, I must say you do look mighty familiar.

Me: 😈

Him: 😎

Me: I think Robert Frost is mad at me.

Him: 'Cause you told him to fuck himself the other day?

Me: Yeah. I didn't mean it. I actually like him.

Him: I think he would've liked you too. And I don't think he was the type to hold grudges anyway.

Me: You don't think Robert Frost held grudges?

Him: Nah. Anybody who writes about trees, leaves, and roads doesn't hold grudges for long. Now T.S. Eliot, on the other hand . . .

Me: Yeah, I bet T.S. Eliot could hold a grudge forever.

Him: Yep. And Emily Dickinson too. She didn't get out much.

Me: LOL. So I wanna tell you something.

Him: Okay.

Me: I wrote a poem for you.

Him: For me??

Me: Yep.

Him: I still have to tell you the rest of my poem.

Me: You will, but only when the mood is right. After the election.

Him: Okay.

Me: But let me tell you my poem. You ready?

Him: Yes.

Me: Don't be too ready. It sorta sucks.

Him: I'm sure it's bacon.

Me: No, no, it's so not. Prepare to be disappointed. I NEED you to think it's gonna suck worse than the suckiest thing ever, so that when you find out it Just Sucks, it won't suck so much.

Him: Damn. I don't think vacuum cleaners use the word "suck" so many times in one sentence.

Me: Before I share it, I need you to promise me you're saying to yourself, "I bet it's gonna suck." Are you telling yourself it's gonna suck?

Him: Yes. It's gonna suck.

Me: Awesome, thank you! Now here it is . . .

> Why do you keep making my soul sizzle?
> Are you a cook?
> Why do you keep stealing my heart?
> Are you a crook?
> Why do you keep lifting me up?
> Are you a hook?
> Why do you keep—

"SALLIE!!!"

I looked up from my phone to see my sister glaring at me.

"Huh?" I said.

She snapped, "Are you going deaf in your old age or what?" She jabbed a finger at Mr. Dranger.

I looked at him and said, "Hm?"

He told me, "I was just asking if you understand everything I just went over."

"Uh, yes," I lied.

He smiled at all of us and said, "Great. So then I hereby proclaim this meeting is over. Let's have a good debate tomorrow, guys."

Uly and I shared a secret smile as we all walked out of Mr. Dranger's office.

"To Be Continued," I whispered to him.

He pointed at me, smiled, and nodded. "Most def."

Things went from sweet to far from sweet as soon as we got out of the office.

Sitting in one of the waiting area's chairs was senior Scott

Smith, John's big brother. I hate to say that somebody looked terrible, but he looked terrible. His hair was uncombed, he had stubble on his face, and his letterman jacket was wrinkled, splotched with stains, and even peeling in places. He was basically the human version of a paper you crumple into a tight ball then uncrumple and try to smooth out. He used to be the captain of the school's wrestling team—and he has the barrel-torso'd wrestler's build to prove it—but he was recently terminated by the coach for inappropriate behavior; that's all I was told.

As we walked out of the office, he stood up and looked at us with red eyes that were the kind of red that people get from either not enough sleep or too much.

"Hey, Scott," Sherry said as she guided her boyfriend over to his brother.

Taking John's other arm, Scott told Sherry, "I got it now. How about letting go of him?"

The words he said and the abrupt way he said them stunned me.

But they didn't seem to stun Sherry. She looked like she was used to it. "Sure thing," she said. She kissed her boyfriend, then slowly let go of his arm.

Scott looked over at Leona and asked her, "You're running for president too?"

"Yeah," Leona said.

Scott said, "What's gonna be your first executive order? That we should add Shopping and Gold-digging to the school's curriculum?"

Before Leona could respond, John's brother shifted his eyes to Regina and asked her, "And you're running for president too?"

"That's right," Regina said.

Scott smiled and told her, "Actually, I like that. I've always wanted someone to change the school mascot to fried-chicken-and-watermelon."

Regina said, "What's your problem?"

"I'm looking at it."

"Fuck you," Regina snapped.

"In your dreams, honey," Scott snapped back.

John said, "Scott, come on . . ."

With his eyes on my sister and Regina, Scott said, "The only thing a woman can run is a vacuum cleaner, and everybody knows it."

John sort of tugged on his brother's arm. "Dude, come on, take it easy . . . We talked about this."

Scott didn't take his eyes off Leona and Regina. "Women are gonna be the reason we fail as a country."

Regina said, "Oh yeah? And *you're* the one who's gonna fix this country?"

Scott said, "If I was running things, every last cunt in this world would be cut up beyond recognition."

Hearing those words made my stomach knot up in shock and anger.

Glaring at Scott, Uly told Scott's brother, "Yo John, you need to check your bro before he's six feet below."

John tugged on Scott's arm a little harder this time and told him, "Come on, let's go home." He turned his dark glasses from his brother to us and said, "Sorry, guys. He's just . . . I'm sorry."

He turned back to his brother. "Let's go."

Scott guided his brother a few paces, then he stopped. And turned around to look back at us for a few moments. His face was blank. Then he turned around and went back to walking with John.

When the two Smiths were gone, Uly said, "What the . . . ?"

Sherry told us, "He's just angry about what happened to his brother."

Regina said, "So that gives him a free pass to be a scumbag? And damn, *we* weren't the ones who crashed the car."

Sherry nodded. "I know, but I guess he's just mad at the world. A couple of years ago, their mom left their dad. For a woman . . .

a black woman. And last summer when John was visiting with his mom and her girlfriend, they let him take their car for a drive, and that's when he had the accident."

"Damn," Leona said.

Sherry said, "I'll see you guys tomorrow."

As she turned she reached out like she was about to grab something, but then she lowered her arm and glanced at us like she hoped we hadn't noticed. She walked off. It took me a moment to figure out what that was about: she was so used to gripping John's arm that gripping his arm had become a reflex for her. Without his arm, her arm almost didn't know what to do with itself. She looked lost as she wandered out of the office, almost like a broken windmill that still spins even though half of itself is missing. And in that moment, I felt almost just as sorry for Sherry as I was for John.

Tonight I did a sort of debate rehearsal with my sister. She stood in the middle of the living room while I sat on the couch and tossed questions at her. Because I didn't know what the actual questions will be in the debate—the questions will be coming from random students in the audience—I had to work in the dark, but I tried my best to predict the kind of stuff that'll be hurled at her tomorrow, and so I asked them tonight:

"Why should we pick you over the other two candidates?"

"How will you make our school a better place?"

"What will be the first two major projects you'll work on as president?"

"If you become president, how will you want to be remembered at this school fifty years from now?"

Leona did a pretty good job answering all the questions. Sometimes I pretended to be Regina or John and I asked her some rebuttal-type questions they might ask (and questions I was curious about too). Stuff like: "How can you say you want the school to be better when you're dating a guy whose club members attacked six students the other day?" or "You sure people won't remember you as the one who said that thirty percent of the kids here should get kicked out just because of the town they live in?" And Leona handled those questions pretty well too.

So I think she's in good shape for tomorrow.

After our rehearsal, I headed over to Dandee's and hung out with her for a little while. Every time I visit her I learn something, and tonight I learned not one but two things.

Looking at one of her many computer screens, Dandee said, "Did you know Ms. MacQuillan is into midget porn?"

I said, "No way."

She said, "Yes way. She's into lesbian midget porn."

I stayed in my seat in the basement's corner. Even though I wanted to see, I just couldn't bring myself to see, because seeing would've made me an official accomplice to what was basically cyber espionage.

I said, "Why would a non-midget woman who's married to a non-midget man be interested in lesbian midget porn?"

She shrugged and said, "Life gets boring, I guess."

Then she said, "Oh, and I found out something about Mr. Dranger."

My heart started thumping harder. I didn't know whether I wanted to make my ears wider so I wouldn't miss a thing or seal them off so I'd miss everything. I braced myself for what I was about to hear. Was it going to be . . . Sex with parakeets? A fetish for Colorado-shaped birthmarks? An unhealthy obsession with *Sesame Street*?

"He likes visiting anarchy websites," Dandee said.

I was relieved. Then I stopped being relieved just as fast. It wasn't as bad as seducing parakeets or plastering every inch of the bedroom wall with Cookie Monster, but anarchy websites? Was he visiting them because he likes anarchy? Or was he visiting them because he dislikes it? Was he visiting them because he wants to learn how to start anarchy, or stop it?

Those nagging thoughts, mixed with the haunting image of

the super-soakers spraying Rainbow Relief with foam, kept nagging at me right up until Uly picked me up at Dandee's. As he walked me home I thought about talking to Uly about it, but then I remembered our pledge to keep the election out of our relationship, so I made sure we kept talking about everything but the election.

When we got to my door, I invited him in, but he said he had to start working on an essay for Ms. Forrester. Knowing that he was about to say goodbye, I suddenly felt the kind of sadness I'd seen on Sherry's face this afternoon.

Putting my hands on his shoulders, I said, "I hate when we say goodbye. It sounds like we're never gonna see each other again, even though I know we will."

"I know."

I said, "So I was thinking . . . Instead of saying goodbye, let's say something else. It'll be a code that only we know about."

He smiled. "I like that."

I said, "It could be one word or two words, but it should be something that makes both of us feel really good."

"Like some kind of food?"

I said, "Yeah! Let's do food. What should it be?"

He said, "How about bacon? It doesn't get better than that."

I winced and shook my head. "I don't wanna say goodbye with something greasy. How about Lollipop?"

He winced and shook his head. "Too cute. And I don't always like lollipops. How about spaghetti?"

I shook my head. "Too many syllables."

He said, "I'm so glad we thought of this."

I laughed.

He said, "Maybe we could do a beverage."

I said, "Yeah! How about, um . . . Orange Juice?"

"Gives me a stomachache. How about Milk?"

"I'm lactose intolerant."

He sighed and said, "Okay, let's just stick to the juices. I really like Gr— "

"—Grape juice?!" I finished.

Smiling, he nodded.

I said, "I like it too!"

"So you wanna make Grape Juice our code?"

"Yes. Let's make it Grape Juice . . . Grape Juice."

"Grape Juice," he said.

"Grape Juice," I said. "That'll be our code for 'Goodbye And I Love You.'"

Behind me the door swung open and Leona said, "Oh *there* you are! You said you were gonna help me bake the Leonite cookies for tomorrow!"

I told her, "I will. I'll be right in. Just give me a minute."

"Hey Uly," my sister said.

Uly nodded and said, "Hi, Leona."

My sister looked at him for a moment, then said, "So Uly, I know there's a lot of stuff going on between your sister and me, but I hope you know that doesn't mean I wanna crash your system too. I think you're a cool dude. Seriously."

"Thank you," he said, probably because he didn't know what else to say.

I guess Leona didn't either because she went back into the house.

The moment might not have been awkward, but it was definitely awkwardish.

Wanting to de-awkward, I smiled at him. Then I moved my face to his and we kissed.

"Grape Juice," I whispered to him.

"Grape Juice," he whispered to me.

And I went inside. It worked: I wasn't sad.

Well, maybe a little sad.

ULY

The Debate was held in the gym. Students sat in the bleachers on both sides while the teachers sat their asses in the court area. Regina, Leona, and John stood behind mics in the middle of the court while, over in a corner of the gym, Mr. Dranger stood his ass behind a lectern with a mic attached to it.

The gym quieted down as Mr. Dranger started speaking.

"Good morning, everyone," he said, "and welcome to our presidential debate. As always, this will be the only presidential debate we'll have. In a national presidential election, however, there are, in fact, three debates: two are conducted by a moderator who asks the candidates questions, and one is in what's called a Town Hall format wherein people from the audience ask the candidates questions. This debate you're about to see will be in that Town Hall format. The reasoning behind that choice is to give you students a chance to ask your candidates any questions that may or may not have been nagging you since their campaigns began. So, in effect, this will be a chance for all of you to get some things off your chest—not just you the audience, but also your three candidates. As for how this works, we've made it very simple. One person from each grade, pre-chosen before this debate, will ask a question of all three candidates. After each candidate answers, I will then ask the candidates if any of them would like to challenge one of their opponents with a follow-up comment or question in regard to the answers just given. The opponent who's challenged will have the opportunity to either address that question/comment or simply state 'No Comment,' at which point we'll then go to the next grade level for their question. After each grade level has had their questions answered, the final question will come from a faculty member. After that question is dealt with by the candidates, that'll be the end of the debate, at which point you'll be dismissed for lunch." He cleared his throat. "Okay, so without further ado, let's start with the first round—the Freshmen."

The other grade levels made anti-Freshmen gagging noises as Ms. MacQuillan handed a cordless mic to a short freckled girl with glasses who stood up from the front row of the freshmen bleachers. "HI, MY QUESTION IS—"

Shorty's voice was so loud the mic screeched and mofos—including Sallie and me—groaned and held their ears.

From the lectern, Mr. Dranger said, "Uh, Monica, there's no need to talk so loud. Just talk in your normal voice, okay? We can hear you."

"Croatia can hear you," someone murmured from the Juniors section and the gym laughed.

"Okay, people, let's settle down," Mr. Dranger said. "Go ahead, Monica—but in your normal voice, okay?"

"OKAY," Monica said. Her voice was still loud as hell. "HI, MY QUESTION IS THIS: WHY WERE THE *TURN KNIGHT TO DAY* POSTERS TAKEN DOWN, AND DO YOU THINK THEY SHOULD GO BACK UP?" She gave the mic back to Ms. MacQuillan.

From the lectern, Mr. Dranger said, "In keeping with alphabetical order by last name, Regina Gates will be the first to answer, followed by John Smith, followed by Leona Walls . . . Regina—your answer."

My sister spoke into her mic. "I'm happy to answer that

question. They were taken down 'cause they were offensive to students of color here. Many students of color—myself included—interpreted the poster to mean 'Let's try to turn this school completely white like it was forty years ago.' The white being symbolized by the word 'day.' And that's why the posters were taken down, and to answer the other part of your question—no, I don't think they should be put back up. Thank you."

Mr. Dranger said, "And now, John Smith . . ."

John pushed his dark glasses farther up the bridge of his nose and said, "Good morning. Well, I just think we should all just try to get along and be positive. School should be a place you're proud to call your own."

He moved slightly back from the mic to signal that he was done.

Mr. Dranger said, "Oh, okay. And now, Leona Walls . . ."

Leona smiled and said into the mic, "Hey Monica. Well, I think your voice might've done a better job of waking up this school than my posters did."

The gym laughed.

Leona held up her hand and said, "Actually, I'm serious about that. All I was trying to do with those *Knight To Day* posters was get everybody to see that things around here need to change. A lot of students come here every day, feeling nervous and scared, wondering when it'll be their turn to get attacked. So, by saying, 'Let's Turn Knight Back To Day,' all I was saying was, 'Let's turn this back into a safe school.' I was using 'Day' to symbolize hope, not the color white. But people like Regina Gates always think in color. With her, it's all race, all the time. You know something? Most of the time, most people aren't even thinking about race. I know I'm not. Most people are thinking about boys, girls, homework, videogames, cars, tests, college. But somebody like Regina doesn't wanna hear that. Because when all you do is look at race, the pay is pretty good. And what do you get paid? Attention, and for some people, that's worth more than even platinum."

She nodded at Mr. Dranger to signal that her ass was finished.

From the lectern, Mr. Dranger said, "And now, which one of the three candidates would like to challenge an answer they've heard?"

My sister raised her hand.

Mr. Dranger nodded. "Go ahead, Regina."

My sister said, "This is for Leona." She looked over at her. "You say I look at race. Actually, I *don't* look at race. Race looks at *me*. Sometimes I try to look away, but then Race grabs my face and forces it back around so I can look at it again. Sometimes I try to pull away from Race, but Race just reaches out, grabs me, shakes me, slaps me, and says, 'Where do you think you're going?' Only someone with privilege would say they never think about race. You're someone with privilege."

Leona shot back, "Yeah, and what's my privilege?—that I'm white?"

"That's right," my sister said.

Leona said, "I lost my mother when I was five. I lost my father when I was twelve. I don't know what dictionary you're using, but that doesn't sound like Privilege to me. I lost both my parents, but I didn't let that stop me from being a High Honors student who's now running for president of the school. 'No Excuses' isn't just a song."

Some mofos laughed and clapped.

Ignoring the mofo feedback, my sister told Leona, "Privilege has nothing to do with how many parents you grow up with. Whenever you shop at a store without constantly worrying if the store-owner is looking at you, that's privilege"

Parts of the gym clapped.

My sister continued: "Whenever you talk back to a cop without once thinking he could take out his gun and blow you away forever, that's privilege."

There were more claps.

Regina continued: "Only someone from a comfy place of privilege would say, 'In order for me to feel safe, I want thirty percent of the kids here to leave and go to some other school and be unsafe.'"

Leona said, "What're you talking about 'unsafe'?"

Regina said, "If the Woodlawn and Oakville kids leave here, where are they gonna go?"

Leona shrugged and said, "Wherever they went before."

My sister said, "Before they started coming here for high school, they went to Montgomery High in Haddington. You got any idea how dangerous that place is?"

Leona didn't say anything.

My sister told her, "You got nothing to say. Sometimes nothing says everything, doesn't it?"

The gym laughed and clapped.

From the lectern, Mr. Dranger said, "Okay, let's settle down. We need to go to the second round now—the Sophomores."

Mr. Schmidt handed a cordless microphone to Zack Zelinka, who stood up from the first row of my section. He spoke into the mic: "Hi, uh, I have a question for only one of the candidates." He looked over at Mr. Dranger. "Can I do that?"

From the lectern, Mr. Dranger said, "Uh, sure. So then, the other two candidates will only comment on the answer. Go ahead."

Zack said, "Okay, then I'm gonna do it now." He turned back to the three candidates. "Uh, my question is for Leona Walls. Uh, last year you and I had the same Enrichment class. It was Room 314 where Mr. Dollinger teaches Geometry, Geometry Honors, and Trigonometry 2. So one day—it was a Tuesday, lunch was spaghetti, green beans, and chocolate pudding—after lunch we were in Enrichment, and you were talking to your friends about how *Sesame Street* added a new Muppet to the cast. And this is what you said—you said, 'They added a Muppet who has that thing. What's it called? When you're retarded but it's the good retarded—you know, the one where you can perform brain surgery but you don't know how much a candy bar costs?' And then somebody said 'autistic,' and you said, 'Oh yeah, autistic, that's it!' Now, as an autistic person, I took offense at what you said. I can't speak on the brain surgery thing, but we know how much a candy bar costs. We're not good retarded or bad retarded, because we're not retarded. So here's my question: Why should we make you president when you once said something like that?"

The gym clapped hard. Leona looked stunned as hell, like her ass had just gotten hit by a verbal Mack truck.

When the clapping died down, Leona said, "Well, first of all, are you sure that was me who said that? There were a lot of people in that Enrichment class and—"

"No, it was you, it was you," Zack quickly said. "You were wearing a green cardigan sweater with beige pants and dark tan penny loafers with beige socks and you had yellow earrings that dangled. It was you."

Parts of the gym laughed.

Leona said, "Okay, well . . ." She was stumped as hell, you could tell. "If I did say it, I don't think I said it that way. Maybe you heard it wrong because—"

"No, no, I heard it right," Zack said. "It happened between 11:17 and 11:20 A.M., April ninth. I heard it right."

Leona said, "Okay, well, I guess we'll have to agree to disagree, Zack. But let me answer your very good question. I think this school needs a president who speaks her mind and is always honest. You might remember, Zack, what I said during the Speechathon last month: honesty is the best gift you can give someone. And honesty will always be my mission. And sometimes things might not always come out of my mouth right, but they'll always come out of my mouth honest. Now, I don't remember saying 'good retarded' or 'bad retarded,' but I *do* remember complaining about *Sesame Street* adding an autistic Muppet. And I stand behind that complaint. I mean, are the ABCs and 123s going to take on some kinda special magical power if they come from an autistic person? Are they gonna make kids sprout wings and fly to Neptune and cure some incurable Neptune disease? The ABCs and 123s are always gonna be the same boring ABCs and 123s, no matter who's saying them. So why do we need an autistic person to say them? It's the same with Wonder Woman. Why does she have to be Jewish all of a sudden? Is making Wonder Woman kosher going to stop crime forever? When our parents were our age, there was this thing that started going around called political correctness. And, unfortunately, it's still going around. Political correctness basically turns life into this big costume party where everybody's brain comes as Martin Luther King. Everybody forces themselves to always say the right things instead of the honest things. Well, that's one party I'll be sitting out."

She gave Mr. Dranger the nod, signaling that she was done.

Mr. Dranger said, "Regina—would you like to comment?"

My sister shook her head and pointed at Zack. "Homeboy said it all."

Parts of the gym laughed.

Mr. Dranger said, "John—would you like to comment?"

"No, I'm good," John said.

Mr. Dranger said, "Okay. And that brings us to the third round—the Juniors."

Ms. Hannigan handed a cordless mic to Cindy Goldman, who said, "This question is for all three candidates. A few months ago my cousin's high school in New York started having trans-friendly bathrooms, where transgender kids can use the bathroom that matches their gender identity instead of their birth gender. Our school was thinking about doing it, but no decision has been made yet. Do you think our school should have trans-friendly bathrooms?—why or why not?"

"Regina—your response," Mr. Dranger said.

My sister said, "Yes, I think this school should have trans-friendly bathrooms. Forcing a transgender boy to use the girls' bathroom just because he was born as a girl is like dismissing his identity. It's like continuing to call him Kathy after he told you he wants to be called Scott."

She nodded at Mr. Dranger.

Mr. Dranger said, "And now—John, your response."

John said, "I just think the goal should always be to keep things positive. School is where we build our future, and so it should be a comfortable place that gives us the tools to build that future."

He stepped back from the mic.

Mr. Dranger said, "Okay, thank you. And now—Leona, your response."

Leona said, "No, I don't think we should have trans-friendly bathrooms."

There was a sprinkling of Boos throughout the gym.

Mr. Dranger told the Boo peeps, "Okay, let's settle down. Remember what Mr. Woolery said about respect . . . Okay, Leona—continue."

Leona said, "I just don't get this whole Trans thing; I swear to God, I don't. Just 'cause you don't like one of the pieces Mother Nature gave you, *we* gotta suffer the consequences and stumble over pronouns and rack our brains trying to remember to call you Nancy after ten years of calling you Robert? The pronouns are the worst. You can't even say 'he or she' anymore. Now you gotta say 'they.' Even if you're referring to just one person. Think about that. That means I can't point to a random girl anymore and say, 'Wow, she looks great in that dress.' Now I gotta point to her and say, 'Wow, they look great in that dress.' And the person you just pointed at is sitting there, scratching their head like, 'When did I develop multiple personalities?' And it's not enough that they're ruining our grammar; now they wanna ruin our bathrooms too. Look, I don't know about other girls here, but I would be *very* uncomfortable having a guy walk into a stall next to mine, especially when some of these ex-guy girls don't even look the part. Just off the top of my head, I can think of three boys here who just showed up to school one day and said, 'I'm a girl now,' but they still look and dress the same way they did when they were a boy. And now they have the nerve to wanna use my bathroom? What's next?—guys with a full beard and mustache, walking into my bathroom and saying, 'Yes, I still have this beard and mustache but I'm a girl now.' How do we know they're not just saying that just so they can get into the girls' bathroom? And as far as I'm concerned, if you've never walked a whole evening in heels, without *ever* taking them off, then you better stay the hell outta my bathroom."

The gym clapped.

When the clapping died down, Leona said, "Um, sorry about the cursing, Mr. Dranger."

The gym laughed.

Mr. Dranger said, "Apology accepted. And now, which one of the three candidates would like to challenge an answer they've heard?"

My sister raised her hand.

"Go ahead, Regina," Mr. Dranger said.

Regina said, "This is for Leona." She looked over at her opponent. "You need to check the hem of your dress."

Confused, Leona looked down at her dress.

My sister said, "Your privilege is showing again. We can always count on people like you to say, 'I'm happy with the gender *I* was born with, so why isn't everybody else? Why should I be uncomfortable just because somebody else is?' . . . How can you be a leader of an army when you can't feel when one of your soldiers is in pain? Not everybody in this room was lucky enough to get the right gender packet when they were born. But you wouldn't understand that. Everything is a label to you. Girls wear heels. Check. Guys have beards and mustaches. Check. Oakville and Woodlawn kids are violent. Check. Black guys look cool with shaved heads. Check. Well, there's a label on your brain, and it has only one word on it: Closed."

Parts of the gym clapped.

Mr. Dranger said, "And now Leona—your response?"

Leona shrugged and told the gym, "What's wrong with labels? Maybe it's just me, but I think they're great. Because of labels, I know not to open a door to a dangerous room. Because of labels, I know not to sit on a bench that's still wet with paint. Because of labels, I know not to eat from a jar of Nutella that's five years old. Because of labels, I know not to wash my hair with Listerine and gargle with Head & Shoulders. What's wrong with labels?"

Some peeps booed while others clapped.

Mr. Dranger said, "Okay, for the sake of time, we need to start moving along a bit more quickly. Let's go to our fourth round now—the Seniors."

Ms. Santangelo handed the cordless mic to Craig Stivic, this chubby futhermucker whose face is always rocking a wiseguy grin. He spoke into the mic: "This question is for all three candidates: Sprite or 7UP, and why?"

The gym laughed.

Smiling, Mr. Dranger said, "Okay, Regina—your response."

My sister's face was so serious you would've thought she was about to answer a question about famine in Bosnia. She spoke into the mic: "Actually, I don't like soda. Not a fan of carbonated stuff. Juice is my jam."

Mr. Dranger said, "And now John—your response."

John said, "I guess I'm more a 7UP guy. Not as sugary as Sprite."

Mr. Dranger said, "And now Leona—your response."

Leona smirked and said, "Seriously, Craig? Okay, I hate both. I prefer a tall bottle of Craig How About Asking A Real Question Next Time?"

The gym laughed.

Mr. Dranger said, "And now, for our fifth and final round—a question from a teacher."

History teacher Ms. Townsend raised her hand from the faculty forest and stood up; the cordless mic was already in her hand. She said, "I'd like to ask all three candidates: Imagine it's twenty years from now. How would you want people to remember you as president?"

My sister said, "That I always tried to keep it one hundred. Not forty, not fifty-five, not seventy-two. But one hundred. One hundred percent real. One hundred percent chill."

John said, "I'd like to be remembered as a president who tried his best to make this school a place you're proud to call your own, a place you didn't hate getting up and going to when that alarm clock sounded, a place that gave you the tools to be comfortable enough at to build your future."

Leona said, "I'd like to be remembered as the first person who tried to make this school better by locking up political correctness and throwing away the key forever."

Mr. Dranger told the gym, "Okay, and that concludes our third annual Presidential Debate."

Peeps started stirring and getting loud.

Mr. Dranger held up his hand and said, "Wait, wait, wait— I'm not finished yet."

Groans peppered the gym as teachers motioned for mofos to get back in their seats and quiet down.

Once the gym was quiet again, Mr. Dranger said, "What I'm about to say next is extremely important. For the first time in the history of this school's presidential elections, we will start doing weekly polls from now till June, to get a sense of how you're feeling about each candidate as their campaign further evolves. The very first poll will be your reaction to this debate you just heard. Between now and 11:00 P.M. tonight, you will simply text to 69797 the first letter of the candidate you feel did the best job in today's debate. So if you feel Regina did the best, you will text *R*. If you feel John did the best, you will text *J*. If you feel Leona did the best you will text *L*. And again: you will text it to the number 69797. The results will be announced tomorrow morning on the Knightly News. I'll give all of you a couple of minutes to do it now. We will dismiss you for lunch shortly thereafter."

As the gym went back to being noisy, I turned to Sallie and was about to say, "My sister kicked ass, didn't she?" But I stopped myself when I remembered that she probably didn't want to hear that shit. Even if she knew it was true.

But now I was stuck. I didn't know what to say. I couldn't say that *her* sister kicked ass, because I really didn't think she did.

So I just said, "Well, that was . . . interesting."

Sallie kind of laughed and said, "Yeah. I'm just glad there's no dust print of my sister on the floor, ceiling, and staircase."

I forced myself to laugh. Then I took out my phone and texted *R* to 69797.

Sallie took out her phone too and texted something. But I'm not sure what it was.

And I didn't want to know.

She didn't ask about my text, either.

SALLIE

The Debate results were announced this morning. Coral Bleeker told us that John and Regina tied with each other, getting 30 percent apiece. My sister got 40 percent. So my sister won the debate.

As her campaign manager, I'm happy. As Uly's girlfriend, I'm sad. As Leona's sister, I'm happy and sad. As a human being, I'm mostly sad.

So it looks like Sad won the little debate that's been going on inside me since the big debate yesterday.

Am I a rotten person for secretly wishing my sister's enemy had won the Debate?

JULY

As the O'Jays' "Forever Mine" fluttered from my sister's phone, I frosted one side of the cake while she frosted the other side. There was some advice I wanted to give her but I had to be careful about how I was going to drop this jam. Leona beating her in the Debate poll had her feeling down—that's why she wanted to make the cake in the first place—and I knew the only thing she wanted with the cake was ice cream, not annoying advice from her little brother. But she needed to hear it. And now it was time to give it.

I said, "So, Jeen, check it out: I've been thinkin'. Maybe it wouldn't hurt if you kinda . . . you know, smiled more when you're up there talkin' to the crowd. You know, crack jokes and whatnot. Mofos seem to eat that shit up, and so far, it looks like Leona's the only one cookin'."

My sister stopped frosting her side of the cake. She looked up and glared at me. "You been datin' this bitch not even two minutes yet and already she's tellin' you how to run my campaign?"

I quickly said, "Whoa, whoa—wait a minute. It ain't that

kinda party. This isn't comin' from her; it's comin' from me. She didn't even say anything about it."

Regina said, "Bullshit. 'You need to smile more.' 'Why are you so serious?' That's some white-people shit right there. So don't stand there and tell me she had nothin' to do with this, 'cause I know she did. Well, you *and* her can kiss my ass."

"Why you bein' so Extra?" I said. "Just chill and hear me ou—"

"You're *that* blinded by that vanilla vag of honor that you're startin' to give advice like them now?"

I said, "Yo, you best back up with that shit. I ain't tryin' to disrespect you, but I sure as hell ain't tryin' to get disrespected. My girlfriend isn't either."

That made her check herself. Her glare switched to a stare, which she moved away from me.

I quietly said, "All I'm sayin' is—maybe you would've done better in that poll if you weren't so serious whenever you speak to the crowd. I took this Public Speaking class last year and Mr. Abrams said that motherfuckers prefer speakers who are funny; he said humor is the best way to get your message across."

My sister said, "A racist bigot is about to be president of our school. Humor is a luxury my black ass can't afford."

I said, "Would you stop with that militant shit? I know things are bad, but they're not *slavery* bad. Come on, Jeen—the only Underground Railroad you've ever been on is the afternoon local from Camden to Philly."

She went back to frosting her side of the cake, but I could tell she was weighing what I was saying.

Putting some more Gentle in my tone, I said, "Look, check it: you're funny when it's just me or your friends; all I'm askin' is that you show that part of yourself to other mofos. There's nothing wrong with bein' serious, but damn: Do you wanna put on a frown or a crown? I want you to *win*."

Frosting the cake, my sister nodded and said, "I hear you."

We frosted the cake in silence.

Then I said, "Vanilla Vag Of Honor???"

We both laughed.

I said, "Shit sounds like a military porno cooking show."

She laughed harder. Then she got all serious again like she was sorry I caught her being human.

By now the cake was completely frosted. She took out three saucers as I started cutting.

I said, "I can't believe Smith was tied second place with you. He didn't do shit in that debate."

My sister nodded and said, "The best job in the world is Being a White Guy. It's amazing work if you can get it. The hours are great, the pay is greater, and the benefits? The greatest. It's like this world is damn near programmed to please white men. Even with all the progress that's been made over the years, this country still kisses their ass, and I'm sick of it. You don't believe me? Check out John Smith: this guy is blind, with the charisma of a piece of lettuce, yet the prettiest girl in the school is on his arm, and he's just two people away from the highest position at Knight High. *That*, my brother, is how great it is to be a white guy in this country. I wouldn't be surprised at all if this school ended up pickin' *him* as president."

Handing her the first saucer of cake, I said, "You trippin' now. There's no way in hell that's gonna happen. He's lucky, but he ain't *that* lucky."

SALLIE

So Uly and I decided to go on what we call a Sister-Free date today. Our sisters have been taking up so much of our time lately—more and more with each day, all but hijacking our relationship, and before the hijacking turns into a hostile takeover, he and I figured we needed to make at least one day a week a Sister-Free Zone. DWOS, we call it: A Day Without Older Sisters. So we started with today's date. Before meeting each other, we turned off our phones, and when we met up, we pledged that we'd keep our phones turned off, allowing only two minutes—toward the end of our date—for a Text-Message Check, to make sure the sky hadn't fallen *too* hard while we were in Uly & Sallie Land.

Today was Saturday, the perfect day to go Sister-Free, and sister-free we went, happily spending most of the day in Philly, checking out a movie at the Rave, food-watching at Reading Terminal, and snuggling against Our Tree at Rittenhouse Park. Not once did we turn on our phones. Not once did we talk about our sisters. Not once did the words "election," "debate," "posters," "Smith," or "speech" invade our conversation. It was a true daycation: a one-day vacation from our lives.

As we rode the PATCO back to Jersey, we looked at each other and sort of sighed because we knew this meant two things: 1. Our date was almost over, and 2. It was time for the Two-Minute Text-Message Check. It was time to see how hard the sky had fallen.

I turned on my phone. Uly turned on his phone.

"Damn," he said. "She left me fourteen messages."

"I got you beat—eighteen."

We spent a few moments scanning the messages.

Eyeing the screen, Uly said, "Wow, she's mad as hell."

Scanning my sister's texted yells, I nodded. "Same here."

Grinning, Uly looked at me and said, "What's the meanest one you got?"

I read one of them: "You Darth Vader-sounding freak, where the hell are you! I swear to God, I'll send him a video of you sleeping so he can see how you snore like a foghorn and drool like a drunk baby! Don't fuck with me! Call me now!"

Uly laughed and said, "Damn."

Smiling, I looked at him and said, "What's the meanest one you got?"

He read one of them: "Motherfucker, I'm trying to give our school some class while a fool is trying to get some ass. Get your sprung butt over here now!"

I chuckled and said, "I think we'll call it a tie. Unless you want to count the exclamation points for a tie-breaker?"

"Yeah, let's do that. How many exclamation points at the end of that one you just read?"

"Let's see," I said as I counted the exclamation points. "I got nineteen. How many did you get?"

"I got eleven. Looks like you're the winner."

We raised our phones and clinked them the way people do with wine glasses. I sarcasm'd, "Both of our sisters hate us, but mine hates me more—Yay!!"

We both had a bunch of voice messages too, but we decided we'd listen to them after the date. We turned off our phones and went back to holding hands.

After a while I found myself listening more and more to this conversation a man and woman were having in the seat in front of us.

The woman said, ". . . Our microwave makes this strange, off-kilter buzzing sound like there's something stuck inside. So the other night, she and I stood in the kitchen and just started dancing to that broken microwave sound. And that's when I knew I was in love with her."

The man said, "You don't think that's weird? I mean, you guys have been living together for three years and *that's* when you knew you were in love with her?"

The woman said, "Yep. That's always how I know I'm in love with somebody: when we can dance to something that's *not* music. My last relationship, we were living in this really old apartment where the radiators always clanked and rattled whenever the heat was on. One winter afternoon she and I danced for fifteen minutes to those clanking radiators, and that's when I knew I was in love. The relationship before that, it was a flickering fluorescent light-bulb."

The man said, "But that doesn't even make any noise!"

The woman said, "Yeah it does. Sounds a little like some-body's getting electrocuted. Well, we danced to that thing like it was Beethoven."

Uly and I looked at each other, raised our eyebrows, and gig-gled quietly.

Just as she started talking about how a humming refrigerator contributed to her very first relationship, it was time for Uly and I to get off.

The train, I mean.

When we were about midway to my house, we passed by a construction site that was a few blocks away, but the construction's sounds—the drilling, the hammering, the mechanical-arming—were so loud it might as well have been a block away.

Uly suddenly stopped, which of course made me stop.

"What?" I asked him.

Looking at me with a small smile, he put his arm around my waist, gently drew me closer to him, held my hand, put his cheek against mine, and we started swaying. Swaying back and forth to the drilling, the hammering, the mechanical-arming. The sounds were ugly and mechanical, not even remotely romantic. But as I listened closely, I could hear a rhythm to it all—hardware turning into harmony.

And for the first time in my life, on a New Jersey street just yards away from a construction site, cheek to cheek with a boy who was setting me on fire without lighting a match, I felt like I was in the most beautiful ballroom in the world.

JULY

Ms. DP (Della Porto) was bacon enough to "lend" her classroom to us so we could use it as Regina's campaign headquarters after school. (I hear Mr. Chadwick did the same with his room for Leona's headquarters and Coach McCrea did it for Smith.) As we were designing new posters and talking strategies one afternoon, Narmeen cannonballed into the room, all out of breath, and more amped up than I'd ever seen her.

"What happened?" Regina asked, standing up.

I probably would've stood up to, but the small smile on Narmeen's face seemed to suggest that the news was more magic than tragic.

Narmeen said, "We might be able to get John Smith outta the picture!"

"What're you talking about?" I said.

Narmeen said, "Lisette Garcia told me he got really rough with her cousin—Rozlyn Lopez—on a date last year."

Regina said, "What do you mean 'rough'?"

Narmeen said, "He tore her clothes, felt her up. She kept telling him to stop, but he didn't. He didn't go all the way or anything, but it's still . . . you know."

The room was quiet as we tried to digest what Narmeen had just fed us.

Narmeen slit the silence with "We go public with this, and he's gone." She told my sister, "All you gotta do is mention it once—on the Knightly News or something—and he's history."

Regina said, "Wait a minute. Who is this Lisette girl? She could be makin' up shit just 'cause she doesn't like Smith. I don't wanna go public with something like this if I can't keep it 100. I mean, this is sexual assault."

Narmeen said, "Lisette told me her cousin's willing to come forward and tell you everything that happened."

My sister's eyebrows went up. "Real talk?"

I said, "Rozlyn Lopez? Does she go here?"

Narmeen said, "She went here last year but after John Smith did what he did, she sat out the rest of the year and now she's going to another school."

Regina asked, "You got Lisette's number?"

That brings me to today. When I got home a teary-eyed Latina girl was leaving just as I was walking into the apartment. I told her hi but I don't think she heard; wiping her eyes with Kleenex, she brushed past me and walked out; I closed the door behind her.

Regina and Narmeen were sitting in the living room: both of their faces were this traumatized tropical punch of shocked, angry, and sad.

"Who's that?" I asked them even though I already had a pretty good guess.

Regina said to Narmeen, "Can you believe that? I always knew his ass was raggedy."

Narmeen nodded and sadly said, "Just goes to show you: some people can't see even before they lose their sight."

"Who's that?" I repeated.

My sister looked at me and said, "Rozlyn Lopez."

Then she gave me the 411 on what Rozlyn had told her. It was hard to listen to. When she was done, any respect I'd had for

John Smith was more gone than Vaughn and out of there like Vladimir.

Regina told me, "Hook me up with a spot on the Knightly News for tomorrow. I'm exposin' his raggedy ass."

I said, "Wait a minute. I'm down with exposin' Smith, but you can't expose him without exposin' Rozlyn too, and she might not want that."

Regina said, "I promised her I wouldn't mention her name. I'll just talk about what he did."

The Brother part of me wanted to throw a Yep Rally, but the Campaign Manager part of me wanted to tie it with a Nope Rope. I guess the rope beat the rally because I said, "But now it's her word against his, and it's not even coming from her, it's coming from you; so now *you* look like the raggedy one, tryin' to cook up something to smoke him outta the campaign."

"Cook up something?" my sister said. "Did you see that girl's face? Are you gonna sit there and tell me you think she's lying?"

"Hell no," I said. "I believe her. But Smith has a lot more friends here than she did, and a lot of mofos ain't gonna be in the Believin' business if you go wide with this. Like I told you— I'm down. I'm just trying to get you to peep the sitch from their window."

Narmeen said, "Does it really matter that we can't give everybody confirmation that it really happened? All that matters is that we're getting it Out There. All you gotta do is *say* somebody stinks, and that's enough to keep people away. They don't have to sniff the person themselves."

I have to hand it to Narmeen: she doesn't open her mouth much, but you never want to miss it when she does, because sometimes silver and gold fall out.

After giving her friend's words some mind time, Regina looked at me and said, "That's it. I'm doin' it. Hook me up with a spot."

SALLIE

It was a surprise to see Uly's sister on the Knightly News this morning, and it was an even bigger surprise to hear what she had to say.

Looking more somber than her trademark somber, she looked into the camera and said, "At first, I wasn't going to tell you this. But then I figured all of you have a right to know . . . It's come to my attention that one of the three people running for the honor of being your leader doesn't have the stuff that true leadership is made of. If Leadership was a cake, two of its most important ingredients would be Respect and Sensitivity. It's come to my attention that candidate John Smith is missing both . . . About a year ago, before his injury, he was on a date with a girl whose name I won't say, out of respect for her privacy. They started kissing and he started wanting more than a kiss. But she didn't. But he still did. When she tried to get outta the car, he pulled her back and tore her blouse. Then he yanked down her pants and started . . . touching her. When she yanked her pants back up and pushed him away he punched her in the mouth, busting her lip. Then he shoved her outta the car and told her to walk home . . . Now, I know this is hard for a lot of you to hear. It was hard for *me* to hear. I'm sure a lot of you think of John Smith as the guy with the sweet smile who broke mad records on the football field. Well, to you, he might be a star, but to that girl he assaulted, he's an asteroid. And her life is still in pieces. Like I said—at first, I was gonna keep this info to myself. I knew how it would look: one candidate trying to throw shade at another just so they can shine brighter. But this isn't about that. This is about me getting sick of guys having their way with girls and getting away with it just 'cause they can throw a mean football or tell a mean joke or make a mean amount of money . . . Because this is a She Said/He Said thing, John Smith probably can't get kicked out of the election. But you can still show him the door by not voting for him. By not supporting him. Don't give this guy a Yes Fest. Give him a No Show. He might not have listened to *her* No, but you can best believe he'll listen to *your* No. And that's all I have to say. Thank you."

Regina's Knightly News report started as a firecracker but as the day went on it became less firecracker and more bomb. Everywhere you went people were talking about it. In the halls, in the bathrooms, in the caf, in the library, in the classrooms. And by the end of the school day, this note was scribbled above the football on some of the VOTE FOR JOHN SMITH posters throughout the school: *He Touched DOWN all right!* And this note was scribbled on some of the other ones: *Chick GAGnet.* And on some others, this one: *Ladies Ban.*

While I came across plenty of John Smith's posters today I never came across John Smith, so I'm not sure how much Regina's bomb hurt him.

The one person her bomb definitely hurt was a person the bomb wasn't even thrown at.

My sister.

I'd just finished my homework and was about to call Uly when Leona called me to her room.

"This is bad," she said, pacing back and forth.

"What's bad?" I asked.

"This John Smith thing."

I told her, "For him, maybe. But not you."

She said, "You don't understand. If he goes, then it'll just be me and her. And I don't want it to be just me and her. *She's* the one who needs to be Backspaced, not him."

Confused, I said, "I'm not Getting this."

She impatiently sighed and said, "*Him* I *know* I can beat! *Her* I'm not so sure."

I said, "You don't think you can beat her?"

"I didn't say that," she snapped. "I said I'm not sure. Beating him is Checkers. Beating her is Chess. Every day I'm hearing more and more people saying, 'Regina Regime! Regina Regime!' That smug bitch. We gotta figure out a way to Backspace her and do a Restore From Trash with him. I mean, with Chess, I'm a decent player, but with Checkers, I'm a fucking Warrior Princess."

She stopped pacing, darted over to me, and grabbed my hands. She said, "Sal, I really need your help here . . . I need you to find some dirt on her."

"What do you mean?" I said.

"What do you think I mean?" she said.

She looked at me for a long time.

I shook my head and quietly said, "I can't do that, Lee."

"Why not?!" she said. "It'll be so easy! You're *right there*! You go to her house every day!"

"I'm not doing it," I said.

She said, "It's not like you have to poison her cocoa or anything. All I'm asking you to do is some searching. You open up enough closets and pretty soon you come across one you can't open 'cause bones are in the way."

"I'm not doing it," I said.

"Or you could just talk to him. He's known her all his life. Ask him about her—things she's said, kids she's made fun of."

"I'm not doing it."

"It's like it's 1944 and you have to fuck Japan up the ass, but you have the key to the bedroom because you're dating Germany!"

I pulled my hands from her hands and yelled, "I'M NOT DOING IT!!"

"WHY THE FUCK NOT?!" she yelled.

I said, "Because this is my boyfriend, not Germany!!! I don't daydream about holding hands with Germany! I don't check my phone every five minutes to make sure I didn't miss a text from Germany! I don't wanna spend the rest of my life with Germany! I'm not IN LOVE with Germany!" Calming down, I more quietly said, "Lee, he's my boyfriend."

"And I'm your sister!" she said.

I said, "I know, but he's my boyfriend."

"But I'm your sister!" She jabbed her finger at my heart. "I was here first, goddammit!"

The door opened and Wilk stuck in his dumb head. "Leo, is everything all ri—"

My sister picked up a blow-dryer from her dresser and hurled it at the door. "Get the fuck outta here!!"

Wilk's head disappeared before the hairdryer could hit it and he closed the door. "Okay, um, so I guess I'll talk to you later," his muffled voice informed from the other side.

My sister went back to storming back and forth. I put my hand on her shoulder, trying to stop the one-person stampede, but her shoulder shook off my hand and she kept stampeding.

"Lee," I said, "you don't have to go all Corrupt CIA just to beat her. You're smart. You're funny. People can't take their eyes off you when you speak. You can beat her that way. Just do you. Just believe in yourself. Why can't you do it that way?"

"Because I wanna win!" she snapped.

It was a response that shocked me so much it left me without a response.

When the quiet got too quiet, she said, "Look, just leave me alone for a little while. I gotta think."

I left her room and headed over to Dandee's for some soothing Best Friending.

Sipping my lime Red Bull, I vented to her about my sister. "And now she wants me to use my relationship with Uly to dig up some dirt on Regina."

Dandee nodded and said, "She wants you to be Leonardo DiCaprio in the *The Departed*."

I nodded. "Without the blue eyes. I swear, I never should've Swiped Right on this whole Campaign Manager thing."

Dandee didn't say anything for a long time—so long that I started to notice it. I looked at her and saw that she was looking at me with this sort of weird expression.

"What?" I said.

She said, "I wanna tell you something, but I'm not sure if I should."

My heart started beating faster. "Tell me. What is it?"

She said, "Remember how you said you hate that your sister wants you to use your relationship with your boyfriend to dig up some dirt on his sister?"

I nodded.

She said, "Well, you're about to be half happy and half sad."

"What do you mean?"

She said, "You won't have to use your relationship with Uly to get dirt on Regina . . . because I already have some dirt on her."

Now my heart *really* started beating fast. "What is it?"

"You sure you wanna know?"

"Dandee, what is it?" I impatiently asked.

Dandee put down her can of Red Bull and went over to one of her many computer monitors. As she clicked away on her keyboard, she looked at the screen and told me, "I recorded this a couple of years ago, actually. We were on a charter bus, heading back to school from a field trip. She had some quite interesting things to say."

With her head she motioned for me to come over to her.

On the screen was a freeze-frame of Regina, looking slightly younger, sitting next to another black girl on a bus.

Dandee hit Play.

And the video started.

In the video, the black girl next to Regina was giggling. She said, "I can't believe you said that."

Regina nodded and said, "And I'll say it again: white men. They're the ones I blame the most."

The other black girl said, "Yeah?"

"Hell yeah," Regina said. "Everything that's wrong with this country, a white man has been behind it. Look at healthcare. It's been a shit show from the get-go. And who's been in charge of healthcare since it started? White men. And look at all the stuff that happened in the 1960s—people sprayed with fire hoses, mothers and kids included. Who was behind that? White men. And it doesn't stop there. Look at Hollywood. Ninety percent of the movies and TV shows suck today. The comedy ain't funny, the suspense ain't suspenseful, and the reality stuff ain't realistic. And everything else is boring and unoriginal as hell. And who are the people who make those movies and TV shows? White men. And who's boring, unoriginal, unfunny, unsuspenseful, and out of touch with reality? White men. So why would they be put in charge of entertainment?? Your guess is as good as mine. I swear, everything white men touch turns to shit. And it always has. But for some reason, nobody wants to tell 'em. Yo, I'm telling you: this world needs to fire white men."

The other black girl laughed and said, "You tripping."

Regina said, "I'm serious, yo. This country needs to give white men a pink slip that says, 'After a thousand years of poor results, we've decided your services are no longer needed.' And then the country needs to start looking at resumes from motherfuckers with higher voices and darker skin. And I'd bet you a *million* dollars that, in just five years' time, this whole country would be a fun, better place to live."

The video ended.

"And that's it," Dandee told me.

I was so shocked I couldn't move.

I couldn't believe what I'd just seen.

Dandee said, "I'll send you the link."

When I finally found my voice again, I asked her, "Why didn't you show me this before?"

Dandee said, "You're dating her brother. It would've been awkward. My name is Dandee Majestyk, not Holly Homewrecker."

My phone vibrated.

"There," Dandee said, "I just sent it to you. You're the only one I've shown it to, so nobody else has to know about it if you don't want them to. It's up to you. But if you want some dirt on her, your phone just got a big scoop."

In a daze, I said, "Thank you." It might've been the first time I ever thanked somebody for giving me something I wasn't thankful for.

The walk back to my place is usually twenty minutes, but tonight it felt like twenty years.

I was happy.

I was sad.

I was confused.

Happy because I now had the dirt my sister wanted on Regina.

Sad because I now had the dirt my sister wanted on Regina.

Confused because I had no idea what the fuck I was going to do with this dirt.

If I gave the dirt to my sister, it would make her happy, but it would also make Regina sad, which would make my boyfriend sad.

Because he loves his sister.

But I love my sister too.

But I love my boyfriend too.

I thought to myself: *Dandee said she wouldn't tell anybody. That I was the only other person who knew. And if I didn't want anybody else to know, nobody would ever know. I could just go into my house and up the stairs to my bedroom and delete the dirt link without ever saying anything to Leona and then enjoy a shitty sleep that wouldn't be nearly as shitty as it would be if I showed the dirt to Leona . . .*

But as I got closer to my house, I started thinking about Regina and her friends at the Rainbow Relief table, ignoring me. Different phrases started echoing in my head:

What's her ass doing here?

I didn't expect you to understand.

I guess I hit a nerve.

As I got closer and closer to my door, Regina's unsmiling, unfriendly face got bigger and bigger in my mind till it was just about the size of the house I was about to walk into.

And I guess that's why I did what I did next.

I knocked on Leona's door.

"Come in," she said.

I stepped in and saw her sitting at her desk, doing homework.

"Hey," she said.

 "Hey," I said.

She took off her glasses, which she only wears when she does homework, and said, "So hey, I'm sorry about all the yelling earlier. It's just—once I'm on fire, it's hard for me to put it out, y'know?"

I nodded my understanding. Then I said, "So, I got something to show you."

I showed it to her.

You know that expression "grinning from ear to ear"? I always thought that expression was bullshit; I just didn't think it was physically possible.

Till tonight. After the video, that's exactly how my sister smiled at me. Then she gave me a kiss on the mouth and yelled,

"You so rock my life! WE GOT HER NOW!!!" Then, doing the Double Middle Finger, she yelled, "Checkmate, bitch!" to the ceiling, which—for some reason—served as a stand-in for Regina.

She played the video again.

After it ended for the second time, she tossed her glasses aside and started putting on her sneakers.

"Where're you going?" I asked her.

"*We're* going over to John Smith's," she said, quickly tying her laces.

"Why are we going over to John Smith's?" I asked.

"There's a rumor going around that he's thinking about dropping outta the race. We gotta tell him it's okay now, he can stay in."

She hopped up and went to her closet for her jacket.

Already I regretted passing the dirt to sister instead of trash bin. I said, "Isn't it kinda late?"

She glanced at her watch and said, "It's not even ten o'clock yet. And anyway, we got good news for him." She pointed at my phone.

After she called John to make sure he was home, we headed out. I wasn't a fan of seeing John's brother again, but I figured I should be with my sister just in case he went red-eyed-asshole again.

John's girlfriend Sherry answered the door and let us in.

John was sitting on the living room couch. Even at home he kept his dark glasses on.

"I hope this doesn't take long," Sherry said as she ushered us toward her boyfriend. "We're in the middle of studying for a Trig test."

Leona told her, "It won't be long but it *will* be good." She sat next to her opponent and put her hand on his shoulder. "How's it going, buddy?"

John smiled and said, "I'm okay. How's it going with you?"

"So listen," my sister said, "I hear you're thinking about dropping outta the race."

John said, "Yeah. After Regina made that announcement this morning, there's just been too much drama. I don't need that."

Leona said, "Well, when there's too much drama, all you gotta do is turn the channel to Reality. And the reality is this: Regina Gates has gotta go. And thanks to something my sister dug up tonight, she *will* be going. Oh John, you have *got* to see this. I mean, um, hear this." She motioned for me to hand it to her. "Gimme the phone, Sal."

As I handed her the phone I tried to tell her with my face that I wish she hadn't told them I was the one who'd handed her the Regina bombshell.

Sherry joined John and my sister on the couch to watch the video.

I couldn't watch it again, so I wandered out of the living room and into the vestibule where a giant framed picture hung on the wall: it showed John, his brother Scott, and their father smiling at the camera. Given the more youthful faces of John and Scott, I guessed the picture was from a few years ago. If framed family pictures had titles, this one would've been called "Three Guys and Three Fish": they seemed to be on a fishing trip or something because the only thing bigger than their smiles was the fish each of them was proudly holding up. My eyes were drawn not so much to John's father but to John's father's T-shirt, which showed a painting of a man playing pool on a pool table that wasn't a pool table but a bikini'd woman in high heels whose body was stretched out to serve as a pool table.

Let's just say I wasn't a fan of the painting.

Suddenly I had to go to the bathroom. I stepped back into the living room and asked, "Um, where's the bathroom?"

Her eyes on the video, Sherry said, "Down the hall, turn right, and you'll see it on your left."

I thanked her and headed for the bathroom.

Just as I was about to step into it I saw another room from the corner of my eye. I turned around and saw someone sitting on the edge of the bed. It was John's brother. He sat there in his letterman jacket, with his hands folded on his lap, daydreamingly staring at the floor while some video was playing in the background. The sight of him instantly made my heartbeat go faster. Because here's the thing: Not long after he'd made the cunt & fried-chicken-and-watermelon comment, I reported it to the principal, and he was written up and had to serve a day in detention. And now, here I was, standing just a few feet away from someone who was just one head-lift away from seeing the person who got him in trouble. And yes, I knew it was possible he didn't know *I* was the one who'd reported him, but what if he did?

But he didn't lift his head up. Just kept staring at the floor. Actually, he seemed to be doing more listening than looking: on his dresser was an open laptop that was playing the video—probably YouTube—where this guy in a suit was talking to the camera, saying, "Men really need to start going their own way. We need to stop depending on women for our happiness. We need to exile them from our lives . . ."

I turned on the bathroom light. He still didn't look up.

Barely believing my luck, I stepped into the bathroom, quietly closed the door behind me, and locked it.

When I was done, I quietly opened the door and saw right away that my luck had run out.

He was staring at me.

And for the first time, I noticed the poster on the wall behind him: it showed a bunch of rifles and guns arranged in the shape of a Valentine heart. My eyes shifted back to Scott, whose mouth slowly stretched into a small smile as he stared at me.

"Hey," he said.

"Hi," I mumbled.

Just as I was about to walk away, he said "Hey" again.

"What?" I said.

"Come here."

"Why?"

"Come here."

"Why?"

"Just come here."

"WHY?"

"You'll find out when you get here."

I said, "I think I'll pass."

As I was about to take another step away, he nodded and said, "Good. It's probably for the best. You're contaminated anyway. You've crossed over to the Dark Side. You're a lost cause now. A failed experiment."

I frowned at him.

He smiled. "Just kidding."

The frown stayed on my face.

He said, "Doesn't anybody have a sense of humor anymore? What the hell's happening to everybody?" Then, never taking his eyes off me, he said, "Y'know, I had a nightmare the other night. I dreamed I was watching a movie about the Joker, only he wasn't called the Joker anymore. He was rebranded as the Woker. It was the most boring movie I'd ever seen in my life. No car chases, no shoot-outs. Instead there were exploding microaggressions that burned down safe spaces where flying social justice warriors spoke truth to power about stopping a genetic mutation of heteronormative values that were rapidly spreading throughout the earth. And the Joker wasn't even killed by Batman. He was killed by an angry Twitter mob who tore him apart for intersection-shaming and being complicit in the embracing of the patriarchy. And a few blocks away, Batman was being rushed to the hospital with a ripped-off dick for forgetting that 'Penguin' was the dead name of Pauline, Gotham's first trans supervillain . . . But you know what the worst part of the dream was? I couldn't even get up and leave the theater 'cause my piece-of-shit girlfriend had chained me to the seat and superglued my eyelids to my forehead so I wouldn't miss a fucking thing." He gave me a bitter grin. "I swear, that's the last time I'll ever eat rainbow sherbet before bedtime."

Not wanting to hear anymore, I started walking away when he said, "I got a question for you."

I turned around and looked at him.

He said, "You know how I know girls are a mistake of nature? 'Cause they don't even have the common sense to date their own kind."

He gave me a long, penetrating stare.

"Class dismissed," he said.

Fighting the urge to spit at him, I walked on.

I was shaking a little when I got back to the living room. John, Sherry, and my sister were talking about the video, which had just finished playing.

"Trust me," Leona told her opponent, "once I show this video to the school, she's so gonna be toast. *Burnt* toast. I can't wait."

John said, "I don't know. I don't think you should do it."

"Why not?" Leona said.

John said, "I don't like kicking somebody when they're down. This whole digging-in-the-past thing is a waste. We should all be moving forward. That's the best way to travel."

Leona said, "The best way to travel is you and me on a plane and her on a bus that just broke down." She looked at him more closely. "Don't tell me you're still thinking about pulling out?"

John nodded. "Every time people look at me, they're gonna think about what she said this morning. Already girls are calling me a creep and messing up my posters."

My sister said, "But John, don't you see?" She caught herself and tried again. "I mean, um, don't you understand?" She held up my phone to him. "She's on video, basically saying that she's a racist! When the whole school sees this tomorrow, then you and that whole girl-out-the-car thing disappears, and so does Regina! This is no time to Swipe Left. You're still in the game, buddy!"

John shook his head and said, "I don't know."

My sister took his hand and said, "John, you might not know it, but you're kinda making a statement by being in this race. You're basically telling kids that a . . . disabled person can do anything they can do, including run for president. If you drop out, you know what kinda message that'll send? It's like you're saying you're Less Than just 'cause you're blind. And think about how it'll look to your brother and your dad. You really want them to think you let two girls chase you away?"

The living room went quiet as John thought about my sister's words.

He looked toward the floor for a few moments; he opened his mouth like he was about to say something, then closed it. Then he looked back up and opened his mouth again.

He said, "Well, maybe you're right."

"So you're back in?" Leona excitedly asked.

John smiled and said, "Yeah, I'm back in."

Leona hugged him. "Oh John, this is gonna be so supremely bacon, with just you and me in the race! We don't have to worry about her muddying up everything. I'd rather compete against a respectable opponent like you than a racist one like her."

Sherry stood up. She didn't seem to share my sister's enthusiasm. "Okay, if there's nothing else, we really need to get back to studying. That Trig test is gonna kick our ass tomorrow if we don't."

As Leona and I rode our bikes back home, I felt like somebody who'd lit a match to burn one sheet of paper but the match somehow ended up burning down a whole building. Thanks to my actions, a likely sexual assaulter had just been pulled back in while a girl whose campaign platform I like more than my sister's—and whose brother I like more than any boy I've ever met—was about to be pulled out. Life sucks.

When we got home I told my sister, "Hey, don't tell anybody else I was the one who showed you the video, okay?"

Leona said, "Why not?" Seeing my sad face made her understand. "Oh. Right. Don't worry—I won't."

I washed up and got into bed. But I didn't go to sleep. How can you go to sleep when rewarding your sister also punishes your boyfriend, his sister's campaign, and an innocent girl who once got shoved out of a car?

Have I mentioned that life sucks?

ULY

Today was straight-up drama without a comma. Flaws without a pause.

It started this morning and it just kept getting worse with each hour.

On the Knightly News Leona with her grinning ass presented a video that somebody had recorded two years ago of my sister throwing serious shade at white men. I'm not going to get into all she said, but look, I ain't gonna front: the stuff she said was raggedy as hell. There's no way around it. She never should've said any of it.

And what makes it worse is that it's a wound I can't even dress up. Her campaign is now bleeding from a bazooka shot and there's this big-ass bloody basketball-sized hole there and all I have are two Band-Aids, if you can feel me on that one. It wouldn't be so bad if it was just a rumor. With a rumor, Hearsay is your savior and He Said/She Said is your best friend. But this is a damn *video*; you can't pretty up the raggedy with a Hearsay suit or deodorize it with He Said/She Said spray. It's just raggedy, straight up and down and sideways, in all its naked glory, for all to see and smell. I mean, what am I going to say?—that it's *not* my sister sitting on that bus, saying all that stuff? That somebody's phone had CGI'd her (and her voice) onto the bus?

All day mofos were rolling up to me and asking what's up with my sister. And all I could do was shrug and say, "I don't know what she was thinking. I'm gonna talk to her."

Even Sallie seemed to be influenced by the fallout. She sat with me at lunch, but she was quiet and a little distant.

By the afternoon most of my sister's posters had been screwed with. Mofos crossed out the letters of her name, leaving the *R*, and they scribbled "acist" next to it.

And rumors were floating around that she was going to be dropped from the election.

As for Regina herself, I couldn't find her anywhere.

Till tonight. As I was doing my homework she walked into the apartment, her face grim as hell. She rarely looks happy anyway, so I didn't know if her sad expression was from some distressing news or just from her being herself.

"Did they shut down your campaign?" I asked her.

Taking off her coat, she shook her head. "Mr. Dranger says I can still run."

I let out a loud exhale. "Damn. Looks like you dodged that bullet."

Hanging up her coat, she said, "I wouldn't go that far." She closed the closet. "They suspended me. For three days."

My eyebrows went up. "Real talk? 'Cause of that video?"

"They said it wasn't, but I know it was," she said and walked into the kitchen.

Following her, I said, "What reason did they give you?"

Putting hand sanitizer on her hands, she told me, "They said it was because I let out confidential information about another student. You know, Smith and that girl he attacked. Her accusation of him was supposed to stay on the DL but I took the shit aboveground and now I gotta go underground for three days."

She wrapped an apron around her waist and took out a big pot and a box of spaghetti. Just as I was about to put the pot on the stove, she motioned for me to move away. "No, I don't need your help. 'Fact, I don't want anything from your ass anymore."

"Why are you mad at me?" I said.

She said, "Because that bitch you call a girlfriend is the one who showed the video to Leona."

My mouth got cold and my heartbeat suddenly felt like it was in my neck. "Bullshit," I said. "How do you know it was her?"

Regina held the pot under the faucet, yanked up the knob, and the cold water blasted out. "No, the better question is: How could you, as my campaign manager, *not* know it was her?"

I said, "She didn't say anything to me about it!"

Keeping the pot under the cold water, Regina said, "Well, somebody said something to somebody about it, 'cause the word is out now. And I might be too." She cut off the cold water and slammed the filled pot onto the front burner, sending up snakes of water that spilled over the sides and splattered on the counter and the surrounding stove surface. She turned on the fire, smacked a lid on the pot, and shook her head while keeping her stare on the stove. "Goddammit, man, you *swore*, you *swore* to me that you weren't gonna let your shit with her interfere with your shit with me."

I said, "And I didn't!"

She whipped around and glared at me. "You did!! You been sleepin' at the wheel 'cause you been sleepin' with the enemy!"

I fired back, "We don't even really know if she was the one who did it! Your head is catchin' a tumor all because of a rumor!"

"Rumor my ass!" Regina said. "She did it. I know she did."

I said, "Did you *see* her do it?"

"There are some things out there you ain't gotta see to know. I don't see the earth movin' around the sun, but I know the shit is happenin'. And I know your girl was the one who dropped that video."

I said, "Look, let's just break through the bullshit and go to Real City here. I know what this is really about. You don't like that I'm dating her."

She said, "You're wrong, bro: I *hate* that you're dating her."

I nodded. "So there it is."

She nodded and said, "And there it always *will* be. It makes me *sick to my stomach* that you're dating her. All the fine, beautiful, smart girls of color roamin' around and all you have a taste for is vanilla. Even the good brothers like you—at the end of the day, y'all are nothing but a bunch of Uncle KJs."

Trying to keep my rage in a cage, I quietly said, "I'm nothing like Uncle KJ. And now, I'm seeing I'm nothing like you either. You know why? 'Cause when I look at Sallie, I don't see a white girl. I see a nice girl."

Regina said, "Well *I* see a white girl, and about a million mirrors agree with me. Okay, maybe she's nice too. But check it out: at the end of the day, all the Sallies are Leonas. And no wonder—look who they're raised by: white men."

I said, "So just 'cause Sallie's sister is racist, Sallie has to be too? You actin' like racism is wet paint or some shit—you brush against it, and it rubs off on you."

Regina said, "It doesn't have to 'rub off' on white girls, 'cause it's already there. Every white girl. When their back is to the wall, other white girls are the only ones they'll call. Even when their back is *not* to the wall." She moved her eyes back to the pot. "I remember when I was in Mr. Walsh's Bio class a couple years ago. I had three of 'em as lab partners and they only talked to each other. Completely shut me out. It was like I was some disease they hoped would go away if they just didn't look at me. And whenever they did look at me, they always put on this big fake smile like they were thinking 'I'm only being nice to you because I have to be.' But when they smiled at each other, it was always a real smile. Natural, you know? Not forced.

But whenever it was me—fake smile again. Sometimes I think all white girls are born with that fake smile programmed into their mouths or something. Because every white girl I've ever known has it." She looked back at me. "Including Sallie. And you know why they have it? Because, deep, deep down, white is their favorite color. White is the only color they're comfortable with. White is the only color they truly love. The cool ones are the best at pretending it ain't. And the raggedy ones are the best at proving it is."

I said, "Regina, are you gonna look me in the eye and tell me you really think that?"

She said, "Brother, I can look you in the eye and tell you I really *know* that. White people really, truly only love each other. Just check out what happened this week. The minute it looked like kids were startin' to show me more love than her sister, Sallie drops that video. And it ain't just the white peeps our age. It's administration too, John Smith assaults a Latina girl a year ago and he's still in the race *and* in school. I talk a little bit about how raggedy white guys are *two* years ago, and my black ass gets suspended. White people only love white people. Always have, always will."

My phone hummed. I took it out and saw SALLIE next to a Heart symbol on the screen. I wasn't ready to talk to her yet, so I put it back in my pocket.

I looked at my sister. I wanted to tell her she was wrong, but her face was a street with only one sign: NOTHING YOU CAN SAY WILL CHANGE MY MIND.

So I went to the living room and listened to music, hoping it would drown out all the echoes my sister's words were making in my head . . . when they weren't bumping into my own bad thoughts about Sallie.

ULY

When I met Sallie on the porch of her house the next morning she kissed me, then said, "What happened to you last night? I called you, like, ten times. You didn't hear the phone?"

I said, "Oh, yeah, I did. But I wasn't feeling well. Sorry about that."

She touched my arm. "Oh no, what was wrong?"

I said, "I guess I had a headache or something."

"Are you feeling better now?" she asked.

I said, "Yeah."

She smiled at me, then threaded her fingers through mine, and we started down the walkway, heading to the movies.

When we were off the walkway and about to go down the sidewalk, I asked her, "Were you the one who gave that video of my sister to Leona?"

Sallie's smile faded and she looked at the ground. "Yeah." It was barely a mumble.

I stopped walking. It felt like somebody had kicked me in the gut with a bayonet-tipped boot.

"Damn, Sallie," I said. "Damn."

She quickly grabbed my arm and said, "But I didn't think she was gonna show it to the whole school!"

"Well, what the fuck else did you think she was gonna do

with it!!—write an essay about it??!! Turn it into a musical??!!"
I'd never yelled at her before and it felt strange as hell.

It must've sounded just as strange because Sallie shrank back a
little—her face was a blender that had just mixed together shock,
confusion, and pain.

She said, "Well you don't have to yell."

"Well you didn't have to screw me over!" I yelled. "Now my
sister's all over my ass, sayin' I dropped the ball and let her down!
I don't wanna hear that shit!"

Sallie lurched forward and got in my face. "My sister would've
said the exact same thing to me if I hadn't shown her that video!
You think *I* wanna hear that shit??!! You think you're the only
campaign manager standing on this sidewalk??"

It was the first time Sallie had ever yelled at me and it felt
even weirder than yelling at her.

As we stood there on that empty sidewalk, glaring at each
other, I felt this foreign, quirky combo of emotions running
through me. I still loved her with a passion that would make a
hundred Hallmark cards go "Goddamn!" But—for the first time
ever—I also disliked the hell out of her. A part of me wanted to
French-kiss her for five hundred years, but another part of me
wanted to make her sleep on a bed made completely of dead rats.

I said, "Fuck it. Let's just go to the movies."

We both went back to walking.

Then I stopped. So did she.

I said, "Why didn't you at least tell me you had a video?"

"Do you tell me everything you do as campaign manager?"
she said. "And didn't we promise to never talk about election stuff
with each other?"

I said, "But this was different!"

"Why?" she said. "Because it's *your* sister's campaign that got
screwed? Because it's all about your sister, right? Because it's all
about *you*, right? The hell with me, right?"

"I never said that!"

"You don't always have to say it out loud to say it!" she said.

I was stumped, so I went back to walking. But not for long. She caught up to me and yanked my arm to a stop.

She said, "Maybe I showed that video to my sister 'cause I thought it was time to finally be *her* campaign manager and not your sister's co-campaign manager!"

"What're you talkin' about?"

She said, "I'm talking about how I've helped your sister's campaign more than you've helped my sister's!"

"I can't believe your ass just took it there," I said.

She said, "You know I'm right! I told you how to get your sister on the Knightly News that time, and I tried to show support for her Rainbow Relief by sitting there almost every day, pretending her and her friends weren't treating me like some three-eyed homeless zombie from Mars! What have you ever done for my sister's campaign?"

"Nothing," I said.

"Oh, so you admit it!"

"Yep," I said. "And you know why I've done nothing for your sister's campaign? Because your sister is a racist."

Sallie looked like I'd just rammed a metal couch into her. Then she said, "No she's not."

"Yes she is," I said.

"No she's not! My sister's not a racist! She just looks at things a little different from the way you and I might look at 'em."

I nodded. "Right. She looks at things like a racist."

"Stop saying that!" Sallie said.

I shrugged and said, "Okay, she's not a racist. She's a bigot. How's that?"

My girlfriend's face got red. She said, "Do you know how much that hurts? When you call my sister a racist, what're you saying about me?"

I said, "Actually, it has nothing to do with you. It doesn't mean you're a racist. But your sister *is* a racist. And the sooner you get that through your head, the sooner your denial can be dead."

She said, "You know what? Fuck the movies. And fuck you. I don't wanna go anywhere with you. Ever again."

I nodded and said, "You just took the words right outta my mouth."

She stormed back home.

So did I.

I don't want to get all corduroy up in here, but my heart suddenly felt the way it feels when you have a hole in the middle of your shirt. As you walk outside, feeling the cold air swarming through the hole and hitting your skin, all you can think about is going home and giving the shirt to your grandmother so she can sew it up, or just throwing it away and putting on a new shirt. But my grandmother's been dead a long time, my father and sister can't sew worth a damn, and you can't pull out another heart from the drawer.

I legit felt like shit.

I was so miserable I went over to my girl Marilyn's, hoping she could cheer me up, but her ass just made things worse. She spent the first hour trying to figure out if it was a Break Up.

"Wait, what were her exact last words again?" Marilyn asked me as she swept her marker across a large sheet, designing my sister's latest campaign poster.

I sighed and said, "I already told you—she said, 'I don't wanna go anywhere with you. Ever again.'"

Marilyn said, "See, actually, that's not that bad. I once had a girlfriend throw a strawberry milkshake at me and say, 'If you ever show your face around here again, I'll cut you.' The next day, we were *sharin'* a strawberry milkshake. It ain't always about the words, bro. Sometimes it's about the tone of voice. Or the eyes. What were her eyes like when she told you to drop dead?"

"Let's just drop it, okay?" I told her.

She said, "Okay. So when are you gonna call her and ask if it's just a Break Up or a break?"

I said, "Damn, Marilyn—I said drop it!"

She held up her hands and said, "Okay!" She pointed at the poster she was designing and said, "Wait, why am I even doin' this? Isn't your sister's campaign pretty much dead?"

"I don't know," I said. I was starting to get a headache.

"She said all white men should die. Trust me, her campaign is dead."

"I'm so glad I came here," I said.

Marilyn said, "But there's a way your sister can bring her campaign back from the dead. All she has to do is march into the school and give everybody a car, like Oprah used to do whenever her ratings got low. White people love when black people are *givin'* them cars instead of takin' them."

She went on and on, and my attention drifted in and out over the next couple of hours. My brain was a neighborhood where every street corner was Sallie Boulevard.

THAT WAS four days ago.

And each day has been worse than the day before.

I feel like a piece of me is literally missing—like I'm minus a hand or leg.

I haven't seen her since the argument.

I miss the hell out of her.

I miss her voice. I miss her laugh. I miss the way she smells. I miss the way she walks. I miss the slow, careful way she chews her food, like as if the next bite she takes might land on some bone or piece of glass. I miss the way she nods whenever a character in a movie or TV show says something she agrees with.

And her eyes. Those dark, dark intense eyes. I miss them so damn much. It's gotten so bad that the other day I was in the living room, watching CNN with my dad, and this female commentator with blond hair and dark brown eyes was on, and even though her face looks nothing like Sallie's, her hair-and-eye color combo still reminded me of her, and I had to leave the room and go into the kitchen till the damn show was over.

This love shit is hardcore as hell. If you ain't a strong mofo, don't fuck with it, 'cause it can't wait to chew you up and wash you down with acid rain.

I keep wanting to call her, but every time I pick up the phone, I put it down. I just can't do it. I don't know if it's my bullshit pride or something else, but I just can't tap the name *Sallie*.

Then came tonight.

I just couldn't take it anymore. I still wasn't ready to call her, but I had to reach out to her in some way.

So I picked up my phone, and decided to text her.

This is what I typed:

Next to you the sun feels cold
In your hand a lump of coal looks gold
You can beat Charm in a race
You can make Hate slow its pace
When you talk, my ears hear a song
When you laugh, my worries don't seem that long
The truth is, you drive me insane
And if Insanity is water, then let it rain.

When I was finished, I put my finger over the Send button.

And just as I was about to tap it, I thought about how she'd taken her racist sister's side over me, and so I moved my finger from Send to the Backspace button, deleted the entire poem-message, and put my phone away.

Maybe I'm better off without her.

But damn, it hurts.

It hurts.

SALLIE

This isn't going to be a long entry because I really don't feel too well right now. I've been sick—like, actually, physically sick—since It happened. When my stomach isn't tied up in painful knots, my throat is sore from crying, and when my throat's not sore, every bone and muscle in my body is sore, like a bunch of Mack trucks mistook it for highway asphalt.

So I really don't feel like talking or writing right now. I'll just throw some numbers at you. Numbers from this week:

6: The number of days that have passed since It happened.

5: The number of nights I've cried myself to sleep. And the only reason why this number isn't 6 is because the sixth night, tonight, hasn't come yet.

4: The number of times Lady M has brought dinner to my bed.

4: The number of times I've turned her away, telling her I don't have an appetite.

5: The number of times I've eaten lunch in the school library instead of the caf where I usually eat lunch with him. And since there are five days in a school week, that's been every day this week.

2: The number of times my sister has told me, "Would you just snap out of it! What is he—the only guy in the world?"

2: The number of times he and I passed each other in the hall at school (before we realized we were about to pass each other) without looking at or speaking to each other, like we were complete strangers.

2: The number of times I ran into the closest bathroom to cry into the sink right after passing by him in the hall like we were complete strangers.

576 (guesstimate): The number of times I've wanted to pick up my phone and call him just so I could hear his voice, then hang up, but changed my mind about doing it, since I knew he'd know it was me because of my phone number.

576 (guesstimate): The number of times I thought maybe I could call him from a pay phone so my number wouldn't appear, but then changed my mind because he'd probably still know it was me.

7:08 P.M.: Two hours ago, when I decided to send him a text.

7:11 P.M.: When I finished writing the message, which was this: **How did everything that was so great get so bad? I miss you so, so much it's killing me. Can we talk?**

7:12 P.M.: When my phone rang, just as I was about to send the message.

7:12 P.M.: When I saw that he was the one calling.

7:12 P.M.: When my whole body trembled as I wondered if I should pick up or just let it ring.

7:12 P.M.: When I decided to just let it ring. So he could leave me a voice message. So I could hear his voice again. (So I could hear his voice again!!)

7:13 P.M.: When I waited for my phone to signal that a voice message was just left.

7:14 P.M.: When I waited for my phone to signal that a voice message was just left.

7:15 P.M.: When I waited for my phone to signal that a voice message was just left, even though I knew that my phone usually signals within seconds after the message is over.

7:16 P.M.: When I figured that maybe he was just leaving a really, really super epic, super long voice message— maybe the longest one ever left on my phone—and I decided to give it just a couple of more minutes.

8:03 P.M.: When I wondered why my phone still hadn't signaled.

8:04 P.M.: When I realized that maybe he just hadn't left a voice message.

8:05 P.M.: When I thought to myself, *Well, if he doesn't have the decency to leave me a voice message, why should I have the decency to send him a text message?*

8:05 P.M.: When I completely erased the text message I was going to send him.

8:06 P.M.: When I put my phone down, put my head down, and cried some more.

ULY

As Marilyn and I chilled in her room, listening to music, I realized that Sallie had been out of my life for a week and a day. And that's when I knew what I had to do.

I stood up and told Marilyn, "I can't take it anymore. I'm headin' over to her place."

She nodded. "Sure took your ass long enough." Then she looked me up and down and said, "Wait a minute—you're missing something."

Looking at myself, I said, "What?"

"Where's your gift?"

"Gift?" I said.

She said, "You can't go over there and apologize without a gift. If you want a woman to forgive, say, 'Sorry.' If you want a woman to forgive and forget, say, 'Sorry, and this is for you.' The End. You better get your black ass over to a flower shop."

My eyebrows went up as the spark of a new idea hit me. I said, "Actually, I can do better than flowers. I'll give her my Special Edition *The Good, the Bad and the Ugly* DVD with deleted scenes."

Marilyn's eyes went wide and she said, "Is you crazy?? No bitch is gonna get wet from that!"

I said, "No, she's down with that kinda stuff. It's our favorite movie."

Marilyn shook her head and said, "You two *better* stay together, 'cause nobody else is ever gonna take your freaky asses."

I hurried over to my place to get the DVD, then I headed over to Sallie's. I probably should've called first, but I was afraid she'd hang up on me.

When I got to her door, I rang the bell and waited. My heart was thumping like a mofo.

The door opened; it was Lady M, with a guitar slung across her chest. She smiled at me and said, "Oh, Uly—what a nice surprise!" She motioned me inside. "Come in." It was hard to tell how much she knew: Did she know about my argument with her stepdaughter? Did she know about my sister saying all white men must go? Did she know about me calling her other stepdaughter a racist?

I smiled and shook my head, declining her invo to come in. "Um, that's okay. I just wanted to have a quick word with Sallie. Is she in?"

"Oh, yes," she said, "I'll go get her . . . I guess you'll wait here?"

"Yes, thank you."

She closed the door, but not all the way. I could hear some faint chatter coming from inside and recognized the voices of Leona and her boyfriend but I couldn't place the other voices, nor could I tell you what the hell they were jawing about.

After a couple of minutes, the door opened again. I braced myself for the reappearance of Lady M, regretfully telling me that Sallie didn't want to talk.

But it was Sallie standing there. She was holding a rolled-up paper tube that I guessed was her sister's new campaign poster. She closed the door behind her, all the way.

"Hey," she said.

"Hey," I said.

As she stared at me, her eyes teared up. So did mine.

Then we hugged each other, hard and tight. For a long time.

Then we let go and looked at each other again.

Just as I was about to open my mouth, she said, "Wait, let's say it at the same time. On the count of three, okay?"

I smiled and nodded.

She said, "One . . . Two . . . Three. I'm sorry."

At the exact same time she said, "I'm sorry," I said, "Nice day, huh?"

As her expression switched to shocked confusion, I burst out laughing.

She play-punched my shoulder and said, "You asshole."

Quickly putting my laughter on the shelf, I said, "No seriously—I'm sorry. I didn't mean to yell at you like that."

She smiled and nodded. "I know."

We stared again at each other for a few moments, then I remembered the DVD. I said, "Oh, I got something for you."

Her eyes went a little wide. "Really?"

I took the DVD out of my bookbag and handed it to her.

"No way!" she said, excitedly running her fingers all over the box.

I told her, "It has audio commentary and a new documentary. And there are some deleted scenes—they were originally filmed without sound, but a few years ago Eastwood and Wallach came back and dubbed their voices over it so we can hear the actual words. They both sound old as hell now, but I still give them props for tryin', you know? Oh, and the Tuco torture scene is extended—they added, like, three minutes to it."

"Sweet," Sallie said. "Thank you so much, Uly."

Then she looked up at me and kind of laughed. "I can't believe this," she said.

"What?" I said.

She said, "Actually, I have something for you too."

"Real talk?"

She nodded and held up the rolled-up paper tube.

"What's that?" I said.

She unrolled it. It was a poster for *The Good, the Bad and the Ugly*, but all the words were in Italian.

Pointing at it, she said, "It's the original 1966 theatrical poster—you know, when the movie first came out. This was the poster that was hanging in all the theater lobbies in Italy. I ordered it a couple of years ago." She handed it to me. "And now I'm giving you custody."

It was one of the best gifts I'd ever gotten.

"Wow, thank you," I said, taking it.

I put my arms around her waist and gently pulled her to me. And we kissed.

Then we put our foreheads together.

"I'm so sorry," she whispered to me.

"I'm sorry too," I whispered to her.

We kissed again.

Then I said, "That stuff I said about your sister . . ."

Sallie put her finger to my mouth like she didn't want me to continue.

"Don't," she said. "Let's not bring that up anymore."

I said, "Okay."

She said, "New pledge: we never, ever talk to each other about the election again, from now till June, and if one of us slips and breaks the pledge, we have to pay the other one two dollars. Deal?"

I laughed and said, "Deal."

Since her kitchen knife wasn't around, we pinky-sweared.

Then she pointed regretfully behind her at the door. "I gotta head back in. Leona needs me to help her bake some more stuff for . . . you know."

I nodded and said, "Okay."

We kissed one more time.

Then she whispered, "Grape Juice."

"Grape Juice," I whispered.

And she went back inside.

As I walked back home, my phone rang. It was Regina. Things have been kind of tense between her and me the last week; not as raggedy as the Sallie & Me sitch, but definitely about twenty miles from rosy. We weren't exactly dying to get each other's autographs at this point, but at least we were back on speaking terms again.

"What's up," I said.

She said, "What's up. I need you to get me back on the Knightly News for Monday morning."

My heartbeat went Olympic sprinter again. All the relief I was feeling from my breakup makeup with Sallie got body-slammed by this new tension my sister was giving me. Why did she want to get back on the Knightly News?

I told her, "Okay. Why?"

She said, "Truthanasia—that's where I live. That's why." Then she hung up.

As I walked the rest of the way home, I tried to bury my worry with a shovel called Just Think About Sallie, but my sister's request kept kicking off the dirt and rising again.

What the hell is my sister going to say on Monday? Is she going to give her campaign an official death blow by throwing more shade at white men? Already kids who used to Nice her are deserting her faster than you can say "outcast," more and more each day.

Is she going to announce that she's quitting?

Is she going to do something even worse?

SALLIE

When Uly's sister appeared on the Knightly News this morning, my guess was that she was going to announce her withdrawal from the race. That was my guess. That was my hope. That was my dream. I knew it was wrong to have that hope and dream, but I also knew that if Regina stopped being Regina The Candidate, then Uly could stop being Uly The Campaign Manager and start being Uly My Boyfriend again, and we could go back to dating in peace. I don't have to tell you how close our relationship came to breaking into a hundred pieces this past week, so peace is something he and I definitely can't afford to lose. I still don't know who leaked out that I was the one who showed the video to Leona. My sister says it wasn't her but might've been Sherry, and Sherry says it wasn't her but might've been Leona. Either way, I was still trying to get dry from the leak's water damage, and I *so* needed some more good news when Regina sat to face the camera this morning.

She didn't give it to me.

But she did give me—and everyone else in the school—this:

"Good morning, Knight High. By now, most—if not all—of you have seen the video where I said this country should fire all white men. I'm not going to front and tell you that my words were taken out of context or that the video was audio-shopped to make me look bad. Truthanasia is where I live, so I wanna keep it real and admit that I said all those words, just as you heard them. I also wanna admit that I was wrong. It was wrong to say those things the way I said them. And even though the words were wrong, they came from a real place. You see, I was very angry at the time, and—in some ways—I still am. Why am I angry? Because I live in a country where a white guy shoots a black teenage girl in the head for trying to get in his lane on the highway and the next day in a news article he's called a 'gentleman' by the county sheriff . . . right across from an article where two black kids who stole some candy from a corner store are called 'thugs.' That's why I'm angry. But that's still no excuse to say what I did the way I did. And for that, I apologize. I never said I was perfect. I'm just like all of you out there. I make mistakes. I guess you could say I think of myself as a work-in-progress. I think all of us are works-in-progress, and the only time we're truly ready to be wrapped and put on the shelves is when there's a tag on our toe, if you can feel me on that. I want to end this by saying: I know there've been rumors that I'll be ending my campaign today. Well, you know what my campaign and this weather have in common? They're both just getting warmed up. I'm still in the race, and when it comes to changing this place, I'm still on the case. And if you're on that team, then join the Regina Regime. Thank you, and peace out."

PART

3

April

When that rope starts to pull tight, you can feel the devil fight your ass!
—Tuco, *The Good, the Bad and the Ugly*

ULY

When Regina, Narmeen, Marilyn, and I rolled into school this morning, we saw something that shocked the shit out of us. Somebody had taped a bunch of Confederate flags to the walls and windows of the second floor. To a white person, the Confederate flag might just be a big square cloth with bars and crisscrossing stars on them. But to a black person, it's a "Fuck You" in fabric form.

Written on each flag, in big, black-magic-marker letters, were the words "LEONA FOR PREZ!"

After five minutes of staring at the flags and giving each other murmured variations of "You see this shit?" and "I can't believe what this school is turning into" and "They ain't gettin' away with this," my sister said, "I got an idea."

Ten minutes later, all four of us—each armed with a jumbo pair of scissors—cut out the stars on each flag. When we were done each of us had two fistfuls of individually cut stars.

Then throughout the rest of the day, we handed a star to every black, Latinx, or Asian kid, to every openly gay kid, to every openly trans kid, to every learning-disabled kid, and we told each of them, "You're a star."

Some of the kids looked at our asses like we were crazy, then looked down at their star like it was crazier. Other kids just laughed, pocketed the star, and kept it moving. And a few kids smiled and taped the star to their foreheads.

Okay, check it out: I ain't gonna front; I know my sister's Star thing was kind of corduroy.

But it was also kind of beautiful.

SALLIE

This morning, anchorgirl Coral Bleeker interviewed my sister about the Confederate flags that some knuckle-dragging asshole hung in the hallways yesterday.

Coral asked her, "So, as one of the three presidential candidates, how do you feel about what happened yesterday, with the Confederate flags?"

My sister said, "I think it was wrong to cut up those flags like that. Whoever put up those flags was just exercising their free speech. Their reward shouldn't have been getting vandalized. The same thing happened to my posters a couple of months ago, and it's not right."

I could feel the color draining from my face. It felt like I was listening to my sister sing a song in the wrong key, and I was—for the first time in my life, maybe—embarrassed to be her sister. I looked around the class, without looking too much like I was looking around the class, to see if anyone was looking at me. I was hoping they'd all come down with a case of group amnesia and had forgotten I was related to her. But kids were either idly texting on their phones, taking a nap, talking to each other, or—worst of all—staring at Coral Bleeker and my sister on the projector screen.

You could tell that Coral was trying to fight a wince as she took in my sister's off-key notes.

"Okay," Coral said, "but a lot of people think those Confederate flags shouldn't have been hung up in the first place, 'cause they represent oppression and hatred. You don't agree?"

My sister said, "The kids who hung up those flags are no more wrong than the kids who vandalized them. Do you know what it's like when something that means so much to you is vandalized? All because the vandalizers think they have a right to destroy something they disagree with. I'm telling you, Coral, I speak from experience. My *Turn Knight Back To Day* posters were totally harmless and it was all because of a misinterpretation that they got vandalized. And the vandalizers won. How is that fair?"

Coral looked confused. "So are you saying that Confederate flags are harmless?"

My sister said, "Yes, basically. I mean, isn't everything, when you really think about it? Every object in this world is, like, neutral. It's us who make it into something more: we make it into something racist if we prefer to be the victim, or we make it into something hopeful if we prefer to be somebody who looks at the brighter side of life. *Turn Knight Back To Day* is a message of hope, to those of us who believe in hope. *Turn Knight Back To Day* is a message of hate to those of us who believe in hate. And I think the Confederate flag is the same way."

AFTER SCHOOL Leona and I sat in the back seat as Lady M drove us home. I looked out the window at the angry throng of parents that lined the block leading up to our school. Most of them were mothers of minority students, but some were white too. One mother held up a sign that said: KKK (KNIGHT KORRUPTS KIDS). Another mother held up a sign that said: KIDS SHOULD READ PRIDE AND PREJU-DICE (one side), NOT FEED PRIDE AND PREJUDICE (the other side).

Another mom waved a sign that said: SAY GOODNIGHT TO BAD
KNIGHT. Another mom: KNIGHT'S MATH = DIVIDE (PEOPLE) +
SUBTRACT (LOVE). Another mom, holding a sign with a drawing
of an alarm clock on it: WAKE UP FROM THIS KNIGHTMARE!!

It was the saddest scenery I'd ever seen. But, in a weird way,
it also made me hopeful.

My sister ignored the passing parental protests; she was
showing me a schedule of campaign activities she wanted to do
for the rest of this week, but I was barely paying attention.

It didn't take long for my lack of attention to get her attention.

"Hello?" she said. She knocked on my forehead. "Is Sallie
home? What's with you today?"

I was sort of glad she asked me. I needed to get this off my
chest. I turned from the window and told her, "That stuff you said
on the Knightly News this morning—it was so not bacon."

She looked surprised. "What do you mean?"

"How could you say the Confederate flag is harmless? This
is the *Confederate fucking flag*, Lee, not a pair of ugly dungarees or
whatever the hell."

My sister turned away from me and sat back; she looked
bored. "Oh my God. Dating one of them has turned you into one
of them."

My face started getting hot; I glared at her. "What's that supposed to mean—'one of them'?"

She looked at me and said, "A whiner. A victim. Another asshole born with a protest sign in their mouth."

"Fuck you," I said. "Do you know how much hate went into
making that flag?"

She said, "The Confederate flag is just a way of honoring the
people of this country who stood by what they believed in and
refused to sell out just 'cause everybody else was saying it was The
Right Thing To Do."

I said, "The Confederate flag is a piece of shit created by dis-loyal pieces of shit who wanted to split from this country so they could continue treating human beings like luggage."

Leona said, "Want some more cheese with that whine?"

"Have I said 'fuck you' yet?" I asked.

Lady M looked at us in the rearview and said, "Is everything okay back there, ladies?"

Leona and I didn't say anything. And we kept not saying any-thing for the rest of the ride.

When we got back home I went to my room, crashed on my bed, and stared at the ceiling. I was feeling so many things toward my sister but the feeling I felt the most was Disappointment. I was disappointed in her.

I turned on my side and my eyes fell on the framed picture sitting on my nightstand. The picture shows Leona and me with our arms around each other standing in front of the Ferris Wheel at Six Flags. My eyes focused on my sister's smiling, thirteen-year-old face. And at the same time I heard my boyfriend's words echoing in my head: *Your sister is a racist. Your sister is a racist. Your sister is a racist.* Those echoing words clashed with the smiling girl staring back at me from the picture. Sort of like the way echoes of *It's so dry* wouldn't make sense if you were staring at a picture of the Atlantic Ocean.

Uly's words stopped echoing, and now the only things filling the silence were my own thoughts:

Could it be true?

Is my sister a racist?

I looked again at her in the picture.

She's not.

Racists are burly, ugly men with bushy beards and backward baseball caps and three missing teeth and Southern accents and plaid lumberjack shirts that smell like stale beef jerky and even staler tobacco.

She's not.

She's beautiful and funny and wears perfume that smells so good I can't wait to "borrow" it and clothes so fashionable I wish I had the taste to buy them. When she was nine she put a snowball in the oven to see how long it would take to melt. Racists burn crosses, not snowballs. When she was sixteen, I had a pair of leather maroon boots she loved so much she paid me fifty dollars for them even though they were two sizes too short for her, then she hacked off the toe part with a hacksaw and turned them into open-toe boots, and a week later, about a dozen freshmen and sophomore girls were walking around with open-toe boots. Racists don't do that. Racists pay fifty dollars to watch other racists hack off actual toes.

My sister is not a racist. And besides, she's from New Jersey.

Wondering if my sister was a racist was so exhausting it made me sleepy, but I couldn't go to sleep because I kept wondering if my sister was a racist.

I wanted something else on my mind, so I took out my phone and called Uly. And not even five minutes into our conversation, I couldn't remember any of the stuff I was thinking about before. And long after I hung up with him I still couldn't remember.

But a few minutes ago, as I was doing my homework, my eyes fell back on the framed picture next to my bed. And now I remember again. And I so wish I could un-remember. But I can't.

I guess it's time to call Uly again.

ULY

Okay, check it out: Knight High has two theaters—one is basically the auditorium, where most of the big musicals and plays (including that raggedy one I was in last fall) are performed, and the other is a much smaller one that used to be something else (either a mini-library or a faculty dining room, I forget which) before it was converted to what it is today: the Black Box Theater. Called the Black Box, for short. It even looks like a box from a distance: it's a giant cube with black wooden walls on the outside. The Black Box is basically where the "special" school plays are performed—you know, the plays that aren't afraid to be a Lyft for the Big Issues that are too heavy for the auditorium to pick up: racism, sexism, homophobia, transphobia, etc. It's the school-stage version of niche networks like BET, Lifetime, and Here. Black Box is student-run, with a faculty member or two serving as the guide-on-the-side, and it gets its funding from any "leftovers that the auditorium was too full to gobble up," to quote my sister, who's been the assistant director of the treasury since last year.

Well, a couple of days ago, in the evening hours after school, a bunch of kids went up to the third floor and painted the entire Black Box white. Then they wrote, in black letters, on the entrance door:

WELCOME TO THE WHITE BOX!
The following restrictions apply:
No Chocolate
No Spice
No Curry
No Rice

Because Knight High's hallway cameras are stupidly timed to shut off every day at three-thirty in the afternoon and come back on the next morning, we don't know for sure who did it, but we have a couple of guesses. One possibility is this racist-ass group called the Day Backers, founded and led by Leona's raggedy-ass boyfriend Wilk. They were the mofos who sprayed foam at our Rainbow Relief station last month before scampering away like the pebble-balled punks they are. Another possibility is this new group called WAP: depending on who you ask, the shit stands for either White And Proud or White American Prince. (I wouldn't be surprised if it's both.) Nobody seems to know exactly how many members they have, but they identify themselves to each other by wearing a small blank white button, which they pin to the inside of the bottom of their shirt: if somebody rolls up to them and whispers, "Are you WAP?" they either say no or they flip up the bottom of their shirt and show the white button.

During lunch this afternoon Regina and I went to the principal's office to complain. Mr. Woolery told us he was looking into it because, "Vandalism will not be tolerated here."

Regina told him, "But Mr. Woolery, this is more than just vandalism. This is a hate crime."

The space between Mr. Woolery's eyebrows did the confusion crinkle and he said, "Hate crime?"

My sister glanced at me the way she does when she thinks the person she's talking to is an idiot, then she looked back at the principal and told him, "Didn't you see what they wrote on the door? It said: '*No Chocolate, No Spice, No Curry, No Rice.*'"

Mr. Woolery looked like he was waiting for a punch line that had already passed him by. He said, "That's food. What does that have to do with a hate crime?"

My sister gave me the Glance again, then told him, "They're basically saying: '*No Blacks, No Latinxs, No Indians, No Asians.*'"

Regina spent the next five minutes explaining to him why "Spice" meant Latinxs, "Curry" meant Indians, and "Rice" meant Asians, and even though he got it, he still didn't quite Get It.

He said, "Okay, I see, but unless they specify Blacks, Latinxs, Indians, and Asians, I can't treat it like a hate crime. Vandalism— yes. Racism—I'm just not convinced."

My sister said, "They changed the color of a whole theater from black to white and called it 'The White Box,' and you don't think it's racism?"

Mr. Woolery kind of shrugged. "Sorry. I just don't." He cleared his throat and shuffled some papers on his desk. "Now, if there's nothing else, I really need to get back to work here."

Shaking her head, Regina stood up. She and I walked out of his office; just as we were about to leave the outer office, I could overhear Mr. Woolery tell his secretary, "I swear to God, I can't wait till this fucking election is over."

As my sister and I headed to the caf, I said, "So what're you gonna do?"

She said, "What needs to be done."

I said, "And what's that?"

She gave it a little mind time, then said, "I need you to hook me up with, like, seven or eight cans of paint of all different colors, but no white. You think you can have 'em for me by lunchtime tomorrow?"

I said, "I don't know. I can try."

As it turned out, I was better at this Trying business than I'd thought, because by the beginning of lunchtime today, there I was, rolling a cart of eight paint cans (and a dozen paintbrushes) toward my sister, who was standing in the middle of the third-floor hallway, just a few feet away from the White Box. As much as I wish I could tell you I got all that paint because I'm the Wondrous Amazing Incredible PaintMan™, I gotta stay in Real City and say that I got it simply because Ms. Daniels, the art teacher, is down with the Regina Regime.

When my sister saw the paint cans and brushes, she nodded and said, "That's what's up."

Then she unzipped her bookbag and took out a blue bullhorn that Narmeen had talked her uncle—an ex-cop—into lending her.

Looking into my paint cart, Regina asked, "What're the colors?"

I pointed at the cans and said, "We got yellow, red, blue, orange, green, pink, gray, and brown."

My sister smiled at me and raised her fist for a bump. "You the man, Ules."

After we fist-bumped, Regina turned on the bullhorn, which spit out a long starter screech that damn near chewed up my eardrums.

Covering my ears, I said, "Damn, that thing's no joke."

My sister nodded and said, "Good, 'cause I ain't trying to make 'em laugh. It's time for this school to get schooled." She pointed at the paint cans. "You do the lids, I'll do the kids."

I nodded and started popping off the lids while she spoke into the bullhorn.

"GOOD AFTERNOON, EVERYONE," she announced. "MY NAME IS REGINA GATES AND I'M ONE OF THE THREE CANDIDATES RUNNING FOR PRESIDENT. AS MANY OF YOU HAVE PROBABLY NOTICED BY NOW, OUR BELOVED BLACK BOX THEATER HERE ON THE THIRD FLOOR WAS PAINTED COMPLETELY WHITE YESTERDAY BY A HATE GROUP HERE AT THE SCHOOL. AND THIS HATE GROUP WROTE ON THE DOOR: 'NO

CHOCOLATE, NO SPICE, NO CURRY, NO RICE.' AS MANY OF YOU KNOW, THAT'S THEIR WAY OF SAYING, 'NO BLACKS, NO LATINXS, NO INDIANS, NO ASIANS.' IF YOU FIND THIS UNACCEPTABLE, IF THIS MAKES YOU MAD, IF YOU WANNA LET THESE HATERS KNOW THEY'RE NOT WELCOME HERE, THEN ALL YOU HAVE TO DO IS MEET ME IN THE MIDDLE OF THE THIRD-FLOOR HALLWAY RIGHT NOW, PICK UP A PAINTBRUSH, DIP IT INTO THE PAINT CAN OF YOUR FAVORITE COLOR, AND FLICK THE BRUSH AGAINST THOSE UGLY WORDS ON THE DOOR. IF ENOUGH OF YOU DO THIS, THOSE UGLY WORDS WILL END UP GETTING COVERED BY EIGHT DIFFERENT BEAUTIFUL COLORS. THOSE OF YOU WHO HEAR ME: GET UP FROM YOUR DESK AND COME OUT HERE TO THE THIRD-FLOOR HALLWAY AND HELP ME COVER THIS HATE WITH EIGHT—EIGHT BEAUTIFUL COLORS. THEN GO DOWN TO THE SECOND FLOOR AND THE FIRST FLOOR AND THE CAFETERIA AND GATHER ALL YOUR FRIENDS AND TELL THEM TO COME UP HERE AND DO THE SAME THING. COVER THE HATE WITH EIGHT. WE GOT YELLOW, WE GOT GREEN, WE GOT BROWN, WE GOT BLUE, WE GOT RED, WE GOT ORANGE, WE GOT GRAY, WE GOT PINK. JUST DIP THE BRUSH INTO YOUR FAVORITE COLOR AND FLICK IT AGAINST THE HATE. COVER THE HATE WITH EIGHT."

As my sister bull-horned, more and more kids started milling through the hallway or out of their Enrichment classes and moving toward her.

In the meantime Narmeen and Marilyn had joined up with us, and they started helping me hand the paintbrushes to the kids.

Following my sister's instructions, each kid dipped the brush into one of the cans and flicked the brush toward the words on the White Box door, peppering the *No Chocolate, No Spice*, etc.

with their color. When they were done, I or Narmeen or Marilyn quickly told them, "Great, now go find as many of your friends as you can and tell 'em to do the same thing!" and they nodded and ran off, in pursuit of other peeps who were down.

In the first five minutes, about a dozen kids rolled up to us and flicked.

Ten minutes into it, about twenty kids started rolling up to us. And as the lunch hour got longer, so did the crowd size.

The bigger the crowd got, the faster Narmeen, Marilyn, and I had to hustle to make sure everybody dipped & flicked.

And the whole time, Regina stayed on that bullhorn, repeating her announcement on a loop, changing it up every now and then with inserts like: "COME ON, HURRY, WE ONLY HAVE THIS ONE LUNCH HOUR TO COMPLETELY COVER UP THE HATE ON THAT DOOR" or "IF YOU'RE TIRED OF PEOPLE BEING MEAN, START WITH GREEN; IF YOU WANT THIS SCHOOL TO BE MELLOW, START WITH YELLOW; IF YOU WANNA BE AROUND PEOPLE WHO THINK, START WITH PINK; IF YOU WANT LOVE TO BE FOUND, START WITH BROWN; IF YOU DON'T KNOW WHAT TO SAY, START WITH GRAY; IF YOU KNOW EXACTLY WHAT TO DO, START WITH BLUE; IF YOU WANNA PUT HATE TO BED, START WITH RED; AND IF YOU'RE LIKE ME AND DON'T KNOW WHAT THE HELL RHYMES WITH ORANGE, START WITH ORANGE."

By the twenty-five-minute mark, you couldn't see the *No Chocolate, No Spice*, etc. words anymore: they were completely sheeted over by red/blue/gray/green/brown/yellow/orange/pink splotches. But kids still kept coming up and flicking. They started targeting their flicks toward the other words on the door: WELCOME TO THE WHITE BOX! and THE FOLLOWING RESTRICTIONS APPLY.

"THAT'S IT," my sister bull-horned, "KEEP FLICKING TILL THIS *WHOLE ENTIRE BOX* IS DIFFERENT COLORS."

At about the half-hour mark, the Knightly News crew, with a microphone-clutching Coral Bleeker at the front, rolled their asses up to us; one of them was holding the camera, which he kept swinging from the flicking crowd to the theater's dripping door and walls and back again. Coral was scrambling through the masses, trying to interview as many mofos as she could, asking them things like, "Why are you doing this?" and "What if you get in trouble?" and, "Who do you think put those words on the door?"

Right about then my sister slipped in a new interjection to her looping announcement: "AND LET'S NOT FRONT. WE ALL KNOW A LEONITE PUT THOSE UGLY WORDS ON THE DOOR. WELL, HERE'S YOUR CHANCE TO SHOW THESE LEONITES WHAT YOU THINK OF THEM."

I saw Zack Zelinka, the autistic kid from the debate who'd taken offense at Leona's "retarded but the good retarded" comment, pushing his way through the crowd, toward the camera and Coral's mic. I was shocked to see that he was wearing a Leonite shirt; it's basically a white T-shirt with #LEONITE magic-markered in red on it. He started talking to the camera as Coral held out the mic to him. I moved closer so I could hear what he was saying.

He told the camera, "Yeah, uh, Leona Walls, if you're out there, I bought this shirt today just so I can do this . . ."

He pulled the shirt off, ran to the paint-can cart, dipped the crumpled shirt into the green paint, then ran over to the theater's door and smeared green over the X in BOX. Then he ran back to the camera and said, "Yep, yep, I did it, I did it. And you know why? Because you're a . . . What do they call that again?—when you're annoying but it's the bad annoying? Oh yeah: ASSHOLE!!" Then he held up the crumpled, green-smudged Leonite shirt and said, "I will *never* be a Leonite!" He spit on the shirt then hurled it to the floor and stomped on it. Some people in the crowd clapped.

By the forty-minute mark, the flicking flock had swelled to about a hundred peeps; I couldn't believe it. We just didn't have

enough paintbrushes for every mofo, and time was running the
hell out, so I asked Regina what she wanted to do.

She bull-horned, "FOR THOSE OF YOU WHO CAN'T GET
A PAINTBRUSH, JUST DIP YOUR HAND IN THE CAN
AND SLAP YOUR HANDPRINT AGAINST THE THEATER
BOX. SLAP THE HATE WITH YOUR COLOR. THAT'S IT.
COME ON—SLAP THE HATE. SLAP IT. SLAP THE HATE
WITH EIGHT."

One by one, brushless kids dipped their hands in the cans,
ran up to the theater box, and smacked their handprints against
the door and walls. Pretty soon, even the peeps who had brushes
dropped them and did the handprint thing. After a while, about
forty kids were beating the hell out of that theater box with their
painted hands. Some of them were even standing on medium lad-
ders—that freak Narmeen, she always seems to know where to get
a damn ladder—and smacking the top of the wall, so that almost
every inch of the white box was a different color. The thumping
of their hands against the wooden theater made the hallway sound
like it had a heartbeat or something.

From the corner of my eye I saw a blond girl rounding a corner
and stopping in her tracks. I turned and saw that it was my girlfriend. She didn't see me. When she saw what was happening, she
looked down, and sadly walked away. Before I could call out to her
she'd disappeared back around the corner.

It felt like somebody had punched me in the chest.

Meanwhile Regina motioned for Coral and the camera kid to
come over to her.

As the theater-box-beating continued, my sister looked into
the camera and spoke into her bullhorn: "TO THE LEONITES
OUT THERE, THIS IS WHAT HAPPENS WHEN YOU MESS
WITH ME AND MY PEEPS . . . AND TO ANY LEONITES
OUT THERE WHO ARE TIRED OF ALL THE HATE-ORADE
YOUR LEADER KEEPS POURIN' OUT, IT'S NOT TOO LATE

TO COME OVER TO MY SIDE . . . STOP BEING A LEONITE, AND START BEING A REGINIAN!"

My eyebrows went up. It was the first time I heard her use that. Reginian. I liked it. A lot.

Regina bull-horned to the camera, "I'LL SAY IT AGAIN. DON'T BE A LEONITE. BE A REGINIAN!"

The theater beaters turned around and started chanting "Reginian! Reginian! Reginian!"

A corner of my eye caught a line-up of teachers standing along the lockers behind us and I damn near jumped. My ass had gotten so caught up in what was happening that I'd forgotten I was in a damn school. I gave the teachers a guilty smile but they didn't notice. They just stood there, watching the paint-splotched spectacle with expressions that were hard as hell to read. My guess is that none of them stopped it because of the dude standing at the middle of their lineup: Mr. Dranger, who was the only teacher with a small smile on his face.

Knowing that Mr. Dranger had our backs, I calmed down and turned to my sister, who was already looking at me. She seemed just as shocked by the large turnout as I was.

She and I both looked at the theater box, which was no longer white. It was now an accidental Jackson Pollock painting of eight different colors zig-zagging all over the place. It was like a rainbow had thrown up all over the theater, but it was beautiful, revolutionary vomit.

Then came the best part: my sister gave me one of her rare good-china/plastic-off-the-couch smiles. I don't want to sound corduroy or anything, but, at that moment, I felt really proud of her.

Mangling the moment was the mental image of my girlfriend sadly walking away.

Why wasn't she happy about the White Box's takeover & makeover?

SALLIE

A couple of mornings after the White Box got rainbowed, Coral Bleeker played footage of the rainbowing along with Regina bull-horning that everybody should become Reginians. Struggling to keep her impartial frown in place and her partial pro-Regina smile out of place, Coral announced the results of the latest presidential poll (the first one given after the White Box's rainbow wash): now, for the first time, Regina Gates was in first place; my sister was in second place; and John Smith was in third place.

And, not for the first time, I felt like my soul had swallowed Dickens's book *A Tale of Two Cities* and was trying to impersonate it: the eastern half of my insides was happy for Uly and his sister, but the western half of my insides was sad that my sister was starting to fall in the polls. I was feeling this same forked-soul feeling when I stumbled across the White Box's rainbowing the other day: a part of me so wanted to join but another part of me didn't want to because I was afraid I'd get into trouble for messing up school property.

I wish I'd joined.

I think Uly wished I'd joined too, because when I spoke on the phone with him that night he seemed distant and quiet.

And after that latest poll was announced, the other special person in my life was mad at me.

After school that day, I went to my sister's "new headquarters"—Mr. Heinbaugh agreed to let us use his Science room after Mr. Chadwick had Swiped Left on us because of my sister's transgender remarks during the debate (his niece is trans)—and before I could even get through the door Wilk and his three goons practically pounced on me, getting ready to frisk me. I know Wilk wants to help my sister but he's been taking it way too far, more and more each day. He's been frisking every visitor to make sure they don't have any recording devices.

I snapped, "You guys don't have to search me. Remember me? I'm somebody called the Sister."

Giving me a hard look, Wilk said, "You also happen to be somebody called I'm Dating The Opposition. They could've slipped a mini-recorder in your pocket when you weren't looking."

He nodded to his pal Jace who was about to touch me when I told him, "You put one hand on me and one hand is all you'll have left."

Jace didn't put his hand on me. None of them did. I guess they were all fans of keeping two hands.

I brushed past them and walked over to my sister, who was sitting in the big swivel chair behind Mr. Heinbaugh's desk; she hadn't even noticed the doorway tension—she was too busy drumming her fingers and silently fuming.

"Hey," I said.

She glared at me and said, "How could you let her get to Number One?!"

My mouth fell open. "What?"

She yelled, "If you were doing your job, she never would've got to Number One!"

From across the room, Wilk said, "This never would've happened if I was your campaign manager."

Leona kept her eyes on me. "You just completely broke my life. You broke my life."

"This never would've happened if I was your campaign manager," Wilk said again.

I felt like exploding, but my sister was already exploding and I knew that me exploding would only lead to nothing but two big explosions, so I kept calm, turned around, and told Wilk and his crew, "Guys, could you please take off for a little while so I can talk to my sister alone?"

Wilk said, "I don't take orders from you."

"Get out," my sister told him.

Wilk and his three friends got up and left.

My sister said, "How could you break my life like this?"

I said, "Lee, the only reason I'm staying calm right now is because you're upset, but if you want us to keep talking, you need to stop saying that. How is this *my* fault?"

"Because you dating *him* has been a distraction!" she said.

I said, "How could you say that? I've been trying to do the best I can as your campaign manager—"

"I'm not talking about a distraction to *you*! It's been a distraction to . . . everybody. You dating him."

My eyes narrowed. "What're you talking about?"

She said, "It just doesn't look good for me . . . My sister dating a black guy . . . It's just too distracting to my campaign . . . And a lot of Leonites are having a problem with it."

I managed to snap out of my shock enough to say, "Well shit, that's *their* problem."

"It's MY problem too!" my sister complained. "Damn, Sal! Why a black guy, of all people?! Do you know how distracting that is? People are starting to see me not as Leona Walls but as the Girl Whose Sister Is Dating A Black Guy. Why couldn't you have picked something less distracting—like a Puerto Rican? A Puerto Rican guy would've been a nice Interracial Starter Kit if that's your thing, and it wouldn't be breaking my life like this!"

To my surprise, I was still able to form words. I said, "He's the boy I fell in love with. What do you want me to do—break up with him?"

"Could you?"my sister asked, giving me a hopeful look.

My throat dried up. "What??"

Leona stood up and took my hands. "Just till after the election! You guys don't even have to break up!—you can just go on a little break, just till June!"

I snatched my hands back and said, "No way I'm doing that!"

"WHY NOT?!" she roared. "Don't you want me to win??!!"

"Yes! But if you winning means me losing the best guy I've ever known, then maybe it's time you find a new campaign manager!"

She slumped onto the edge of Mr. Heinbaugh's desk and gave the floor a mopey pout.

I told her, "And how would you like it if I asked you to stop dating that poor excuse for a human *you* call a boyfriend? *He's* the one you should be pointing the finger at. If him and his thugs hadn't gone all Jim Crow on that Black Box Theater, maybe you'd still be at Number One."

Leona plopped back into Mr. Heinbaugh's big chair and sank back, looking at the ceiling.

I said, "How could you date somebody like that? You don't think *that's* distracting?"

She said, "He means well. He's just a little too over-Into me. He and I are gonna have to have a long talk after the election."

Slumped in the big chair, my sister looked at me for a long time.

"What?" I said.

She said, "Hey, I'm sorry. You know, for what I asked you to do earlier."

I nodded.

She said, "Are you still my campaign manager?"

I said, "Yes. But you're gonna have to promise you'll never ask me to do something like that again."

My sister nodded. "I promise. I'm sorry. I was just mad about being Number Two. I hate losing, Sal."

"I know." I pulled one of the student desks up to her big chair and said, "So I've been thinking. You know how you can get back to Number One? Stop talking about race and transgender stuff and autistic Muppets and Jewish superheroes. It just divides people. Start talking about the stuff you're going to do when you *are* president. Like, what kind of exciting things do you have planned for next year?"

Her eyes got wide, and not just any wide, but lightbulb-clicking-on wide.

Then came the next day at lunch.

She gave a speech that almost made me lose my lunch.

She promised the crowd she'd do the following things as president: 1. Create Kissing Booths, where the guys can kiss a pretty girl, who'd be standing in the booth, for five dollars a smooch, 2. Ban Sadie Hawkins dances because "the guy should always make the first move; we should let men be men," and 3. Add boxing to the roster of sports so that students can watch fights the same way we currently watch basketball/baseball/football games. What was even more nauseating than her ideas was the thunderous applause she got in response to her ideas.

Three days later, Coral Bleeker reported that my sister was Number One in the polls again. (Regina slipped back to two and John was stuck at three.)

Then, after school today, something happened that made me want to lose my breakfast *and* lunch.

While Leona and I were sitting in headquarters, Wilk poked his stupid head into the room and said, "Leo, I got a surprise for you! Close your eyes!"

"What surprise?" my sister asked.

"Just close your eyes!" Wilk urged again.

Leona closed her eyes.

Wilk motioned to somebody in the hallway.

And five seconds later, his buddies Jace and Larkin wheeled in a human-size clay statue of . . . my sister.

"Okay, now open your eyes!" Wilk said.

Leona opened her eyes.

When she saw the statue, she got up and slowly walked over to it. Her face was blank.

I waited for her to make fun of it.

But when she touched it, her mouth stretched into a grin and her whole face went happy.

She gave her boyfriend a long kiss and told him it was the best gift she'd ever gotten.

PART

4

May

If you save your breath,
I feel a man like you
can manage it. Adios.
—Blondie, *The Good,
the Bad and the Ugly*

JULY

This month is actually almost over, but before y'all get mad at me for not writing, let a brother explain. May was filled with so much drama even Hulu would've been like, "Damn!" There was so much going on I just didn't have time to write. Because we were a month away from not just Election Day but the end of school too, it seemed like everybody wanted a piece of me. Teachers started giving out homework like the shit was about to be outlawed—I had to write *three different* research papers this month. And my sister had damn near turned into a Demand Machine: "Proofread this." "Make copies of this." "Tell her I need it by . . ." "Tell him I need it by . . ." "Tell Marilyn I need six more sheets." "Make sure my lunchtime rally doesn't overlap with . . ." "Listen to this . . ." "Find out if Staples has . . ."

This campaign-manager shit is no joke, and that's straight from the headquarters of Real City. I don't know how the professional campaign managers out there can stand it. Being campaign manager for the last three months is the reason I'm gonna die at seventy-two instead of eighty-one, straight up and down.

But check out the worst part of this job: it had me hopping and flopping so much I hardly got to see Sallie. Everything she and I did this month we had to do fast because we had to get back to either our homework or our sisters. It was like our relationship was suddenly an orchestra conducted by crystal meth.

So let me give you a rundown of what you missed this month. Settle in, 'cause it's a lot.

- Campaign shirts suddenly seemed to be everywhere. You couldn't walk three steps down the hall without seeing a shirt saying #LEONITE or LEOKNIGHT or REGINA REGIME or #REGINIAN. And if you're wondering where they got the shirts from, they just did it themselves. They took a plain white T-shirt and wrote their message on the front or back with a black magic marker. Done. I swear, because of this election everybody is suddenly a bunch of Coco Chanels with pimples.

- The cafeteria has turned into the Red Sea, with kids instead of water: the students who identify as Leonites sit on one side, and the students who identify as Reginians sit on the other side. I've been trying to see which side is thicker, but it's hard to tell; they both seem about even. The other day somebody from each side even put up a big banner—one saying LEONITES, the other saying REGINIANS—over their section, to make the civil war official. As for the middle, it's been unofficially reserved for either John Smith's peeps, or peeps who bring their appetite instead of an opinion, or Sallie and me. In fact, the both of us try to get there early as hell so we can get a seat in the middle before the Smithees or the Appetites beat us to it.

- Some mild controversy jumped off around the middle of the month when Leona introduced the hashtag

#LeeOwnHer to replace the original *#Leona* on her Twitter account. LeeOwnHer. Leona. Get it? My sister sure did, and you can best believe she wasn't happy. She complained to Mr. Dranger about the slavery implications, but Leona insisted that she was using "own" to mean "defeat." Leona's explanation won, and Mr. Dranger decided to let *#LeeOwnHer* live. So now, whenever Leona gives her lunchtime rallies, she sometimes gets the crowd to chant "Lee Own Her!" You've really got to hear it to believe it.

- Once a month Coral Bleeker, the Knightly News anchorgirl, does what's called a Field Report, where she leaves her news desk and goes out through the halls, interviewing mofos about some topic that's been getting a lot of heavy play. So it made sense that the topic for this month was our election. Coral asked two simple questions: Who are you voting for, and why? It was interesting to hear the different answers. The people showing love for John Smith gave reasons that ranged from: "I admire his bravery" to "He's the only one I trust" to "Somebody who can tackle the toughest football players can also tackle the toughest issues" to "Because he's the only guy running. Girls are too unstable. That's why there are no female pilots." The peeps showing love for my sister gave answers that ranged from: "She's the only one who takes it serious" to "She cares about other people, not just herself" to "Rainbow Relief really helped me" to "I liked what she did to the White Box." The kids showing love for Leona said everything from: "Because she's hot" to "She's funny" to "She's the only one honest enough to say what she really thinks" to "I wanna go to a school with a Kissing

Booth." The kids who fell outside the Regina/Leona/Smith zone gave answers ranging from: "All three of 'em suck" to "Doesn't matter, they're all the same" to "Who's running again?"

- Toward the end of last month Leona's boyfriend Wilk got some Leonite sophomores from Sculpture class to build a Leona statue made of fucking clay. If that wasn't bad enough, all this month the statue has been standing at the end of the third-floor hallway, just outside the library, for all to see. When Regina and I complained to Mr. Dranger, he said the statue was appropriate because it was part of the election's democratic process and that if we wanted to combat her statue with our own statue of Regina, that would be part of the process too. I looked at my sister and told her, "Sorry, but I ain't about to make a damn statue for your ass." But check it out: I haven't even gotten to the really disturbing part yet. All this month Wilk with his freaky, sprung ass has paid different pairs of kids to guard the statue during their free periods and lunch hours; so whenever you see the statue you're also seeing a pair of kids sitting at the base of it, texting on their phones or talking or eating.

- As for the weekly polls, they've been doing enough up-and-downing to make seesaws seasick. The first week of this month, Leona was at First. Then the second week my sister was back at First. Then the third week Leona was top dog again. The fourth week? My sister again. We're now in the fifth week and the latest poll hasn't come out yet, but I've been catching more and more kids paying close attention to the screen whenever Coral makes the poll announcement. No one knows what the hell is going to happen from one week to the next.

And that brings me to the raggedy portion of this Rundown program.

This month some things have gone down at this school that make the White Box shit from last month look like something out of Dr. Seuss. I don't even like thinking about it, but I don't want to give you the runaround on this Rundown, so check it out:

- A swastika was drawn on two lockers: one on Cindy Goldman's and another on Barry Sokoloff's.
- Somebody wrote on the bathroom wall NO ROOM FOR NIGHT AT KNIGHT. Get it? Think about it for a bit, and you will.
- On the tiles above the toilet in one of the bathroom stalls was written: GO BACK TO AFRICA with an arrow pointing down at the toilet.
- Written in soap on the mirrors above the bathroom sinks was UNITE WHITE.
- Not all of it is from the Leonites. Somebody, probably a Reginian, wrote on one of the staircase walls: YOU KNOW SHE'S WHITE, SO BEAT A LEONITE.
- This next one is still trying to sink in. A few weekends ago, Krystal Simmons and her friends started having what they call Banana-Peel Parties: if you're darker than a banana peel, you're not invited and you definitely can't come in. Last weekend, four Reginians—two were biracial, one was Indian, and one was Latinx—gathered a bunch of rotten banana peels, put them in a paper bag, and knocked on Krystal Simmons's door. When Krystal opened the door, the Reginians each held a rotten banana peel to their face and told her, "See?—we're lighter. You gonna let us in?" Krystal closed the door on them and they

dumped all the rotten banana peels on her doorstep
and went home.

- Somebody egged Ms. Lawson's car and drew a hanging
  monkey in white chalk on the car's black hood. Ms.
  Lawson is the only black teacher at Knight High.
- About a week ago two trans students were attacked in
  the staircase during the lunch hour. One was punched
  and kicked; the other one was thrown down the stairs.

So I've told you all of that to say this: when I think about
all the raggedy shit that's gone down this month, I don't even
recognize my school anymore. Not that it was all Yay before
May—I've never felt completely comfortable in this jawn—but
this month showed me that maybe my sister was right about
the Leonas outnumbering the Sallies in this world. Before this
month, I always knew my school had bad breath and crust in its
eyes, but May showed me that it also has strong underarm odor,
lice in the hair, and a smelly discharge from its ears, if you can
feel me on that.

But none of that broke a brother's heart as much as what happened today.

While I was hanging at my girl Marilyn's after school, a
couple of quarters had slipped from my grip and rolled under
her bed. While my hands were on coin patrol, they stumbled
across an unexpected criminal: the corner of a big poster. When
I slid it out from under the bed I saw *#LeeOwnHer* in big glit-
tery letters above a drawing of Leona in a red cape and boots,
with one hand on her hip (basically the drawn version of her
damn statue).

As my whole body was starting to lock with shock, Marilyn
came back from the bathroom. When she saw what I was looking
at, she kind of winced and said, "Damn. You weren't supposed to
see that."

I pointed down at the betrayal in glitter & red and asked her what was up.

She shrugged and told me, "Leona said she always liked my designs and she asked me if I'd do a few for her if she paid me. The price was right so I said, 'Let's Make A Deal.' The End."

My throat felt dry as hell but I managed to say, "How can you Nice her after all that shit she said about trans people?"

She shrugged and said, "Insults fade when you get paid."

I said, "So that's all it's about with you—the money?"

"Yes indeed, honey," she said, looking me right in the eye. "Welcome to the world. You meet my price and I can play real nice. I don't give a shit who it is."

I said, "Two trans kids are in the hospital right now, all 'cause of her bullshit. What if one of 'em was you?"

She shrugged again. "I can handle a broken eye socket, as long as I have five Andy J's in my pocket."

I stared at her and couldn't think of anything to say. Up till that moment, I'd always thought I could get at least an 89 on any pop quiz about Marilyn Ramirez; but right then I realized I'd be lucky to score a low D. She was suddenly the most familiar-looking stranger I'd ever seen in my life.

When words found me again, I said, "I'm gone like Vaughn, yo."

As I was about to head out of her room, she said, "For real? You doin' a Game Over on our friendship all 'cause of some bullshit school election nobody's gonna remember in five years?"

I turned around and looked at her. I guess my eyes said it all because she told me, "Okay, fuck you then."

I said, "You probably wouldn't. I don't have enough money."

I left.

PART

5

June

Every gun makes its own tune.
—Blondie, *The Good, the Bad and the Ugly*

SALLIE

This morning I opened my locker and saw a dead rat, and that was pretty much all I saw. I'm more a shrieker than a screamer, so I shrieked, slammed the locker shut, and sort of buried my head into Uly's chest. Wrapping his arms around me, he kept asking, "What's wrong? What happened?" but all I could do was point at my locker. My tongue had forgotten how to talk.

He opened the locker, and a second later, I heard him say, "Holy shit."

As it turned out, somebody had tied a note to the dead rat's foot, and on the note was this typed message: IF YOU DON'T STOP SEEING HIM, YOU'LL NEVER SEE HIM AGAIN.

Uly and I figured there was probably a matching rat-corpse-message with his name on it too so I went with him to his locker and, with shaking hands that tried not to seem too much like they were shaking, he twirled his combination lock's dial, unlocked the latch, then pulled open the locker . . . and saw nothing but books and a sweater.

It didn't take us long to figure out why I was the only one who got a rat: for the last three months, my locker's combination lock had been broken, and I was too busy and lazy to ask Mr. Rezigno for a replacement. But I wasn't too busy or lazy today.

After my new combination lock was in and the dead rat was out (Mr. Rezigno held on to the message), I still didn't feel relaxed. It really creeped me out that someone (or someones?) had been watching me closely enough to know that my locker's combination lock was busted. If they watched me opening my locker, what else were they watching me do?

And if they were bold enough to either kill a rat or find a rat already killed and put it in my locker, who's to say they weren't bold enough to not be joking about hurting my boyfriend?

By dinnertime my fear had morphed to anger with fear-flavoring. I was angry that I went to a school where two people with a simple pigmentation difference couldn't date without one of them worrying about a dead rodent with a death-threat shoe ending up in their locker.

And that anger is the only reason I can think of for why I decided what I decided tonight.

It started with a casual comment from my sister. We were all sitting at the dinner table—Leona, me, Wilk, Wilk's sister Ashley, her boyfriend Skip, and Lady M—and Leona was talking about a bad experience she'd had with a Staples worker the other day.

Leona told us, "Oh my God, it was such a nightmare. I didn't think a cashier could be so nasty. I mean, she wasn't just rude—she was, like, black-girl rude, you know?"

Ashley looked confused. "She was black?"

Leona said, "No, she was white. But she was black-girl rude, you know. So I asked to speak to the manager and . . ."

I barely heard the rest of what she said. Because the words "black-girl rude" kept echoing in my head. Suddenly everything else sounded like I was hearing it underwater.

All I could hear clearly was *black-girl rude* . . .

Black-girl rude . . .

Black-girl rude . . .

I got up from the table and wandered out of the kitchen.

". . . rything all right, Sallie?" Lady M underwatered.

But I didn't say anything. Just kept walking.

When I got to my room I picked up the framed picture of my sister and me at Six Flags and sat on the bed with it. The echo continued:

Black-girl rude . . .

Black-girl rude . . .

As I slid my finger down my thirteen-year-old sister's face in the picture, I could feel tears stinging my eyes. And then I felt the same tears stinging my cheeks.

Because that's when I knew.

That's when I knew what I'd been forcing myself not to know all these months and even the last couple of years.

Other comments she'd recently made started echoing in my head.

Describing Shirelle Willows, one of the most beautiful girls at our school, to a student who'd never seen Shirelle before: *She's black, but she's really pretty.*

Telling our cousins that our car was almost too full: *One more person and it's gonna get Puerto Rican in here.*

Expressing her shock at Celeste LaGuardia's high Math SAT score: *She scored a 650?? She must've had an Asian in her purse.*

As my tears continued to splat onto the framed picture, I knew what I had to do.

I dried my face, wiped my eyes, went back to the kitchen, and told my sister I needed to speak with her in the living room.

When we were both in the living room, she said, "Sal, what's wrong?"

I said, "I quit."

She said, "You quit what?"

I said, "Being your campaign manager. I quit."

She stared at me for a moment, then she said, "This is a joke, right?"

I said, "No."

She said, "Did Uly tell you to do this?"

I said, "It has nothing to do with him."

"Then why are you quitting?" she asked.

I said, "Because of what you said in the kitchen."

"What did I say?"

"Black-girl rude."

My sister rolled her eyes and said, "Aw, come on, I don't need this shit now."

With tears refilling my eyes, I said, ". . . Leona, you're a racist." It was the worst thing I'd ever said to my sister, and it didn't exactly roll off my tongue; it sort of limped off my tongue. I suddenly felt nauseous.

I could tell it shocked her but she tried her best not to look shocked. She sighed and shook her head. "Can't you just wait till after the election to pour Woke-a-cola all over me? You can't quit now. We still got two more weeks! I need you!"

I shook my head and said, "I'm out."

She gave me a long stare, then said, "So you're choosing your boyfriend over your sister?"

I said, "I'm choosing not to be a campaign manager for a racist."

She sort of narrowed her eyes. "How could you call me that?"

I said, "Leona, you basically turned 'black girl' into a synonym for rude. You said ninety-five percent of the black kids at our school should leave our school. You're dating a guy who's just two white-paint-cans away from being a KKK member. This isn't the way you and I were brought up. Where's all this coming from? I mean, who *are* you?"

She said, "I'm just someone who tells the truth. You should try it sometime. You think I'm the first person to say I don't wanna go to school with black people? People were saying that hundreds of years before I was born, and people will still be saying it hundreds of years after I'm dead. They're toxic people. Just look at the news. You wanna ruin a place real fast? Just invite *them* in. Even black people don't wanna be around black people. The minute they get enough education and make enough money, what's the first thing they do? Move to a neighborhood where there's mostly white people. I'm not a racist, Sal. I'm just someone who pays attention."

I nodded. "Me too. And that's why I'm not your campaign manager anymore . . . You and your campaign ruined our school. It's a prejudiced hellhole right now, 'cause of you. I so regret the day I came up with the word Leonite."

She nodded as her face turned sort of red. "So you're deserting me, is what you're saying."

I said, "I'm not deserting you. I'm just moving on."

She shrugged and said, "You say tomato, I say kiss my ass."

Then she turned around and went back into the kitchen.

I went up to my room and started doing my homework, but it's hard to do your homework when you've just realized your sister is a racist.

And it's even harder to do your homework when you suddenly realize your boyfriend's life might be in danger because of your sister's presidential campaign.

| ULY

Yesterday spit on me, but today kicked my ass. Straight up and down.

Even before I woke up yesterday, I was in a bad mood. For the last three days Sallie's been acting weird and distant as hell, so the last thing I needed yesterday morning was this text from Marilyn: I know we're not friends anymore, but I just wanted to tell you: watch your back. Rumors are going around that there's a target on it.

I didn't text her back.

When Regina and I got to school, we saw that *all* her posters looked different: someone had replaced her face with a sticker of a gorilla face.

I'd never seen my sister so mad before. She was actually *trembling*—that was how furious she was.

It didn't take her long to start talking retaliation.

I spent the rest of the day trying to calm her down and cut the fire in her gut—telling her that she'd come too far in this election to blow herself up & out over some bullshit—but she wasn't buying what I was selling. While we were walking home she said, "I'm tired of this world givin' black women shit just 'cause it can, 'cause it knows we're the best at takin' a punch. I'm sick of us bein' the goddamn mules of the world. It's time for us to start bein' the fucking *mountain lions* of the world."

I kept trying to common-sense her, telling her this whole thing wasn't that deep and that retaliating would actually make Leona happy: it would be proof she'd gotten under Regina's skin. By the time my sister went to bed she finally seemed to be back to her calm self, and there was even more sage than rage on her face, so I thought the whole thing was squashed.

Till this morning.

While I was sitting in Mr. Connor's History class, I got this text from Narmeen: Uh, Mr. Campaign Manager, can you explain why Jeremy Kaminski just smuggled in an ax for your sister?

I immediately texted Regina: Did Jeremy Kaminski just give you a fucking ax??? Call me!

She didn't reply.

After class I tried to find her but couldn't. She wasn't in any of her classes and she stayed MIA for the whole lunch hour. I must've sent her about ten texts, telling her "Don't do nothing stupid" ten different ways, but she never responded. I tried finding Jeremy Kaminski's freaky ass too but he was more gone than Vaughn.

During the next to last period, while I was sitting in Ms. Ledbetter's class, I got this text from Narmeen: Somebody just saw Regina on the staircase, walking up to the 3rd floor, carrying something in a long plastic bag. Leona is in Room 307. I'll meet you there!

My heartbeat jumped to my throat as I sprung up from my seat and dashed the hell out of Ms. Ledbetter's class, ignoring her calls of "Young man, where do you think you're going without a pass?"

When I got to the third floor, I saw the back of my sister in the distance, marching down the hall, with a long white plastic bag in her left hand. She was just three steps away from Room 307. I was about to call out her name, but then a strange thing happened.

She moved past Room 307.

Then I noticed what was at the end of the hallway. Leona's statue.

And that's when a brother understood.

I stayed put as she snatched the ax out of the bag.

The two guys guarding the statue jumped out of the way so fast I'm surprised they didn't leave dust clouds.

My sister stormed up to the statue, raised the ax, and went to work whacking the hell out of Leona's clay body. She chopped off the head, then the arms.

Just as she was hacking off the left arm, I was so hypno-horrified that I jumped when I felt a hand on my own arm. I turned to see Narmeen there. In a confused daze, she whispered, "You think we should stop her?"

I whispered, "Are you crazy? That's an angry black girl with an ax."

My sister swung the ax again and split Leona's torso into two half torsos. Another swing separated the legs from the waist.

By the time she started whacking away at the already-whacked, fallen pieces on the floor, a crowd had gathered in the hallway, watching her. Some peeps clapped, but most just stared in shock.

I could only see my sister's back during most of the chopping, but I caught a glimpse of her face a couple of times and the thing that surprised me the most was how calm she looked.

Suddenly I heard a girl's scream crackle from the crowd: "Oh my God!"

A tall blond girl pushed her way out of the thick blanket of people and ran up to the puddle of pieces. It was Leona.

Seeing her opponent, my sister stopped swinging the ax, and let it hang at her side. She watched as Leona slowly dropped to her knees and scooped up some pieces from the pile that used to be her.

As Leona slowly buried her face in the pile, my sister put her other hand on the ax-handle, tightened her grip, started raising it, and for a terrifying-ass moment, I thought she was going to lift the ax higher and sink it into Leona's skull. But instead she lowered the ax, kept it at her side, and, without looking at or saying anything to anybody, calmly walked out of the hallway.

Leona's boyfriend Wilk scrambled over to Leona and put his arms around her as she buried her head in his chest.

Leona Statue: may you Rest In Piece(s).

Mr. Woolery gave my sister a five-day suspension, not for chopping down the statue—which, after all, wasn't school property—but for using an ax to do it. He also wanted to terminate her campaign, but my sister was saved once again by Mr. Dranger, who argued that Regina was under duress—fueled by the racist vandalism of her posters—when she did the downsizing by ax.

So the election is still next Thursday, my sister is still in the race, Leona's statue is gone, and so is my sanity. Don't even ask a brother where the ax is.

SALLIE

My sister paced back and forth in the kitchen tonight like some caged beast without the cage. Uly's sister destroyed her statue seven hours ago, but you would've thought it was seven minutes ago, the way my sister kept huffing and puffing about it.

"I can't *believe* she did that to my statue," Leona fumed. "But why am I even surprised? That's the way they are, deep down. That's the way they all are. If they disagree with you, they don't sit down and talk it out like a rational human being. They switch back to their true, savage, violent, animal selves. That's why my statue is gone."

There was something in her eyes—maybe it's called blind fury or something—that was making me more and more nervous. I said, "You need to calm down."

"Calm down??!!" She yelled in my face, "MY STATUE IS GONE!! BECAUSE OF HER!!! And you're dating her brother!!! Do you have any idea how totally pathetic this makes me look now??!!"

Trying to keep my voice steady, I said, "Even if your statue was still standing, you'd still have a problem with me dating Uly, and you know it. You've always had a problem with it."

She nodded hard and said, "That's right. It actually makes me wanna throw up when I think about you kissing him. Because it's not natural."

Still trying to keep my voice steady, I told her, "You really need to try being quiet right now."

"Fuck you," she snapped. "It's time you heard the truth. You and him dating—it's not natural. That kind of thing is *never* natural, and you know it. If you truly thought it was natural, then why'd you wait so long to tell me and everybody else about it? 'Cause deep down, you knew it was wrong; you knew it was going against what nature intended!"

I couldn't eat my fruit cup anymore; I'd so lost my appetite. I slid it away and told her, "Shut up."

But shutting up was the last thing she was interested in. Her chewed-up-lipsticked mouth stretched into a smile that mingled with her running mascara and tear-stained cheeks. "I'll let you in on a little secret: I knew you two were dating when it first started. *Way* before you told me. Why do you think I made you campaign manager?"

It felt like a linebacker had just line-backed into me. When I finally got my breath back, I said, "What?"

Still sort of smiling, she said, "What, you didn't think I did it because I thought you were some brilliant mover & shaker, did you? Even on your best day, you sucked as a campaign manager. I could've spit and hit five girls who would've been a better campaign manager for me than you. But I figured once he found out you were my campaign manager, he'd Swipe Left on you and it would be curtains on the You & Him Show."

I gave her the saddest triumphant smile ever given and said, "Yeah, and how'd that work out for you?"

She looked away from me and went back to pacing.

I swallowed, then told her, "I never thought I'd ever say this to you, but it makes me sick to my stomach right now that you're my sister."

She stopped pacing and stared at me. Then she darted over to me and grabbed the shoulder part of my shirt like I was a piece of laundry she was about to fling into a laundry basket. I tried yanking myself away but her grip was tight. Still gripping me, she muttered, "Yeah? Well maybe you better think of me as God now because one snap of my finger and my boyfriend and his crew can do enough damage to your boyfriend to make him break out in hives for the rest of his life whenever he just *hears* the words 'white girl.'"

"Get off me!" I said, practically beating her off until she finally let go.

After collecting myself, I squinted at her and said, ". . . So all of that was you?—the gorilla stickers, the White Box, the foam?"

She said, "What do you think?"

After a long moment, I said, ". . . Why?"

"Because I hate her." She said it so matter-of-factly that I wished she'd screamed it instead or even written it in blood; it would've been so much less scary. Then she said, "And you know why else? Because it's time for white people to stop being ashamed to be white and start being proud of it. If they can have a Black Box Theater, then why can't we have a white one?"

There was another question I had to ask, no matter how much I didn't want to ask it. Trying to keep my voice from shaking, I said, ". . . And the dead rat—that was you too?"

She gave me the kind of stare that had more Yes-flavoring than No-flavoring.

Right then all I wanted to do was get out of that kitchen and, preferably, out of her life, but since you can't divorce your sister, I decided to just get out of the kitchen, but not before I said one more thing. "Lee," I quietly said, "I hope Regina wins next week, and I hope she wins in a landslide. And if you do anything to hurt Uly, *you* will break out in hives for the rest of your life whenever you hear the word 'Sallie.'"

I moved past her and left the kitchen.

JULY

I always thought Election Day morning would arrive with trumpets blaring and red, white, and blue chariots riding us from the bed to the breakfast table, but this morning had Regular all over it. Regina fixed us the usual toast and eggs, which we ate while Dad checked out his *Daily News* and my sister and I tapped away on our phones. The only giveaway that today Wasn't Like The Others was what Dad said to my sister before we walked out: "Good luck today, honey. And check it out: no matter what happens, you're always a winner in this house. Don't ever forget that." Regina gave our father a tight hug and said, "Thanks, Dad," punctuating it with her good-china/plastic-off-the-couch smile.

When Regina, Narmeen, and I rolled into Knight, everything and everyone around us seemed to reek Regular too. Except for the giant beige banner saying ELECTION DAY, which stretched wall-to-wall above the middle of the entrance hallway.

That one simple banner was enough to make it real to my sister, who looked at me and nervously raised her eyebrows. "Well, I guess this is it, huh?"

"You're gonna kill it," Narmeen said, kissing her cheek.

"You're large & in charge," I told my sister before hugging her.

She gave my hand a final squeeze, then the three of us went our separate ways to class.

As I sat in first period class, listening to the projector-screened Mr. Dranger instruct us on the voting procedure, I wished Sallie was sitting next to me. It really bothered me that we'd cut our daily chats from fifty to two in the last week, but I figured she was just focusing on helping her sister and that things would get back to normal after the election results were announced.

After Mr. Dranger's long-winded ass finally shut the hell up, the screen went black and Ms. Hannigan turned off the projector. Then, following Mr. Dranger's guidelines, she instructed us to open our Chromebooks and go to the voting ballot on Google Classroom.

The voting ballot showed a vertical lineup of three smiling faces, each inside a circle: Regina Bernadette Gates, John William Smith, and Leona Priscilla Walls; next to each face was an empty square. Fourth in the vertical lineup wasn't a picture but a phrase, also inside a circle: DON'T KNOW/DON'T CARE. And that was next to an empty square too.

I clicked inside the empty square next to my sister's face and a check mark appeared.

Then I hit the green Submit button at the bottom of the screen.

WE HAD to wait all the way till the next-to-last period, Period G, to hear the results.

At exactly 12:40 P.M., Ms. Ledbetter turned on the projector screen, which showed an empty news desk.

After a couple of minutes, Coral Bleeker appeared with a single sheet of paper. She sat behind the news desk and looked into the camera. Her face was hard as hell to read: no smile, but no frown either.

"Good afternoon, Knight High," she said. "All the votes have been tallied and the results of Knight High School's 112th Presidential Election are now in . . ."

The whole classroom was so quiet it made a cemetery sound like Grand Central Station.

Coral continued: "Coming in at Third place is our new secretary—John William Smith . . ."

My heart started beating faster. There was a sprinkling of claps but it stopped just as fast as it started because nobody wanted to miss anything Coral said.

"Coming in at Second place is our new vice president—Regina Bernadette Gates . . ."

There were more claps.

Coral continued: "And the winner of this year's election is our new president—Leona Priscilla Walls . . ."

Half the class cheered. The other half stayed quiet.

The cheers turned to gasps when Ms. Ledbetter broke into tears, mumbled, "Excuse me," and rushed out of the room.

Coral said, "Mr. Dranger and the school council express their gratitude to all of you who voted and took the process seriously. To the three candidates: congratulations; you have until end of day tomorrow to report to Mr. Dranger and officially accept your elected positions. This has been a special afternoon edition of the Knightly News. Thank you and have a good day."

I just sat there, continuing to stare at the screen even after it faded to blank.

Okay, check it out: Was I surprised? A part of me was. But another part of me wasn't. I guess you could say I felt like my school was a patient who'd been showing all the symptoms of a serious disease, and I was a relative sitting in the waiting room, waiting for the doctor—Coral Bleeker—to come out and give me the diagnosis. And when Coral finally came out, I hoped for the best, but wasn't surprised when she confirmed that it was cancer. The terminal kind.

After school all I wanted to do was hug my sister, but I couldn't find her. I even went to Mr. Dranger's office to see if she was hanging there, but she wasn't. Mr. Dranger was, though, and he motioned for me to come in. He tried to keep his face Switzerland, but if you looked hard enough, you could see Grimbabwe.

"So how's she taking it?" he asked.

I shrugged. "I can't find her. Maybe she left early or something."

He nodded for a long time, then said, "It probably won't bring much consolation, but tell her it was really close. The closest I've ever seen, in fact; and I've been doing this for over ten years. Leona beat your sister by nineteen votes. Just nineteen."

I wanted to curse, but he was a teacher.

He said, "The tally was 101 for John, 156 for Regina, and 175 for Leona. And 489 for Don't Know/Don't Care. So, actually, the real winner of the election was Don't Know/Don't Care. If just twenty kids out of those 489 Don't Know/Don't Cares had voted for your sister, she would've won." He gave what he said some mind time, then told me, "On second thought, maybe you shouldn't tell her that. The Delaware River doesn't need any new bodies. But here's something you can tell her: she can still accomplish quite a lot as vice president. I hope she considers it."

When I got home my sister was lying on her bed, staring at the ceiling. Dad said she hadn't moved for hours.

I pulled a chair up to her bed, and told her Dad had ordered some pizza and we were waiting for her, but she told me she wasn't hungry.

I said, "Come on, Jeen, you can't lie here forever."

She said, "She won . . . She actually won . . . To misquote *The Usual Suspects*: The greatest trick a racist ever pulled is convincing the world that he doesn't exist . . . She actually won."

A tear spilled from the side of her eye and slid down her cheek; she quickly wiped it away.

Pretending I didn't see it, I told her, "Mr. Dranger says you can still get a lot of stuff done as vice president."

My sister shook her head. "Fuck that. I'd rather chop off my arm than be second in command to somebody like her. Mr. Dranger can take his vice president offer and stick it up her ass. I don't mean to be an asshole, but I don't mean it that much."

After failing to get Regina to rejoin the land of the living, I called Sallie. She didn't sound happy about her sister winning. She didn't sound happy about much of anything. This was the saddest I'd ever heard her.

"Uly," she said after a few minutes of small talk, "I quit being her campaign manager a week and a half ago."

"For real?" I said.

"Yeah," she said. After a long pause, she said, "You were right."

"About what?" I said.

"What you said about her . . . You were right." She sounded like she was crying. "Why didn't I see it?" It sounded more like she was asking herself that. "All this time, it was right there in front of me and I didn't even see it. Or maybe I did see it but pretended I didn't. That makes me just as bad as her."

"No it doesn't," I said.

"Yes it does," she said.

There was a long pause.

I said, "Lemme come over."

She quickly said, "No, no. It's nighttime . . . I don't want anything to happen to you . . . Meet me after school tomorrow—Newton Park. Okay?"

"Bacon," I told her.

THE NEXT day me, Regina, Smith, Leona, and Smith's girl Sherry stood in front of Mr. Dranger's desk. Leona looked happy as hell; the happiest I'd ever seen her. She was so jittery and giddy I thought she was going to hand out cigars or some shit.

Leaning back in his chair and resting his chin on his two index fingers, Mr. Dranger looked at us and said, "So, what's the verdict?"

Leona quickly raised her hand and said, "I happily accept the position of school president."

Smith nodded and said, "And I happily accept the position of secretary."

My sister didn't say anything.

Mr. Dranger looked at her. "And Regina?"

My sister said, "I respectfully decline. But thank you for the offer."

Awkward Silence was suddenly the sixth guest in the room.

Then Leona said, "Um, Mr. Dranger, could I have a minute alone with her please?" She was pointing at my sister.

Mr. Dranger looked just as shocked as I felt. He asked Leona, "Oh, you mean . . . you want me to leave my office while you . . . ?" He pointed at her and Regina.

Leona said, "Yes, if you don't mind."

"Oh, okay, sure," he said, getting up.

He walked out of his own damn office, followed by Sherry and Smith, but I hung back.

Leona looked at me and said, "You too, if you don't mind."

Regina told her, "He minds. What do you have to say?"

You could tell Leona wasn't thrilled about me staying, but she closed the door anyway and stepped to my sister.

"Look," Leona said, "I know you don't like me, and you're definitely not my favorite person in the world. But I think you and I had the most passion in this race. Definitely more than he did." She pointed at the door to indicate Smith. "I think if you and I maybe put our passion together, we could be this, like, unstoppable, powerful force that this school would never forget. We got the brains to make all kinds of changes. I'm telling you— when you and I get through, we could be legendary. Next year could go down as the Best, Most Lit School Year Ever, because of you and me. Come on—be my vice president. It'll look great on your college application. And if you don't, John and I can pick somebody else, but, no matter who we pick, I already know they won't be as talented and smart as you are." She reached out to touch my sister's arm, but then she drew her hand back, either because she didn't want to touch my sister or she thought my sister didn't want to be touched. "Come on. What do you say?"

Regina looked at her for a long time. Then she said, "You finished?"

Leona seemed surprised by the question, but she nodded and said, "I'm finished."

My sister stepped over to the door, opened it, and said to Mr. Dranger and the crew, "Y'all can come back in now."

When Mr. Dranger, Sherry, and Smith were back in the room, Regina shook Mr. Dranger's hand and said, "Thank you for letting me run. I had a great time. And I look forward to being vice president next year."

If I guzzled twenty lightning bolts I don't think I'd be as shocked as I was at that moment, straight up and down.

My sister looked at Leona, nodded, and said, "You were right about one thing, honey: there *will* be all kinds of changes."

Mr. Dranger gave his own version of a good-china/plastic-off-the-couch smile as he put his arms around Leona, my sister, and Smith, and ushered them to the outer office.

Greeting us were student council advisor Ms. Bradley and John's brother Scott. They were standing next to each other, but that was the only thing they had in common. Ms. Bradley's face was rocking a warm, friendly grin, but Scott looked tore up from the floor up: his clothes were all wrinkly and he looked like he hadn't slept in days.

With his arms still around Regina, Leona, and Smith, Mr. Dranger said, "Ms. Bradley, I'm proud to announce that it's now official: John will be our secretary, Regina will be our vice president, and Leona will be our president."

Ms. Bradley smiled and said, "That's wonderful news . . . Hey, do you have a minute?"

Mr. Dranger said, "Sure, come in."

As he guided Ms. Bradley into his office, he looked at Regina, Leona, and John and said, "A job well done, kids. I know you'll make our school proud. And remember—the Inauguration's in four days. Make sure you're in your Tuesday best."

After Mr. Dranger closed his door, Scott looked at his brother and said, "What, you accepted the third spot?—the secretary?"

Smith said, "Yeah, it's cool."

"No, it's not," Scott snapped. He grabbed his brother's arm, pulled him closer, and sort of whispered through clenched teeth, "Dad raised us to be Number One, not Number Three!"

John said, "Scott, come on . . ." He sounded embarrassed as hell.

Scott told his brother, "You just lost your dick. You wanna get it back?" He pointed at Mr. Dranger's office. "Go in there and tell Dranger there's no way in hell you're serving under two girls."

John said, "'Look, let's just go home . . ."

Keeping his grip on his brother's shoulder, he looked at my sister and Leona and suddenly seemed to be in a daze. "They're trying to take over now . . . This is how it starts."

John said, "Scott, let's just go home—"

Scott snapped at his brother. "You're really gonna let yourself get cucked like this?"

"Calm down, come on . . ." John said.

"You're really gonna let them turn this school into some girlie Woke fest?" Scott snapped.

John jerked his arm away and said, "Scott, would you shut up!" It was the first time I ever heard him yell.

Looking like he was sorry for yelling at his brother, John took a breath and softly told Scott, "It's not about boys and girls, dude." He pointed in the direction of my sister and Leona. "They're just two people who happened to beat a third person, okay? Stop being an asshole."

"I'd take that advice if I was you," I told Scott.

Scott glared at me for a moment, then took John's arm again and said, "Let's go home."

John tugged his arm away and firmly said, "No. I want Sherry to take me home. You need to cool off."

Scott looked stunned, like he wasn't used to his brother rejecting him. For a split second, he looked like the saddest eighteen-year-old in the world. But when his eyes met mine again, his face switched back to angry, and now he looked like the maddest eighteen-year-old in the world.

After staring at me for a few seconds, he slowly turned around and walked out of the office.

Nobody knew what the hell to say after that, so we just See You Later'd each other and went our separate ways.

AS I walked to the park to meet Sallie I heard some rustling like somebody was following me, but when I turned around it was just squirrels skidding up a tree. My heart was beating faster than I wanted it to. I felt like I was being watched or something.

When I got to the park I saw Sallie in the distance, sitting against a tree.

Smiling, I put some race in my pace so I could get to her faster.

"Hey you," I said when I was a couple of feet away from her.

She didn't move. I noticed that her eyes were closed.

Getting closer to her, I said, "Sallie?"

She still didn't move. Her eyes stayed closed.

Then I noticed something around her waist. A thick red ring.

Fighting back panic, I ran up to her and grabbed her shoulders.

Her chocolate eyes snapped open and went wide when she saw me. "Shit! You scared me!" she said with a little laugh.

I took a closer look at the red ring and felt stupid as hell when I realized it was her red sweater, wrapped around her waist.

Just when I was about to ask why she hadn't answered me when I called out to her, I saw the telltale black strings hanging from the sides of her face and felt stupider when she yanked out her earbuds.

She touched my face and said, "What's wrong? You look weird."

I forced a smile and said, "No, I'm all right."

After a moment, she said, "So, is it over?"

I said, "Yeah. Regina decided to—"

She gently put her index finger to my lips. "No, don't. I don't even wanna know. I don't wanna talk about it, ever again. I just wanna know if it's over . . . Is it over?"

This time I gave her a smile that was straight from the headquarters of Real City. "It's over," I told her.

She nodded and said, "Then let's start again."

And she put her arms around my neck and gave me a long, long kiss. Just like the one she'd given me in the Franklin Institute stomach.

SALLIE

Uly and I snuggled in Newton Park for a couple of hours this afternoon, then we decided to go to Ben Franklin Bridge. This time, we wanted to walk the whole way from the Jersey side to the Philly side.

As we rode the PATCO to the bridge, it felt so nice to sit with him without the election sitting between us, like it had for the last three dreadful months. With each passing month, it felt like the election kept crashing our two-person party, and it kept growing bigger and bigger until it was too big to fit through the doorway whenever we tried to shove it out of our party; and then we were just stuck with it.

When we got to the bridge, Uly and I walked from the Jersey end to the Philly end, just like we'd planned. As we walked, we talked about the summer and how we were going to try to see each other every day and catch up on all the hours the election had snatched from us.

When we reached the Philly end, we turned around and walked back toward the Jersey end, never letting go of each other's hand.

Midway, we stopped and, keeping our fingers threaded

together, we watched the Philly skyline, just like we'd done that Valentine's Day night. Every now and then the bridge trembled from the speeding cars, trucks, and trains, but it didn't bother me; I was gripping the hand of the most beautiful boy in the world. He and I kept watching the skyline until the afternoon sky started turning dark. Then we turned around and continued walking back to New Jersey.

PART

6

Nine Years Later

ULY

At first I wasn't sure it was her. But something about the way she tilted her head as she read her phone screen told me I should take a second look. And I'm glad I did, because that's when I saw those dark, dark eyes.

It was her.

The blond hair was shorter now, almost like a bob, but I knew it was her.

"Sallie?" I said.

She sharply turned her head to me, the way people do when they're stunned to find out they're not completely surrounded by strangers.

When she saw me she kind of shrank back and put her hand over her mouth. "Uly?" she said through her fingers. It was almost a whisper.

I nodded.

We smiled and hugged each other. The hug was strange. The last time we'd been that close to each other, it was a kiss—and a mighty long one—not a hug. But it still felt nice.

When she moved out of the hug, I could see tears in her eyes. She touched my face and said, "Oh my God, you still look the

same." She tapped my mustache. "Well, maybe except for this."
She laughed.

"You look great," I said.

"Thank you. So do you."

We stared at each other for a few moments.

Then I pointed at the convention center hall we were standing
in, and I asked, "What the hell are you doing here? Are you a
teacher too?"

She nodded and said, "Thompson Elementary in Palo Alto.
How about you?"

I said, "Overbrook High in Philly."

She laughed and said, "Wow. It's so weird that after all this
time we see each other again in Baltimore."

Chuckling, I said, "I know. I mean, damn. How long has it
been—nine years?"

Nodding, she said, "Nine years."

The huge leather double doors of the lecture room we were
standing in line for opened and the attendant announced that we
could come in.

Because Sallie and I were near the back of the damn line
many of the seats were taken by the time we entered the room
and we couldn't sit together. We told each other we'd meet
up again right after the lecture and have lunch. We kind of
touched each other's hands then she went left and I went
right.

Don't ask me what the lecture was about because the whole
time my head was in another bed, if you can feel me on that.
Seeing Sallie brought Everything back. Knight High. The election. Our sisters. Inauguration Day.

Inauguration Day.

The worst day of my life. A day I still haven't recovered from,
even after thousands and thousands of dollars in therapy. And I'll
probably never recover from it.

After the lecture, I found Sallie in the moving crowd and hurried over to her.

"Don't I know you from somewhere?" I asked her.

She laughed, then squinted at me and said, "Hmm, you do look familiar."

We decided to have lunch at the Diamond Tavern, a restaurant inside the Hilton, where she was staying.

On the way there, we did some small-talking, mostly about the convention and our jobs.

By the time we sat down in the restaurant, we'd been quiet for about five minutes. I think we were both ready to Talk—I know I was: there was so much I wanted to talk about with her, but I also knew most of it was stuff we couldn't talk about.

I studied her face: it had become more contoured, with slight lines beginning to form on the sides of her mouth, but not much had changed. The biggest change was in her eyes. They were the same color, of course, but now a permanent sadness was there. The kind of sadness that can only come from the persistently relentless echoes of a nine-year-old trauma.

As she opened the menu, I noticed the wedding ring on her finger.

"So, how long?" I asked.

She looked up and said, "Hm?" When she saw what I was pointing at, she said, "Oh, four years."

I nodded and asked, "What's his name?"

"Elliot," she said. "We met in college." She pointed at the wedding band on my finger. "How about you? How long? What's her name?"

I said, "Oh. You remember that girl Narmeen?—the one who helped out with my sister's campaign?"

Sallie's eyes went wide in shock. "Holy shit! You're married to her? I didn't even know you two were into each other like that."

I kind of laughed and said, "We weren't at first. But around the end of junior year, we started spending more and more time with each other, found out we had a lot of things in common, one thing led to another, and by senior year we were official."

Sallie said, "Wow. I just can't get over that . . . Narmeen. You once said she reminded you of a serial killer."

I laughed. "Yeah, well, thankfully, the only thing she's killed is my fear of her."

She smiled. That was something else about her that stayed unchanged. The smile. That smile turned her back into my sixteen-year-old girlfriend from nine years ago.

Our eyes locked again.

I wanted to bring It up.

Inauguration Day, the last time I saw her.

We needed to talk about it.

But then again, did we really?

I glanced around at the other eaters and wondered if they could tell that Sallie and I were damaged. Could they see the permanent scars under our skin? I call them freak-show scars because, like the eight-foot man and the woman with three feet, these scars piss on nature's rule book: after nine years they still hurt just as much as they did when they were fresh, they can never heal, and they'll still be going strong when we're weak from old age.

It's amazing how something that started and ended in less than a minute can cause never-ending pain.

I still can't believe how quickly it happened.

The gym. The entire school in the bleachers, watching. Mr. Dranger called up Leona to the platform first. Then he called up my sister. John Smith, escorted by his brother Scott, was last. Before Mr. Dranger could open his mouth again, Scott whipped out a 9mm, yelled "White American Prince forever!" aimed the gun at my sister's face, and pulled the trigger. Then he thrust the gun into Leona's face and shot her point-blank too.

Leona died instantly.

My sister held on for five hours, before her heart decided it had enough and let go.

As for Scott: I actually thought he was going to shoot himself too, but he didn't. Right after shooting my sister and Leona, he just stood there in the middle of the gym, frozen, until some teachers and school security tackled him and kept him pinned down till the police came.

I know the exact address of the prison he's serving time at. Do I sometimes fantasize about mailing him a cake with bomb filling? You better believe it. But it'll never go beyond fantasy. For one thing, a bomb would give him an early release, so to speak; and I want him to stay there as mandated so he can slowly go from cot to rot. But most of all, I realized a long time ago that it's better to grow up than blow up.

Seeing her sister gunned down like that threw Sallie into a deep shock that eventually sent her to the hospital, where she had a nervous breakdown. She never returned to Knight High after that day, and sometime that summer she and Lady M packed up and moved to California. I sent her dozens of cards and wrote her hundreds of messages but they all went unanswered, as were all calls; it wasn't long before she changed her number.

Zombies looked more alive than my ass when I returned to school that fall. Losing my sister was a machete slice across the neck and losing Sallie right after that was a salty spit on the wound. For a big chunk of that year I barely noticed what was going on around me. But some things were hard not to notice. Hoping to help heal the school from the bloody wound inflicted by his brother, John Smith accepted Mr. Dranger's offer to be president and then he chose two of his former football buddies to be vice president and secretary. If the three of them accomplished anything that year, I guess I must've missed it. And so did a lot of other people.

Later that year, my father and Lady M sued the school for

negligence. Personally, I didn't think their cases were strong: How was the school to know that a former Honor Roll student and wrestling-team captain visited the gym that morning with a handgun in his pocket and a hatred-on-steroids in his heart? I guess the judge gave my uncertainty a Like because all my father and Lady M got from the school was a small cash settlement and an agreement to rename the gym after their deceased daughters.

It took a few years to get all the paperwork in order, but now, whenever I visit Knight High (the principal has been inviting me to come there every year and talk to the school about tolerance), I pass by the gym and see REGINA GATES & LEONA WALLS GYMNASIUM over the entrance; the kids nickname it Gates & Walls Gym. Every time I see that sign I can't help but internally shake my head. Only when they're not existing are my sister and Leona able to peacefully coexist; it makes so little sense that it makes perfect sense.

Something that's made me feel a bit better is the fact that, during my visits to the school, I see that Rainbow Relief is still going strong. A couple of years after my sister died, a girl named Minerva Delacruz ran for school president and won, and decided to bring back Rainbow Relief. She was a freshman at the time of my sister's campaign and she told me that Regina's station had helped her and her friends so much that her first presidential correction was Rainbow Relief's resurrection. Over the next few years Rainbow Relief got so popular that it was recently turned into one of the official clubs at the school.

Almost as if she was reading my thoughts, Sallie started tearing up as she sat across from me at the Diamond Tavern.

"What's wrong?" I asked her. It was probably the dumbest question of the day.

Sallie took a breath, then said, ". . . I just wanted to say sorry."

I was stunned. "For what?" I asked.

She said, "For not writing back to you. For not answering your calls . . . It's just . . . I wanted to turn my back on everything that reminded me of . . ." Her voice trailed off and she swiped her tears with some tissue. She looked at me with red-streaked eyes and said, "I'm sorry . . ."

I nodded. "It's okay. I understand."

She said, "I just don't wanna think about that part of my life anymore . . . It's too painful . . . Except for you. You were the best part of it." She gave me a tearful smile.

I put my hand on hers and said, "You were the best part too."

She put her hand on top of mine. Then she moved it away, and the rest of our hand sand castle fell apart.

Wiping away the tears on her other cheek, she said, "I just want to concentrate on moving on, you know? Building a life with my family. I have a beautiful daughter now—she just turned two."

My eyebrows went up. "Real talk?"

Smiling, she nodded and showed me a picture on her phone: a handsome blond man, presumably the husband, was sitting on the couch with an adorable blond, dark-eyed girl on his lap.

"She's such a cutie," I said.

"Thank you."

Pointing at the guy, I said, "And I'm guessing that's Elliot?"

She nodded.

I wasn't about to call him a cutie, so I said nothing.

The picture made me happy and depressed at the same time.

I pointed back at the girl and asked, "What's her name?"

"Cindy."

"That's pretty," I said. "Any middle name?"

Sallie was quiet for a few moments. Then a fresh set of tears filled her eyes as she said, "Leona."

I nodded and told her with my eyes that I understood.

Sallie put away her phone and asked, "Do you think you'll ever have kids?"

"I have a daughter too, actually."

Sallie's face rocked the same shocked expression that had greeted the Narmeen news. "Really?? Lemme see!"

I took out my phone and showed her a picture of my one-year-old daughter.

"Oh my God, she's so beautiful, Uly!" She looked up at me and said, "I can see you in her."

"Thank you. She's my sunshine."

She asked, "What's her name?"

It took me a moment to collect myself, then I said, "Regina . . . Regina Dharma Gates."

This time, Sallie put her hand on mine and gave it a small squeeze.

It wasn't long before it was time to go. She had to get back to her room where her husband was waiting and pack up for the evening flight back to Cali.

We exchanged phone numbers, but I think we both knew we'd never talk to or see each other again. To each other, we were cotton candy that couldn't be eaten anymore because it was too caked with the dirt of things we wanted to forget.

As we walked out of the restaurant, I told her that New York City's revamped Film Forum theater was going to show *The Good, the Bad and the Ugly* in a couple of weeks. "I was thinking about checking it out," I told her. "I've never seen it on a big screen."

She said, "I haven't seen that movie in years. I have a hard time watching violent movies now, after . . ." She couldn't say it.

I nodded. "I understand."

As I walked with her to the hotel lobby I wanted to tell her so many other things.

I wanted to tell her that she's the only person that's ever come close to feeling like my true soulmate.

I wanted to tell her that I couldn't believe a school election ended two lives and one relationship.

I wanted to tell her that I visited the Rittenhouse Park tree with our initials on it at least once a year, until two years ago, when I saw that it had been cut down.

I wanted to tell her I hate that six months were all we had.

I wanted to tell her that I still loved her.

But when we got to the elevators, all I told her was, "It was nice seeing you again."

She smiled at me and said, "You as well."

We hugged, then waited for her elevator.

When its door opened, she stepped on, along with a mother and her little son.

"Mom, I'm thirsty!" the boy said.

Digging in her handbag, the mother said, "You want some grape juice, honey?"

As the mother handed the juice box to the boy, Sallie and I looked into each other's eyes and smiled. But this smile was different. It was a private smile. A secret smile.

Then our smiles faded just as quickly.

The elevator closed, shutting off her face.

I walked out of the hotel and started strolling toward mine.

On the way, I stopped at a wastebasket.

There was really no need to hold on to it anymore.

So I took out my wallet, dug inside, and took out the purple paper square. It was wrinkled and severely dog-eared from almost ten years of handling and wallet-hopping. But I could still make out the faded decade-old words, written in a fifteen-year-old girl's handwriting: *The Good, the Bad and the Ugly?*

Just as I was about to drop it in the garbage, the weak adhesive clung to my thumb, and I kept the Post-it suspended above the rim. Then I tucked the elderly paper square back into the confines of my wallet, closed it, stuck it back in my pocket, and continued heading toward my hotel.

AUTHOR'S NOTE

I've never been an overly political person. In fact, when it comes to politics, I'm probably a C student, at best. In the case of assassinations, for example, I know that the vice president would replace the president, and that the House Speaker would replace the vice president, but if the bloodbath also claimed the House Speaker, I don't remember who'd be next. (I seem to vaguely recall something to do with a "pro tempore," but that sounds more like an Italian dessert than a political position.) So I've always known just enough about politics to Pass for the year. And, for most of my life, I really wasn't much interested in fixing that.

Then the 2016 election season happened. And I found myself increasingly drawn to the fact that the two competing candidates' daughters, Chelsea Clinton and Ivanka Trump, managed to hold on to their friendship in spite of the combative, increasingly nasty rivalry between their parents. More and more, I found myself wondering exactly how the election was impacting the two women's bond: Were their conversations more awkward? Did they pretend that everything was normal whenever they talked? Did any of their friendly interactions switch to tense, resentful fulminations as a result of each one's loyalty to their parent? All of those ingredients just seemed way too delicious not to cook into a full-blown stew that could be a novel.

Being a writer for teenagers, I of course needed to reconfigure and rearrange those ingredients into a story that would be appropriate for YA, so I decided to turn Chelsea and Ivanka from two women into two teenage girls; and instead of having their parents run for president, I decided to make their older siblings, also teenagers, run for school president. But as I began brainstorming, I sensed that the story could be even more impactful if I raised the stakes: What if the school election interfered not with a friendship between two girls but with a romantic relationship between a boy and a girl who were each falling in love for the first time? And what if the boy was black and the girl was white? With those story adjustments, I now saw the stakes soar to the sky. For a high schooler, everything is magnified: they don't just fall in love—they *plummet* in love; and their heart doesn't just break— it shatters into a thousand pieces. And with the often-awkward, always-complicated component of race relations added to the mix, I was now more confident that I had the elements of an interesting story. And that's how my book was born.

Lastly, I'd always wanted to write a story where school could be a microcosm for America, and the book you're holding in your hand is the fulfillment of that wish.

—Kwame Ivery

ACKNOWLEDGMENTS

If you Google "Penelope Burns," you'll see that she's a literary agent. And even though that's true, what Google won't tell you is that she holds a few other titles as well: Optimist, Hard-worker, Funny Tweeter, Proud Sports Enthusiast, Fast Responder To Emails From Clients, and Fixer Of Writers' Broken Spirits. I can especially attest to that last one. In January 2019, I was pretty much down & out: forty agents had said "No" to *The Problem with the Other Side*, one agency had said "Yes" then said "No," and now it was looking more and more like "Maybe" was the answer to the question I was starting to ask myself—"Could it be that you're just not good enough to be published?" Then Penelope offered representation, and four months later, she landed a book deal for me. And suddenly Maybe and No both packed their bags and took the next train out of my life. In other words: Thank you, Penelope Burns, for believing in me when it felt like so many other agents didn't.

I also want to thank Daniel Ehrenhaft and Alexa Wejko, the two editors who made sure the roads my book walked were smooth, the waters my book sailed were serene, and the skies my book flew were bright blue. Dan, I'll always be grateful for the lunches, for your personal stories, for your great sense of humor, and for your overall down-to-earthness. Alexa, I'll always be grateful for your reassuring emails, your attention to detail, your insight, and your perpetual professionalism.

My gratitude toward the Soho Press team is bottomless: Rachel Kowal, thank you for shepherding me through the copyediting and for making the book-production process understandable; Stephanie Cohen and Stacy Silnik, thank you for your precise, hawk-eyed manuscript probing; Amanda Howell Whitehurst, thank you for that striking, visually arresting cover; Janine Agro, thank you for the thematically perfect interior design; Steven Tran, thank you for your clarity and communicativeness. And to the rest of the Soho team: a thousand Thank Yous for helping to make my book ready for the world.

I'd be remiss if I didn't give a shout-out to Soho publisher Bronwen Hruska: thank you for not only opening the doors of your company to me but also offering some additional editorial guidance and encouragement.

To the early champions of my book: Jessie Devine, thank you for your helpful, valuable input. Author Alyssa Wees, thank you for gifting me with the first ever blurb: the generosity of your comments will never be forgotten. Author Preston Norton and librarian Rachel Simon: thank you for taking the time to read my novel and write an enthusiastic, kind blurb about it.

On a more personal note:

Thank you, Collingswood High School, for continuing to be my occupational home. A special shout-out to: English department supervisor David Olivieri—thank you for your encouragement; music teacher extraordinaire and the coolest of the cool, Nathan Ingram—thank you for your advice and words of wisdom; vice principal Doug Newman—thank you for your avid curiosity about my publishing journey; librarian Kimberle Madden—thank you for your boundless, bountiful enthusiasm; principal Matthew Genna—thank you for your ceaseless support-iveness; former district superintendent Scott Oswald—thank you for shocking me with the discovery that it's actually possible for a school superintendent to be funny, creative, engaging, and inspirational (sometimes all within the same minute).

To my fellow CHS teachers: thank you for getting up every morning to do a job where the results of your labor usually happen offstage, unseen by you, or they happen many years later when your name is forgotten but not your face, or your face is forgotten but not your name. What matters most are the Results themselves. And they'll never be forgotten.

Special thanks to CHS teachers Sara Dominiak, Cristin Introcaso, and Taryn Silverman: I will be forever touched by the way you gave me the shining light of your support during a dark time.

To all my students—past, present, and future: thank you for listening (or at least pretending to listen), even when listening was the last thing you wanted to do. A special shout-out to Owen Faupel: you were the first student to show me that my words were more influential than I'd thought. And another special shout-out to Claudia Celia: you were the first student to think one of my stories was interesting enough to summarize, out loud, to her classmates. And a deluxe shout-out to Ryan Trout: even though I've never felt especially heroic, thank you for always trying to make me feel like a hero.

Special thanks to students Ayanna Jones, Asia Yarbrough, Lanna Dawson, Dion Chen, Carly Irwin, Abigail Walker, Vivienne Koory, Taylor Hinson, Amylia Tra, Jasmine Clervil, Alysha Terry, Hailey Spencer, Christy Ngo, Dayanara Fuentes, Catherine Abacan, and Maya Schoeffling: thank you for showing me that sometimes students can provide spiritual support for teachers. You provided that support for me during Fall 2020 and I will be eternally grateful.

To my favorite literary peeps: J.D. Salinger, Richard Wright, Anne Tyler, Tom Perrotta, August Wilson, Lorraine Hansberry— thank you for the inspiration & motivation.

To my brothers, Marcus Ivery and Mathias Ivery: thank you for your respect and for your genuine interest in the things I do.

To my late grandmother Ella Bunch: thank you for instilling in me a work ethic built on punctuality, diligence, and courtesy.

To my mother, Leah Ivery: my character Sallie says that her best friend Dandee is the closest thing to a superhero she knows. Well, you're the closest thing to a superhero I know: you raised my brothers and me while working nights as a corrections officer in a prison filled with murderers, rapists, armed robbers, and several assorted psychopaths, and your smile is still as sunny today as it was on the very first day I saw it. You often tell me that you wish you'd given me more things when I was growing up, but you actually gave me the best gift a parent can give a child, something that's too big for a barcode and too rare to put on a store shelf: unconditional love. And I will always thank you for that.

And finally, to all the struggling writers out there: I know it often feels like you're stuck in a hot, stuffy, windowless room called Rejection and there's no Exit sign in sight; but even that room has a door somewhere. Keep searching and you'll find it. If it could happen to me, it could happen to you.